Praise for the novels of

BELLA ANDRE

"The perfect combination of sexy heat and tender heart."
—Barbara Freethy,
#1 *New York Times* bestselling author

"Bella Andre writes warm, sexy contemporary romance
that always gives me a much needed pick-me-up.
Reading one of her books is truly a pleasure."
—Maya Banks, *New York Times* bestselling author

"Sensual, empowered stories
enveloped in heady romance."
—*Publishers Weekly*

"Loveable characters, sizzling chemistry,
and poignant emotion."
—Christie Ridgway, *USA TODAY* bestselling author

"I'm hooked on the Sullivans!"
—Marie Force, bestselling author
of *Falling for Love*

"No one does sexy like Bella Andre."
—Sarah MacLean, *New York Times* bestselling author

"A great combination of smokin'-hot sex,
emotions, and a great secondary cast.
I am absolutely smitten with…the Sullivan family.
I can't wait to read the rest of their stories."
—*Guilty Pleasures Book Reviews*

"The Sullivans will be a great family to follow."
—*Happily Ever After Reads*

BELLA ANDRE

Always On My Mind

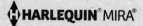

Recycling programs
for this product may
not exist in your area.

ISBN-13: 978-0-7783-1617-6

ALWAYS ON MY MIND

Harlequin MIRA/May 2014

First published by Bella Andre

Copyright © 2013 by Oak Press, LLC

Printed in U.S.A.

Dear Reader,

The first time Lori Sullivan opened her mouth, she made me laugh. Over the years, I've written strong heroines, sassy heroines and sweet heroines, but I've never written anyone quite like Lori. Naughty has never been afraid to take a risk. Even after failing. And even when it turns out that falling in love just might be the biggest risk of all.

But there's another reason why I absolutely loved writing this book: Grayson Tyler. Out on his farm, in his cowboy hat and boots, he couldn't have seemed more wrong for Lori. But I promise you that he is the only man who could have captured her heart (and mine, as well, while he was at it!). I hope he captures your heart, too.

Happy reading,

Bella

One

Lori Sullivan wasn't looking for trouble. She swore she wasn't.

Just because her nickname was Naughty, and trouble seemed to follow her wherever she went, didn't mean she wanted any today. On the contrary—for the first time ever, she was looking for some peace and quiet.

No one in her family knew she was back in San Francisco, having just flown in on the red-eye from Chicago. Even though she loved them more than anything else in the world, she just couldn't face them right now. Her six brothers, her twin sister and her mother were the best family a girl could have…and yet, if they found out that she was back in town, they'd not only want to know why she'd walked out on her show halfway through its run, but they also wouldn't back off until they'd wrung every horrible detail out of her.

How did she know that?

Because that was exactly what she'd done to every

one of them over the past twenty-five years whenever they'd faced a crisis—personal or otherwise.

So, instead of wheeling her suitcase from the San Francisco Airport baggage claim area over to the taxi station to head home to her apartment, she impulsively headed for the rental-car desk.

"Good morning, how can I help you?" chirped the blonde woman behind the desk.

Lori guessed the two of them had to be around the same age but, by contrast, she felt at least a decade wearier than her. "I need a car."

"Great! Where are you headed and how long do you need it for?"

The woman's smile was so bright, Lori felt her eyes tearing up from the glare. Fortunately, after her bleary-eyed flight across the country, immediately upon landing she'd put on her sunglasses to deal with the blinding sunlight pouring in through her small airplane window. She was glad she was still wearing them as she'd hate for the woman to think she was crying.

No, Lori refused to cry over anything that had happened in Chicago. Or during the year and a half before that.

She wasn't a crier, damn it. Never had been, never would be.

The world would have to do a heck of a lot more than give her a cheating scum of a boyfriend and take away her entire dancing career to make her cry.

She was young. She was healthy. She had her whole life ahead of her.

Somehow, some way, she'd figure out what to do with the next seventy years.

Which brought her back to the woman's questions. Where was she going? And for how long?

Blaming lack of sleep for the fact that all her brain could come up with was blanks, she asked, "Where's *your* favorite place to go?"

The woman was momentarily surprised by Lori's question, but then her face got all dreamy. "Pescadero."

Lori slipped her sunglasses down her nose so that she could peer at the woman over the frames. "Pescadero?"

Having lived in Northern California her entire life, Lori figured she must have driven through there at some point, but as far as she could recall, Pescadero had been nothing more than a bunch of farms strung together.

The woman nodded happily. "I just love the green rolling hills that seem to go on forever, all those sheep and cows munching away, and the fact that the ocean is at the end of nearly every farm road."

Lori loved living in the city. She loved working in cities, too, especially since her dance career had always been intrinsically tied to the movement all around her. A sleepy farm town was the last place she would ever have thought to choose for an impromptu vacation.

"It sounds perfect. How long can I have the car?"

Again, the woman gave her a slightly strange look before saying, "One month. Longer than that and I'll have to fill out additional paperwork. But it's really more of a day trip. A shortish one, at that. I can't imagine how you could possibly spend a month in Pescadero."

Even though Lori was silently wondering the same

thing, she handed over her credit card and signed a dozen forms promising that she wouldn't damage the car. A few minutes later, she was holding the keys and was about to walk away from the rental desk when she turned back.

"Any idea how to get to Pescadero from here?"

An hour and a half later, Lori was wondering if the farmland was ever going to end when she saw a roof. Feeling like a sailor who had been out to sea for months before finally catching sight of land, she put her foot down harder on the gas pedal and sped toward what she could now see was the teeny-tiny Pescadero Main Street.

The car rental lady had been right about the pretty green fields and the cute sheep, but she'd somehow forgotten to mention how quiet the silence was…or how lonesome.

Lori had filled her world with loud music and tall buildings and vibrant people for so long that it was strange to be surrounded by complete quiet. She'd flipped on the car radio at one point, but it had felt akin to turning on a boom box in the middle of a church, so she'd immediately turned it off.

Still, for all that her mood wasn't exactly at its best, it was the first sunny day she'd seen in weeks and she was determined to enjoy the warm sun and blue skies. Plus, just as her auto-mechanic-slash-mogul brother Zach had always claimed, there really was something about getting in a car and going for a drive. Granted, she thought as she looked down at her little rental car, he usually did his joyrides in a Ferrari. Besides, he didn't do them alone anymore, now that he and Heather were in love and engaged.

Lori pulled up in front of the Pescadero General Store just as a little girl walked outside carrying a big bag of dog food and wearing a huge smile. A man Lori easily assumed was her grandfather was barely a beat behind her holding a brand-new dog crate. Wearing cowboy boots and well-worn blue jeans, they both fit perfectly into the farm town.

As she got out of the car, Lori saw the girl's puppy. His leash had been tied to a nearby post and when he caught sight of the little girl, the black-and-white dog started wagging its tail so hard its whole body looked like a kite flying in the breeze. The girl immediately dropped the bag of dog food on the ground and picked up the puppy in her arms to give it kisses. The grizzled old farmer said in a gruff voice, "You're going to spoil him," but his eyes were full of love.

For the second time today, Lori felt her eyes begin to tear up. She'd gotten used to the bright sunlight and had flipped her sunglasses up on top of her head a while ago, but now she plopped them back over her eyes.

As she stepped onto the sidewalk, both the man and the girl stopped to look at her, each of them doing a double take. She couldn't figure out what had shocked them so much...not until she finally looked down at herself.

Oh, yeah, this was why. The formfitting, sleeveless, bright-pink top covered in multicolored sequins that ended at midthigh, and nearly opaque tights combined with the glittery heels she'd been dancing in, were a little strange to be wearing in the middle of the day. Not just here, but anywhere, really.

She'd completely forgotten what she was wearing when she'd stormed out of the Auditorium Theatre in Chicago, thrown her things into her suitcase, then headed to the airport to catch the next plane to San Francisco. She'd wrapped an oversize scarf around herself on the plane and in the airport, but it was so warm and sunny during her drive that she'd stripped it off and had left it on the passenger seat.

Of course the puppy didn't care what she was wearing, and when she reached for it, he wriggled his furry body toward her. "What a cute puppy," she said to the little girl. "What's his name?"

"Jonas."

"That's a great name," Lori said as she smiled and patted the dog, but just as her fingertips stroked the soft fur between the puppy's ears, the girl's grandfather dragged them away.

A moment later, when Lori turned to head for the General Store's front door, the ground felt as though it was moving beneath her. Bracing herself against the wall, Lori realized she hadn't had anything to eat for nearly twenty-four hours. Despite what most people thought dancers' lives were like, she had a healthy appetite and a fast metabolism, and knew she shouldn't have gone so long without eating.

It was just that food hadn't sounded very good for a while now....

With renewed purpose, she pushed through the door. Animal feed and farm supplies ran the length of one side of the store. In the middle was a display of knit-wear, jeans, cowboy boots and what looked like pack-ages of underwear and socks. The other side of the store had a deli counter, several refrigerated units holding eggs and cheese and milk, plus shelves weighed down with canned food.

She grabbed a bag of chips and walked up to the reg-ister. The teenage boy behind the deli counter turned bright red. "Wh-what can I get y—" he swallowed hard and reached up to loosen the neck of his T-shirt "—you."

Even as it occurred to her that maybe she should have gone back to the car for her scarf to wrap around her dance outfit, she enjoyed the appreciation in his eyes. Just because she was done with men didn't mean she didn't still want to be *wanted* by them. That way she could have the pleasure of kicking them all to the curb—except for sweet teenage boys, of course.

"What's the best sandwich you've got?"

His eyes went wide at her question, as if she'd asked him for the answer to how the earth rotated on its axis rather than just about cold cuts and bread. And boy, was he working hard to keep his eyes on her face rather than letting them drop to her breasts, which were pretty much on full display in her outfit. He was so cute that she wanted to leap across the counter to hug him for making her feel pretty again, at least for a few seconds of adolescent adoration.

"Um, I don't know." He swallowed hard again be-fore turning to scan the list of sandwiches handwrit-ten on the board behind him. "Maybe the Muffuletta?"

"Sounds good." She put down the chips on the counter as he started to ring her up. "I'll also take the strongest cup of coffee you can brew."

Who knew how much longer she'd be out driving these farm roads before she found a place to stay for the night? She did have the rental car for an entire month, after all.

He took her money with a shaking hand and when she asked, "Could you tell me where the bathroom is?" he dropped it all on the floor, then hit his head on the open register drawer when he went to pick it up.

Clearly not trusting himself to speak this time, he simply knelt on the floor and pointed toward the back of the building with a shaky hand. Lori figured it was a good idea to give him a break while he made her sandwich; she'd hate for him to slice off the tip of a finger with the meat cutter just because she was standing too close in barely there spandex and glitter.

After quickly taking care of business, she looked at herself in the mirror and would have laughed if she hadn't been so horrified by the mess she found in the reflection. With quick and efficient professionalism she fixed her hair and makeup. She'd always subscribed to the idea that if you looked good, you felt good, but today she had a feeling mascara and lip gloss weren't going to fix much of anything.

After leaving the bathroom, she took a few moments to look around a little bit. On second glance, the General Store was pretty cute inside, a little farm "superstore" with groceries and clothes and chicken feed, clearly all of equal importance to the people who lived here. One table had a Local Authors sign on it and she stopped to scan the books of poetry, novels and a couple of non-fiction tomes on farming techniques. The books gave her a sense of the community that this store supported, likely made up of farmers and their families who had been here for generations.

She'd been part of the dancing community for so long she hadn't ever looked for any other world to belong to. Especially not when Sullivan family events with her mother and seven siblings were frequent enough to take up any free time she had.

But now, even the thought of dancing made her sick to her stomach. Her ex had wooed her with dancing… and then betrayed her with it. Once upon a time, she'd danced for herself, for the pure joy it had given her. Until these past few months, when she'd been little more than Victor's puppet, dancing to try to please him. By the time she realized that nothing pleased him, she'd forgotten how to dance for any other reason. And now, it felt as if there was a dead, numb zone inside her where her heart used to be.

She supposed she'd find another community to belong to in time.

Lori was just about to head back to the deli counter to pick up her sandwich when she noticed a large board filled with flyers. She'd always been interested in strangers' lives and devoured biographies as fast as her librarian sister, Sophie, could give them to her. Looking at a community posting board was such a perfect window into lives she'd never live. And the truth was that as she'd driven the short Main Street, she'd been surprised by how cute the town was. The storefronts dripped with old Western charm and she'd even passed a farm stand that looked like a picture out of a magazine.

In the middle of the board was a piece of white paper with the words *Farmhand Needed* in a strong, clearly masculine hand. Not for one second of her life had she ever thought about living or working on a farm. For her entire life, she'd known exactly what she was and what she would be: a dancer.

Only, since she wasn't going to dance anymore, why not try something completely different, something that could very well turn out to be her second calling?

Maybe if she had gotten more than a dozen hours of sleep all week, she might have taken a clearer, more coolheaded look at the decision she was making.

Because she wasn't looking for trouble. She swore she wasn't.

The thing was, for the first time in a very long time, Lori felt a stirring of excitement. Of anticipation.

And a thrill that felt a little bit like fear.

She'd always liked the scary rides at the amusement park, and had been the one to drag her siblings to horror movies. But what could possibly be scary about working as a farmhand?

Especially when she'd already decided she was going to be the best damn farmhand the world had ever seen. Not to try to please anyone else, but to please *herself,* and to know that at the end of a long day on the farm, she'd done good work that she could be proud of.

Lori ripped the ad off the board and put it down in front of the deli boy. She was impulsive, but she wasn't stupid, so she asked him, "Do you know the guy who posted this? Is he a nice man?"

The boy nodded. "Sure, Grayson is nice."

Lori liked the sound of that name. *Grayson*. Probably some old farmer like the grandfather she'd seen on the sidewalk—someone who'd been married for fifty years and needed extra help with his chickens and cows. She had no idea what that help would entail, but she'd always been a fast learner.

She grinned and asked, "Can you tell me how to get to his farm?"

As he made his way across his thousand acres of land, Grayson Tyler knew this was just the kind of day he liked best—quiet, and filled with backbreaking work from sunup to sundown.

When he'd bought this Pescadero farm three years ago, the barn had been on the verge of becoming firewood and the farmhouse had been a mice-infested shell. A hundred and fifty years ago the first landowner here had started to work this land and it'd had a good run for many decades. But the latest generation had been more interested in their fancy cars and IPOs than the farm their great-great-great-grandfather had spent his life cultivating.

Grayson had spent seven days a week for the past three years bringing the farm back to life. His family had thought he was out of his mind when he'd moved from New York City to what they called "the middle of nowhere," even though San Francisco was only an hour away. Not that he'd been to the city, though. He knew too many people who flew between New York and San Francisco on a regular basis. There were too many potential opportunities to meet someone from his past.

That was one of the great things about a farm: the past didn't matter. All that mattered was the animals that were hungry now, and the future you could build one plowed field, one well-fed cow, at a time.

His horse nickered as the farmhouse came into view. "Yeah, boy, we're home," he said as he patted his horse.

Earlier that morning he had started working on rebuilding the chicken coop, so right now his chickens were in the field at the front of his house.

After putting the tack away and turning his horse out to pasture he got busy hammering in one of the final two-by-sixes for a new roost in the chicken coop. Just then he heard the sound of a car engine. His house and the coop were far enough from the road that he couldn't hear the traffic heading to Pescadero, which meant this car was coming up his drive.

Grayson gritted his teeth at the unexpected interruption. People in town knew by now not to drop by without letting him know ahead of time. Only once in a blue moon would a delivery truck come by with a package from New York.

He put down his hammer and turned to deal with whoever had come uninvited, although he didn't recognize the car. The sun was shining on the windshield so he couldn't see the driver's face, but through the open driver's-side window he saw a lock of long, dark hair blow out.

A woman? What was a woman doing at his farm?

Damn it, this was the last thing he wanted to deal with—some tourist who must have gotten lost on the way to the only bed-and-breakfast in town and was coming to get directions.

His chickens weren't used to being out around cars and the stranger was coming up the long dirt drive so fast that one of his prize Buff Orpington hens squawked and opened her wings to get away from the vehicle. Unfortunately, the chicken was nearly fileted under the spinning tires when the driver swerved to the left to avoid hitting her…and then crashed her car into one of his brand-new fence posts.

Two

The car door flew open and the driver got out. "Oh, my God, I'm so sorry! That chicken came out of nowhere. I'll fix your fence."

Grayson heard what she said, but he couldn't manage a response. Not when he couldn't believe his eyes.

He'd never seen a woman this beautiful in all his life. Long, dark hair spilled down over her nearly bare shoulders to her waist, and her big eyes, high cheekbones and full, red mouth were every man's wet dream. She was wearing something tight and soft looking and in the sunlight it was almost as if she were naked with every one of her spectacular curves on display.

And those legs...even though she wasn't particularly tall they went on forever, ending in spike heels that had no place whatsoever on a farm.

Shit. What the hell was wrong with him? Even if it had been a while since he'd taken a woman to bed, he'd never had any problems controlling his reaction to one.

"Who are you?"

She blinked up at him and simply stared for a few moments, before her gorgeous lips finally curved up into a smile.

Grayson silently instructed his heart to keep beating, his chest to keep pumping air. He just needed to survive the next few minutes, send her on her way and then his life could go back to the way it needed to be.

Quiet.

Simple.

Completely devoid of gorgeous women with smiles that knocked him flat.

She was clutching a piece of paper in her hand and she uncrumpled it before answering, "The new farmhand, I hope."

Another man might have laughed at her ridiculous statement.

He didn't.

"Who put you up to this?"

She frowned. "No one." She took a step toward him and he nearly took a step backward in response to all those luscious curves coming at him. "I'm here to apply for the job." She smiled again. "My name is Lori. Lori Sullivan."

Was she really serious? He schooled himself to forget how pretty she was as he studied her earnest expression.

Crap. It looked like she was. Which meant that instead of only wasting five minutes of his day, it was likely going to take him a good half hour to get her out of here.

"Is Grayson around somewhere?" She looked past him, expecting to see someone else.

"I'm Grayson."

Her eyes widened. "Why aren't you older?"

He had no idea how to respond to that. Not, of course, that he had much of an idea how to respond to any of the conversation he'd had thus far with the stunning woman who had blown into his life without even the slightest hint of warning.

Instead of answering her strange question, he told her, "My ad wasn't a joke."

"I'm not joking," she said with a stubborn tilt of her chin.

His heart raced again from nothing more than seeing the flush in her cheeks while she stood her ground in front of him.

"Look, I've got a lot of work to take care of today before the sun sets." He gave a pointed look at the fence post. "Like fixing the post you smashed into, for one."

Anyone else would have left by then, given the way he was snarling at her, but did this beautiful woman get the hint and get back in her car to leave him the hell alone?

No.

Instead of leaving, she took another step toward him on the most gorgeous pair of legs he'd ever seen in his life. "I can help you."

He made himself sweep a hard, unimpressed look over her, even though in his previous life he would have drunk her in with extreme pleasure.

"What experience do you have working on a farm?"

When she bit her lower lip, his blood pressure shot so high he could actually hear it rushing in his ears over the ongoing complaints of his chickens, who were still in high excitement over the car, the crash and the very unexpected visitor in her glittering outfit.

"Well," she said slowly, "none yet. But I'm very determined."

He laughed out loud at that, a rusty sound that held absolutely no pleasure in it.

"Determination isn't going to get the new coop finished or the fence post replaced. I need someone who can actually do the work I need them to do." Jesus, he couldn't believe he was actually standing here debating her qualifications with her. "You can't be my new farmhand."

She looked momentarily distraught as she stared at him and then back down at his want ad clutched in her fist. He could almost hear the gears churning in her pretty head before she nodded as if she'd made a decision.

"Tell me something you need done and I'll do it. Right now, in front of you, so you can see that I'm serious." She faced him squarely. "I want this job, Grayson."

The sound of his name on her lips, her slightly husky voice playing out the vowels a little longer than the other letters, made his gut clench tight. He didn't like the way he was reacting to her.

Didn't like the fact that he was reacting at all.

He looked down pointedly at her shoes. "You're telling me that you're going to get to work on my farm in those?"

She glanced down at her sparkly high heels as if

she'd forgotten she was wearing them. How, he wondered, could she have possibly forgotten when her feet had to be killing her?

She shrugged. "Sure. So what do you want me to do?"

He scowled as he scanned his property for something she could try to do without hurting herself—he wasn't interested in wasting the time it would take getting her to the doctor if she got injured. Glancing at his watch, it looked as if the thirty-minute delay had just turned into an hour. At least.

First chance she got, Lori was going to give that kid at the General Store a piece of her mind. Why hadn't he told her that Grayson was not only young, but also one of the most ridiculously good-looking and virile men she'd ever set eyes on?

Not, of course, that she'd asked, but she could guarantee that if the sandwich maker had been a teenage girl, she wouldn't have forgotten to mention those very important details.

Only, it didn't matter that he was good-looking, did it? Not when she was completely done with men.

Done.

She didn't trust them anymore, unless she was related to them. They were all cheating, manipulative scum. Still, it wasn't exactly easy to remember all of that when she was standing in front of two hundred pounds of muscle, piercing brown eyes and a square jaw liberally dusted with dark stubble. Any woman in her right mind would want to reach out to run her finger-tips over that jaw right before she leaned in for a ki—

Lori forcefully shook the thought out of her head. Okay, so maybe the second she set eyes on the magnificent *Grayson* she should have climbed right back into her car and gotten the heck out of here. After leaving her insurance information for the busted fence, of course. But it had felt like every word out of his mouth was a challenge.

And Lori had never been able to back down from a challenge.

"So," she said, "what's first on your list?"

Just as she asked the question, a chicken decided to peck at one of the sparkles on her shoes. She tried to step out of the way, but it just followed her and pecked harder at her foot.

"Pick up the hen and put her in the coop."

She knew the joke was supposed to be on her, that he thought she was going to screw this up, but how hard could it be to pick up a chicken?

"Sure, no problem."

As Lori squatted and reached for the small body, the chicken was so focused on trying to eat her shoe-sparkle that she didn't have any trouble getting her hands around its middle. Only, just as she was about to actually lift the bird off the ground, it looked up at her with alarm, squawked its displeasure, then wriggled out of her hands and started running in the opposite direction.

She didn't think before muttering a curse word as she stood up to go after the hen. "Come here, you," she said in what was supposed to be a soothing voice, but was tinged with more than a little frustration. "Time to go back into your coop."

When she was only a couple of feet from the bird, she made herself wait until it focused on something crawling on the drive before reaching for it again. But it was smarter about her intention this time, and before she could even get a hand on its feathers, it let out another loud cry, then half flew, half ran away from her.

Lori brushed her hair out of her eyes. She was sweating now and had dirt smudged across the front of her top and along her tights. But she wasn't even close to giving up. No, sir. If Grayson thought this was enough to send her packing, he was sorely mistaken.

She was already heading after the chicken again when Grayson cut her off at the pass. "I can't let you upset her any more than you already have. It'll throw off her laying cycle."

"I didn't mean to upset her," Lori protested, immediately feeling guilty about having done irreparable damage to the chicken's egg production.

He reached down to pick up the hen, and rather than reach for its tail or wings, he cupped his hands in a gentle V on either side of its body and lifted it. With one hand firmly under the chicken, he used the other to hold it close to his body as he carried it into the coop.

Well, she thought with more than a little irritation, he could have told her how to do that *before* she screwed up the hen's life. While his back was turned, she bent down and reached for another chicken. This time around, it was a different—and much happier—story as she scooped up the hen and carried it over to the coop.

Grayson turned around just as she was about to put the chicken inside. "What the hell are you doing?"

She stopped right where she was and gathered the bird a little closer to her chest. The warmth of the plump body against her helped soften the sting of Grayson's fierce glare.

"I figured you wanted all the chickens inside," she said in a voice pitched low so that she wouldn't spook her new feathered friend. "Don't you?"

"Yes," he bit out, but his frown deepened rather than softening. "How'd you pick her up?"

Wasn't it obvious? "I watched what you did."

He moved his glare from her to the chicken and she felt a little sorry for bringing the bird into this.

"Fine. Put her in the coop and then collect the rest. I've got to see how badly your car damaged my fence."

This time, Lori was the one scowling at Grayson's too-broad, far-too-muscular back. So much for getting a thank-you or maybe even a little bit of praise for how easily she'd managed to rectify things with the chickens. It was, she thought, a very good reminder that it was never a good idea to do something to try to please a man.

Still, she didn't let her frustration with him impact her gentle handling of that first chicken. Or the next dozen of them. Unfortunately, even though she knew what she was doing now, it didn't mean the chickens necessarily felt like cooperating. And she had to admit her heels weren't exactly the best footwear for a muddy, gravelly, grassy farm, as the spikes kept getting stuck in the sod. Fortunately, she spotted a plastic dish with what looked like dried corn in it that the chickens seemed to have an inordinate interest in. Picking up the dish, she shook the "treats" and was thrilled when the rest of the chickens came running at top speed toward the coop. Moments later she had them all safely inside.

All but one, darn it. This one responded neither to the treats nor to the actions of the rest of its chicken friends.

After the hen dodged her one too many times, Lori kicked off her shoes and, with renewed determination, used her years of quietly gliding across a stage to stalk the chicken.

"Aha! Gotcha!" she exclaimed when she finally had it safe and sound in her arms. The chicken let out a matching sound that had her laughing out loud. "Had a good time messing with me, did you?"

She was almost at the coop when she looked up and saw Grayson staring at her with such an expression of shock that she almost stumbled with the chicken in her arms.

"What's wrong?" She looked down at her feet. "Is there a snake in the grass?" She couldn't keep the horror from her voice as she went completely still.

"No," he said quickly, "there isn't a snake."

"Thank God." She let out a harsh breath, utterly exhausted from the past twenty minutes of chasing chickens on top of her red-eye flight and sleepless night. Heading again for the coop, she took every barefoot step only after careful consideration of the ground in front of her. "I'll just go put her in the coop and then you can tell me what you want me to do next."

Three

Next? She wanted him to tell her what to do *next?*

Get the hell off his property—and out of his life, taking her laughter with her—that's what he wanted her to do next. At least, it was what he should have wanted.

But for some strange reason he didn't understand, Grayson couldn't bring himself to put her back in her car and order her to leave. Plus, after her rough start, she'd actually done a good job with the chickens and he couldn't justify penalizing her for that.

She shut the coop door for the last time, then walked straight over to the hose and washed off her hands before wiping her hands on her hips and turning back to him. Unfortunately, that drew his attention back to her spectacular figure. Not, of course, that his attention had ever wavered from it. His heart would have to stop before he could ignore the fact that he had a live, in-the-flesh pinup girl on his farm.

One who wanted to be his new farmhand.

Damn it, he needed to figure out a way to get her

to leave before she could get under his skin any more than she already had. Because even in her ridiculous outfit, streaked now with dirt, she was still heartbreakingly beautiful. And, given what he knew of women, she seemed to be shockingly low maintenance when it came to dirt and animals. Why wasn't she losing it over the state of her clothes, her torn tights or the fact that her heels were now covered with wet dirt and grass stains? Clearly, something must have gone really wrong in her life for her to think this was a step up.

Unfortunately, it also wasn't difficult to recognize in her an urge to leave her old life behind and start over someplace where no one would ever think to look for her.

Because that was just what he'd done himself after his wife had died three years ago. And for the past thirty-six months his farm in Pescadero had been his refuge from the past and from ever having to think about what had happened to his wife...or his role in it.

Damn it, he didn't want this woman to think he cared, but he needed to know. "Are you in any danger?"

"Danger?" She looked at him as though it was the strangest question in the world.

"Are you hiding from someone who's trying to hurt you? Is that why you're here?"

A flash of emotion crossed her face before she masked it with a smile that he didn't buy for a second. "No, of course not."

She moved like a prima ballerina even while chasing chickens, but obviously she wasn't an actress because she couldn't lie worth a damn.

"Then should I be expecting an angry husband or boyfriend to show up with his shotgun loaded, demanding to know what I'm doing with his woman?"

"No." She all but yelled the word at him before taking a deep breath—one that made it hard for him to keep his gaze from dropping to her chest. "I'm not in trouble. No one is after me. I just want a job working on your farm."

"Why?"

This time she didn't so much as hesitate before saying, "Because it looks like fun."

Okay, so she clearly wasn't going to tell him the truth. But while he didn't believe for a minute that working on a farm had been her lifelong dream, at least he felt fairly confident that she didn't have an angry guy on her tail.

Still, she had to go. And he had just the plan to make it happen.

"I need to see how you do with some basic farmhouse chores."

He had to give her credit; even though she had to know exactly the kind of chores he was talking about—ones that included toilet brushes and floor mops—she didn't let her smile waver.

"That sounds great," she said, though it was clearly anything but great. But instead of following him into the house, she added, "And if I do a good job with those chores, you'll give me the job?"

Stubborn didn't even begin to describe this woman. Working not to feel too much respect for her determination, he studied her carefully for a few moments. Her nails were long, and while there was dirt under them now, they were well manicured, and her hands were soft and smooth. He'd bet all one thousand of his acres that she hadn't done a lick of cleaning in her entire life. With those legs, and that body, she'd probably spent it as some rich man's pampered mistress.

"If you make it all the way through the list of farm-house chores," he said as easily as he could despite the twisting in his gut at the thought of Lori in another man's bed, naked and breathless as she came for him, "you can have the job on probation." He turned away before she could see the reaction he was having to her.

"Probation?"

He shot her a look over his shoulder. "One hour at a time, Lori. That's how we'll take it before I know whether or not I can count on you."

After he quickly told her what he'd be paying her for each hour that she managed to keep the job, she said, "You can count on me," then blew past him and into his living room. And then, suddenly, she was making a happy little surprised sound.

"Oh, look at her." Lori rushed over to his mangy, ratty old former barn cat, who was nearly done with her ninth life. "She's beautiful!"

"Are you sure we're looking at the same cat?" Frankly, he was amazed Lori had even been able to tell the thing was female.

"She can hear you, you know," she said in a chiding tone, and then, "What's her name?"

He wanted to remind Lori that she was gunning for the role of farmhand, not new best friend who would chat with him all day long. He liked his solitude, damn it. Still, he'd already figured out that not answering one of her pointless questions wouldn't make her stop asking them.

"Mo."

She raised an eyebrow. "Your cat's name is Mo?"

"That's right."

She turned back to the cat and cooed as she stroked it. "How could anyone call such a pretty little girl such an ugly boy's name." She scowled up at him. "One of the Three Stooges, no less!" Again, she focused on the cat. "You were waiting for me to come here, weren't you, so that I could give you love...and a good name."

Love. The word hit him hard right in the center of his solar plexus, knocking the air from his lungs. He thought he'd known about love once upon a time, but he hadn't known a damn thing about it at all. The only thing he knew for sure now was that his life was better off without it.

His voice was fiercer than it needed to be as he said, "You're not going to rename my cat."

But it was as though she couldn't hear him...even though he knew she had—he was standing only a handful of feet away from her and the cat.

"I've got the perfect new name for you!" She looked so excited that the cat actually raised its tired head and blinked at her. "Sweetpea."

Grayson refused to think any of this was cute. "Mo," he repeated. "Its name is Mo."

"*It* is a *she*. And *her* name is Sweetpea." She bent

over to press kisses to the cat's head, then promptly started sneezing.

"You're allergic to cats." The statement came out as an accusation. He told himself he didn't care if he was being too harsh with her. He didn't want her here, anyway.

"No, I'm not." She sneezed again, but continued petting the cat. "Your house must be dusty."

It wasn't, but he said, "Good thing cleaning it is part of my farmhand's job description, then, isn't it? I'll show you where the cleaning supplies are so you can get started."

She seemed to deflate a little bit at the housecleaning reminder, but instead of leaving the cat's side, she said, "How old is she?"

He'd worked with bulls for long enough to know that sometimes it was easier to wait for them to come to him than it was to try to shove them into the breeding chute. He leaned against the doorjamb and tried not to notice how pretty Lori looked sitting cross-legged on the floor petting the cat. As the sun streaming in through the window hit her hair just right, the glossy, dark brown strands held as many shades of red as the leaves on the maple tree in the fall.

"Old."

Her expression didn't change at his terse response. She didn't shrink back, or even look particularly irritated with him. Irrationally, it made him want to see what he could do to get a response out of her.

"How old?"

"I don't know."

"Well, then, when did you get her?"

"I found her in the barn when I bought the place." Since he knew the question was coming, he added, "Three years ago." He looked down at the animal that had purred its way into his heart, even though he'd refused to have one again. "She wouldn't leave."

"You're lucky she stayed with you."

"Lucky?" He had to laugh at that, a rough and jagged sound that held no joy at all. "She'll only eat wet food, she coughs up hairballs the size of tennis balls and she sheds all over everything."

"I've never had a pet."

Lori's pout only served to make her lips look more kissable. Helplessly, he found himself wondering what she would taste like if he ran his tongue all along her full lower lip. What would she do if he bit lightly at the flesh? Would she shiver and moan against his mouth?

He had to forcefully shake the sensual visions out of his head before he could focus on what she was saying. "…Mom always said eight kids were more than enough to contend with."

"You have seven brothers and sisters?"

Crap, he hadn't meant to ask her anything personal, but the question had slipped out in his surprise at what she'd just said. If she had all those brothers, why wasn't one of them out here dragging her back to her real life?

She smiled up at him from where she was sitting, still cuddling his cat, and yet again, he felt the beautiful force of her smile in every cell.

"Seven siblings and a whole bunch more cousins. I've got family pretty much everywhere."

The word *family* slapped into his heart like she'd let loose a taut rubber band against it, just the way it had when she'd been talking about *love*.

What the hell was he doing? He couldn't make the mistake of letting her think they were going to be friends. *If* she managed to make it through the rest of the day, she wasn't going to stay long. As quickly as she'd blown in, she'd blow out again. He couldn't make the mistake of getting attached to her.

Which was why he knew better than to let Lori get attached to anything here, either.

"Mo is going to die soon," he told her in a matter-of-fact tone. "Real soon."

Lori lifted wide eyes to him, then immediately pulled the cat all the way onto her lap, which prompted a fit of rapid-fire sneezes. Of course, good old Mo was so old and tired that she barely reacted to the loud sounds as she settled deeper into Lori's arms.

"How can you say that about your own cat? It's like you don't even have a heart."

He preferred it that way. Not having a heart meant nothing could hurt him again.

Grayson didn't care one bit for worrying about this beautiful stranger becoming attached to his dying cat... or to him.

"She has leukemia," he said, his voice gentler now simply because, for all that he might want her to think it, he wasn't a monster. "The vet expected her to go months ago. He doesn't know how she's managed to hang on this long."

From out of nowhere, he was struck with the thought

that maybe Mo had held on until Lori came—that she'd needed a softhearted woman to make a fuss over her in her final days.

But that was crazy. As totally, completely nuts as Lori actually thinking she could be his farmhand.

He pushed away from the door. "Time to clean."

Four

Lori had never thought she'd need to call on her dance training to clean a toilet or make a bed, but in order to clean Grayson's house perfectly she'd needed every ounce of the precision and focus that she used in her choreography, rehearsals and performances.

She washed her hands, then took a step back to the doorway to survey her work. The sink, tub and shower sparkled the way they would have in a TV ad; the mirror didn't have a single smudge or speck of dust on it; and she'd folded the fresh towels she'd found in the linen closet the way they did in high-end hotels. Grayson, fortunately, wasn't a particularly messy man, which was surprising considering how much dirt there was all around him on the farm. And while the farmhouse hadn't been changed from what she guessed was turn-of-the-century architecture, the bathrooms were gorgeous and completely luxurious.

What she wouldn't give for a soak in the claw-foot tub, she thought as she stretched out her back and legs.

But she could only imagine what Grayson would do if he found her in one of the tubs. Then again, he'd been so grumpy from the moment she showed up on his farm that it was more than a little tempting to mess with him like that.

Only, it would end up messing with her, too. Because if the way her body was heating up at just the thought of Grayson finding her taking a bath was anything to go by, she had a bad feeling that being naked in one of his tubs would lead to nakedness in other places... like his bed.

And that she'd like it too much for a woman who had sworn off men and relationships.

Forcefully pushing away the heady vision of the two of them naked together, she walked out into his bedroom and ran her hand over the dark blue bedcover. Everything in his room was simple. Clean. And purely masculine.

Lori left the master bedroom and slowly made her way through the rest of the house to verify that her work had been top-notch. She'd not only swept and mopped the floors, cleaned both bathrooms and made both the master and the guest beds, she'd wiped down the refrigerator inside and out and cleaned the oven, too, for sheer shock value. Lord knew, she had been shocked by just how toxic the oven cleaner smelled. Fortunately, she'd been wearing thick yellow gloves at the time, so she hadn't seared the skin off her hands.

Cleaning a farmhouse wasn't the most enjoyable job she'd ever had, but at least she felt the satisfaction of a job well done. Sure, it wasn't a job she'd ever planned

on doing, but she'd always figured that if she was going
to do something, she should take the time to do it right.

She'd kept her shoes off and had taken her tights
off, as well, when they'd started to shred at the knees,
so that she was left wearing only the stretchy pink top
that came to the middle of her thighs like a miniskirt. It
was just as well, considering what sweaty work cleaning was. She was just stretching the bodice away from
her skin to fan herself when Grayson walked into the
kitchen through the back door.

He stopped dead in his tracks as he stared at her in
her barely there outfit, the top pulled halfway down
the swell of her breasts. She dropped the fabric like it
was on fire, but the damage had already been done. It
wasn't as bad as if he'd found her in the bathtub, she
supposed. But that was little comfort when he was looking at her with such intense heat that she couldn't believe she wasn't spontaneously combusting right where
she stood.

It was only natural in a tense situation like this that
she'd fall back on years of being a motormouth. "I was
just about to come get you so that you could take a look
at what I've done. I cleaned the whole house, and I can
take you back to look at the bathrooms or you could just
stick your head into the oven to see how I even clean—"

"What happened to your pants?" His words sounded
like the gravel she'd driven over to get to his farmhouse.

"My tights," she corrected as she swiped her tongue
across her suddenly dry lips, "were a mess after the
chickens, so I took them off."

She realized now that maybe that hadn't been her

best decision of the day as she looked down and saw how much bare skin she was showing Grayson. As a dancer, she'd long ago gotten over feeling self-conscious about showing off her body. It was not only a part of her job, but frankly, it was also a large part of her identity as a pretty, desirable woman.

Only, she wasn't dancing here in Grayson's kitchen... and she didn't want to make him want her.

At least, she silently corrected, she *shouldn't* want him to want her.

Grayson's jaw was tense as he shifted his gaze from her bare legs to her face. He hadn't ogled her, clearly didn't even want to be looking at her bare skin, and yet, with nothing but that one quick glance she felt as if she'd stripped away all of her clothes rather than just her tights.

"Don't you have other clothes with you?"

"In my car," she told him, "but I didn't want to waste any time changing into them."

At her honest answer, he sighed, looking momentarily worn out. And more than a little pained. She also refused to drop her gaze any lower than his face. That was gorgeous enough for her teeter-tottering peace of mind. If she let herself appreciate his broad shoulders, or his large hands, or his well-muscled hips and thighs—

Ugh, she needed to stop letting her hormones run away with her. Why couldn't he have been a grizzled old farmer?

Because if there was one thing that Lori had never excelled at, it was self-control.

She thought he muttered a curse—one she agreed with heartily—before he said, "Show me what you've done."

Working to fight her awareness of him as she took him through the house, room by room—especially in the bedrooms, where she couldn't believe she actually started blushing—she knew he couldn't fault her on one single aspect of the job she'd done.

Then again, Victor shouldn't have been able to fault her dancing or choreography, either, but somehow he'd managed to do it, anyway, hadn't he?

When they made it back to the kitchen and Grayson was just closing the oven after running his finger along the inside walls and having it come up clean, rather than covered in grease, she said, "I did a good job." It wasn't a question; it was a statement.

He turned back to her, his expression utterly unreadable. "You did."

"So, where are my quarters going to be? That cottage I saw out back?" She tried not to sigh as she said, "I'm guessing I'll need to clean that, too, won't I?"

He looked surprised by her questions. "You don't have anywhere to stay?"

She gave him a surprised look of her own. "Of course I don't. I figured a farmhand would need to live on-site to help with all the—" she had no idea at all, really, about what the list of chores would be, apart from cleaning and dealing with chickens "—farming." When her comment fell into a weighted silence, she said, "If you don't need anything else right now, I'll go get my things out of my car and take them to the cottage."

"You can't stay in the cottage."

She stopped halfway to the door. "You can't kick me out. We had an agreement. If I did a good job with the chores, then I could have the job." She lifted her chin. "And we both know that I did a kick-ass cleaning job."

He ran his hand through his hair, leaving the dark strands standing on end. Darn it, even that was sexy. Clearly she sucked at being immune to gorgeous men, even when it was imperative for her mental and emotional health.

"The reason you can't stay in the cottage," he gritted out, one tense word a time, "is because it doesn't have a roof on it."

It only took a second for alarm to hit her. "I can't stay here. In this house." She swallowed hard. "With you."

Without saying another word to her, he picked up the phone and made a quick call to what sounded like a local bed-and-breakfast. He was polite enough to the person he was speaking to, but when he hung up a minute later, the phone slammed so hard into its cradle that the whole thing vibrated.

When all she could do was shake her head at the idea of sleeping here with Grayson, he said, "If you can't stand the thought of staying here with me, you're welcome to the barn. Mo used to like it just fine."

God, what had happened to her life? All afternoon, he had been trying to get her to give up on her farmhand goal, but she was far too stubborn to give in. Only, she hadn't counted on sleeping one wall away from a man she knew next to nothing about besides the fact that he was grumpy, and gorgeous, and didn't much seem to like her.

But she'd already walked away from one job this week. She couldn't stomach leaving another one so soon. Besides, she was the one in charge of her life, damn it, and right now she was hell-bent on trying her hand at farming.

So she was going to stay.

And didn't people always say that everything looked better in the morning?

"While the barn sounds simply lovely, I'll bring my bags into the guest room."

At least she knew the sheets were clean, because she'd had the privilege of changing them herself. And even though any man with a hint of manners would have insisted on carrying in her heavy suitcase, Grayson let her drag it from her car and up the porch steps all by herself.

Five

Grayson couldn't believe the way things had turned out. Not only had Lori dealt well with the chickens, but she'd also cleaned his house as if she'd been working as a maid at a five-star hotel her entire life. He'd searched every corner for dust, had prayed for so much as a pillow to be out of place, but he hadn't been able to find one single thing to complain about.

And now, based on that stupid deal he'd made with her, he had to let her stay.

He hadn't shared a house with a woman in three years, and had been perfectly happy to have the farmhouse to himself until today, when a beautiful stranger had blown into his life like a hurricane. And now he was going to have to put her up until she found another place…or until she gave up on her ridiculous farmhand dream. Frankly, at this point, he wasn't sure which was going to come first. Hell, he hadn't thought she'd last this long.

He silently cursed as he watched her struggle with

her bags and had to forcefully push away the urge to help her. The last thing he needed to do was to make things easy for her. Or, God forbid, let her think he actually wanted her here.

Just because she was the most beautiful thing he'd ever seen didn't mean that he was softening toward her. The exact opposite, in fact. All that beauty made him wary, made him remember another beautiful woman....

He couldn't go there, couldn't fall back into memories of his wife. Not tonight. Not when he needed to stay completely on his toes to make sure Lori didn't get under his skin any deeper.

The best thing would be to keep his distance from her. Completely. But after the work she'd done all day, he knew he had to at least feed her. Which was going to mean sharing a meal together on top of everything else, damn it.

He heard the water go on in the guest bathroom and scrunched his eyes tight to try to force away the vision of Lori stripping off her clothes and getting into the bathtub. Bad, bad, bad. Those kinds of thoughts were evil. He knew it...and yet he was still a man, with a man's needs. Needs that he'd gone out of his way to ignore for three years, with only a few random moments of stolen pleasure along the way when he'd known there was no chance of any serious connection or lingering attachments to the women he'd slept with.

He was covered in dirt, too, and would have gone into his master bath to take his own shower, but the thought of being only a wall away from Lori while both of them were naked did things to him that he couldn't deal with rationally. On a curse, he went back outside to use the outdoor shower he'd installed at the far end of the barn. It was a cold night and showering outside didn't sound even remotely good. But it was either that or slowly lose his mind at every sound he heard while thinking about Lori in the tub with soap and—

Shit. He needed to stop thinking about her like that.

He stripped off his shirt and threw it on the porch, unbuckling his belt as he walked past his animals. Even they seemed to look confused by what he was doing, coming out in the dark to wash off in their space.

How, he wondered as he yanked off his pants and boots and hung them over the wooden wall he'd erected to give the outdoor shower a little privacy, could a person cause so much havoc in just one short afternoon? Was it because she had so many siblings? Was she that afraid of being invisible that she went out of her way to be louder, more stubborn and just plain more *there* than a normal person?

As he scrubbed himself hard with the bar of soap, keeping the water just this side of cold so that his growing arousal couldn't come fully to life, his stomach started growling. He cranked off the shower and shook his hair out like a dog before grabbing one of the towels he always kept in a nearby container for just such an occasion. He'd been planning on a steak tonight, and grilling up some vegetables with it. If she didn't like red meat, too bad.

When he was fully dry, he pulled his jeans back on and stuck his feet into his boots. He still couldn't believe she'd been running around with bare feet. City girls like her should be afraid to get their feet dirty, or mess up their pedicures or, God forbid, get a cut from something sharp like the edge of a rock. Pampered girls also shouldn't know how to clean.

The only way he could deal with having Lori around, even just for the short time it would take for her to give up her crazy plan and leave him alone again, was to view her as a spoiled woman out for a lark in the country for a few days.

He wished like hell that it wasn't so hard to ignore the evidence to the contrary.

Dinner. That was what he'd focus on now, rather than the fact that she was probably also drying off from her bath and slathering her toned and smooth legs with lotion.

Grayson took off his muddy boots on the porch, stepped into the kitchen via the side door and stopped so quickly that it slammed into his back. "What are you doing?"

Lori was supposed to be in her room, damn it, not already out of the bath and in his kitchen looking and smelling better than anything he could remember. Her dark hair was still wet, falling past her shoulders almost to her hips as she stood at his kitchen island chopping a bell pepper. She'd put on a pair of jeans that did shocking things to her ass, and even though her T-shirt shouldn't have been the least bit sexy, he now realized that anything she wore would be sexy. Hell, he could have given her a burlap sack to wear and he'd still be salivating over the curve of her neck, the bright paint on her toes, the spark in her big blue eyes that never quit.

"Making dinner."

She said it without turning to look at him, clearly still pissed off at their conversation about where she was going to stay. And possibly the fact that he'd been a jerk about not helping her with her bags.

He hadn't expected her to clean his house *and* make him dinner tonight, but now that she was, he certainly wasn't going to complain. Unless, of course, she didn't actually know how to make a decent meal, and was just doing this to get back at him.

"Do you know how to cook?"

She sighed, deep and long, at his question, seeming to be at least as irritated with him now as he'd been with her earlier. "I wouldn't be making dinner if I didn't." She'd found the steak he'd had marinating and sliced it up, along with the vegetables. "I thought I'd make a stir-fry."

When he didn't respond, when he couldn't seem to get his throat to work right, when he couldn't seem to do anything but stand there like a fool in the doorway and stare at her, she finally turned to him.

"Look, I'm starved and I didn't think it would be a problem if I made us din—"

Her words fell away and her eyes widened as she finally looked at him. As her gaze moved over him, she licked her lips and he nearly groaned aloud at the sight of her tongue coming out to wet her gorgeous lips. She wasn't wearing makeup anymore, having washed it all off during her bath, and if anything, she was even prettier than she'd been when her lashes had been darkened with mascara and her mouth had been glossy with lip-stick.

"Grayson." His name was little more than a husky breath from her dampened mouth. "You're not wearing your shirt."

He'd completely forgotten that he only had his jeans on, without the top button even done up, for God's sake. Defensively, he told her, "You weren't supposed to be in the kitchen."

"And you weren't supposed to be walking around without your clothes on!" she shot right back.

He shouldn't like the way she looked at him, as though she was barely able to keep herself from reaching out to touch him. But since he wouldn't be able to hide just how much he did like it for more than the next couple of seconds, he finally got his feet to obey the order to move again and headed for his bedroom.

Damn it, he thought as he barely stopped himself from slamming his bedroom door shut, he needed another cold shower even though he'd just gotten out of one. Fat lot of good it did, though, when all it took was one look at Lori, one breath of her hair, her fresh clean skin, one lick of her tongue across her lips, for him to forget every rule he'd lived his life by for the past three years.

Normally, Grayson made it a point to keep his memories deeply buried. Tonight, he deliberately pulled them out and made himself face them. He'd known his wife, Leslie, since college, had fallen for her on the first day of English Lit in freshman year. They were supposed to be the perfect romance, the ideal fit—the finance major and the elegant girl who had grown up in a world where she'd learned how to be the perfect hostess and fund-raiser. She was a woman who never said the wrong thing, who was always there for him for whatever he needed.

Their college years were good, but once they'd graduated and entered the real world, both of them had been miserable. Because even though the world of finance wasn't nearly as interesting as he'd hoped it would be—and he missed being outside for more than the hour it took him to do his daily run through Central Park—he'd worked longer and longer hours at his firm to avoid coming home to her false smiles, to perfectly made dinners he had no appetite for, to one event after another full of people he didn't know…and didn't want to get to know.

Somewhere in there, his perfect wife had begun to drink. Of course, she'd hidden it from him. From everyone. Yes, she'd have the requisite bubbly in her hand at her parties, but to the naked eye, it would look as if she'd barely sipped it all night.

A thousand times over, Grayson wished he'd had the balls to make Leslie sit down and talk with him before things got bad. But she'd been just as good at hiding from the mess of their marriage—and their lives—as he was.

The day the call had come in from the police was forever imprinted in his mind. There had been a crash, just her car on a lonely road. Leslie had been drinking. She'd died on impact. He'd seen a picture of the scene in the paper the next day…and the same bile that had risen in his throat then rose now.

He'd grieved for her, deeply. He was pretty sure they hadn't been in love anymore by the time she'd died. But they'd always been friends, and he'd cared about her happiness, had wished that she'd been able to find some.

Only, so much worse than his grief was the guilt that lingered. Guilt that had never—and would never—go away. If only he'd loved her better, if only he'd been the husband he'd pledged to be, then maybe he would have known about her drinking.

And maybe he could have saved her.

An invisible fist was clenching his gut tightly when Lori hollered, "Dinner's on!"

Grayson's memories were a grim weight deep in his chest as he headed out to the kitchen. His stomach growled again, this time at the incredible smell of the stir-fry Lori had put together. She'd set the small white table by the kitchen window, as well, with his simple white plates and some colorful napkins he'd forgotten he had. Now, as he looked at the bright flowers stitched on the napkins, he remembered that they were a farm-warming gift from the family whose property adjoined his. The teenage daughter had stitched them by hand, she'd informed him with pride. But he'd been too dead inside to appreciate her workmanship.

The table—hell, the entire kitchen—felt too small as Lori served them both. Her scent, her beauty, were everywhere. Even his bad memories didn't seem to be enough to drown them out.

And when he took the first bite of the stir-fry with

rice that she'd put on his plate, it was all he could do to stifle a groan of pleasure. For three years he'd been a bachelor, cooking for himself. He was pretty good with a grill, and during the summer he had an endless supply of fruit and vegetables to fill up on, but everything else was simply fuel. It had been years since he'd eaten anything this good.

They both ate in silence and he was more than a little surprised to watch Lori mow through a plate of food that was nearly as big as his own. Then again, she'd worked her perfect little ass off today, hadn't she?

He was reaching for seconds when she finally broke the silence. "Is your stir-fry okay?" Her question had an edge to it, one that clearly said, *A thank-you wouldn't kill you, bastard.*

But he hadn't asked her to come to his farm. He sure as hell hadn't wanted her to stay. And making dinner hadn't been on her list of chores. So even though her stir-fry was so good that he wanted to drop to his knees and worship at her spatula, all he said was, "It's fine."

She glared at him. "It's not *fine*. It's *great!*"

He couldn't help but be struck by how different this dinner was from the ones he'd shared with Leslie. His wife had been a master of small talk, of filling silences with chatter about weather and gossip and the garden. And she hadn't been able to cook, not in the slightest, so they'd had a personal chef supply them with fresh meals.

He was just about to finish his second helping when Lori stood, took her plate over to the sink and started washing it. Knowing he couldn't stand to be in the same room with her for much longer, Grayson said, "You cooked. I'll deal with the plates."

Instead of taking the hint and going to her bedroom, she shook her head. "I work for you now. It's my job to cook *and* clean."

God, she was stubborn. But if she wanted to add to her list of chores, he wasn't going to stop her. Of course, he needed to remember not to get too used to meals this good, since he was sure she'd be gone and heading back to her pampered real life by lunchtime tomorrow.

But just then, the plate went slipping from her hands and crashed to the floor. She cursed as she quickly bent down to clean up the shards.

Grayson moved to help her, but not quickly enough to stop her from cutting herself on one of the sharp edges of the broken plate. He grabbed her hand as it began to bleed.

"Damn it, Lori, I said I would deal with cleaning up."

She tried to yank her hand back, saying, "It's just a little cut," but he was already pulling her up and running her finger beneath the faucet.

He didn't care how little the cut was, he didn't like to see her hurt, or to know that she'd done it to try to prove a point to him about how hard she could work. "You need to be more careful," he growled as he wrapped a clean dish towel around her little finger and applied pressure to it, "especially when you're tired."

They were standing close enough now that he finally saw the dark smudges beneath her eyes. And given the fact that, for the very first time, she hadn't come back with a quick retort, he knew she had to be exhausted.

"Go to bed, Lori. I'll deal with this mess."

"I'm fine."

The urge to stroke his hand over her cheek to find out if her skin was as soft there as it was on her hands made his voice more gruff than it needed to be as he told her, "The day starts early here on the farm. You need the sleep."

Her full mouth tightened down before she shrugged and said, "You're the boss."

She looked at their hands and he belatedly realized he was still holding hers. He took a step back and let her go. Of course, she couldn't just head to her bedroom; she had to make a pit stop to make a fuss over the cat again, with a promise of making her some "yummy treats" soon. It wasn't until she started sneezing uncontrollably that she finally wished Mo good-night with a kiss to the patchy fur on the cat's forehead.

He purposely kept his mind blank as he cleaned up the floor, did the dishes and then headed into his bedroom to hit the sack. He could hear Lori banging around in her room, knew she was pissed off at him, but he tried not to feel guilty about his behavior. Hell, if she'd been the male college-age kid he'd planned to hire, he wouldn't have been worrying about being nice or trying not to touch his new farmhand. And he sure wouldn't be practically tiptoeing around in his own bedroom because he was worried about waking her up when she obviously needed the rest.

What the hell was wrong with him? How could he have considered letting her stay even for one night? Tomorrow, he decided, one way or another she had to go.

Grayson was just pulling back the covers when he heard something that had him standing stock-still.

Crying.

She was crying, damn it.

Grayson clenched the covers tightly in his fist as his heart—the one he swore he didn't have anymore—broke for her.

He had no idea what, or who, had hurt Lori Sullivan. But given how strong she'd proved herself to be all day long, he knew it had to be bad if it could force her to the point where she couldn't hold back her sobs.

Especially since he knew the last thing she'd want would be for him to hear them.

It took every ounce of his self-control not to go to her, and in the end, the only thing that kept him from leaving his room for hers was the absolute certainty that she would hate for him to see her with her walls down, vulnerable and hurting.

And by the time her bedroom finally fell silent a short while later, Grayson knew he wasn't going to make good on his promise to himself, come tomorrow.

He was going to let her stay.

Six

So much for everything looking better in the morning.

Because even though Grayson had let her sleep in past sunrise, when Lori got out of bed to deal with the call of nature she was shocked by how much everything hurt. She'd danced for hours every day for nearly her entire life, yet she still ached from the cleaning and stooping and kneeling on the floor. All for someone who didn't appreciate any of it, and who clearly had never uttered the words *thank you* before.

Why had she ever thought it was a good idea to start over in Pescadero? Instead of renting a car at the airport and driving into the boonies, she could have hopped onto another plane and headed off to Hawaii. She could be lying on the beach right now sipping drinks under an umbrella with the sound of soothing waves lulling away her sadness.

Only, she'd always hated lying around on the beach. Besides, she would have gone absolutely crazy in Hawaii with all of those happy couples on their honeymoons and anniversaries walking hand in hand and kissing in the moonlight.

She hadn't bothered to blow-dry her hair last night after her bath. She could jump into another quick bath and blow-dry, but why should she when she was just going to get all dirty and sweaty again cleaning and cooking and dealing with chickens? It was much easier just to run a brush through her hair and pull it back into a ponytail. She gave another thought to pulling her makeup bag out of her suitcase, but what was the point of that, either? The farm animals wouldn't care what she looked like.

And she certainly wasn't trying to attract Grayson. In fact, it would be better if she didn't look pretty. That way, he wouldn't get the wrong idea about her and actually start looking at her as a woman, rather than a farmhand.

Still, it was weird to forgo makeup, considering that even when her brothers had dragged her out camping a couple of times, she'd brought the basics with her. But as Lori studied herself in the mirror, she was surprised to realize that she didn't look half-bad with a perfectly clean face—apart from the fact that her eyes were a little puffy and red around the edges.

She still couldn't believe she'd cried last night—that she'd actually lain in the guest bed and sobbed into the pillow to make sure the sound didn't carry to the rest of the house. Her twin sister, Sophie, had always been the crier—over sad books or when someone got hurt or even when one of their brothers did something

really great like win the World Series or an Oscar—
but never Lori.

She'd rather hug or kiss or dance. Anything but cry.

She tried to tell herself that they had been angry
tears. Frustrated tears. Exhausted tears. But it was no
use, not when she knew there had been plenty of self-
pitying tears mixed in, too. And those were the ones
that she absolutely wouldn't stand for.

Lori Sullivan wasn't someone who felt sorry for herself. She didn't have time for that nonsense.

Moving quickly, she pulled on her jeans and T-shirt
from last night and looked through the shoes in her bags.
Mostly heels. The closest she had to farm-appropriate
shoes was a pair of ballet flats. She sighed at the thought
of just how quickly they would get ruined in the dirt
and mud and grass. But she slipped them on, anyway.
Just then, she finally looked out her bedroom window
and her breath caught at the view of Grayson's land in
the morning light.

My God, it was beautiful here. She'd noticed the
beauty yesterday, of course, but every moment since
she'd gotten on the plane in Chicago had felt like such
a battle, and she'd been so tired that she hadn't really
seen Pescadero clearly.

With wonder, she drank in the open sky, grass so
green it almost hurt her eyes and—

Oh, my. Grayson was working without his shirt on,
sweat gleaming on his incredible muscles as he chopped
wood like a man possessed.

The natural beauty of his farm was breathtaking, but
once she caught sight of him, she couldn't pull her gaze

away. Not when he had to be the most perfectly built man she'd ever seen. Which was saying a lot, considering that as a choreographer and dancer she worked with amazingly chiseled men on a daily basis.

And then, suddenly, he paused and turned his face toward her window, catching her with her mouth watering and her body reacting to him even from a distance.

Normally, she would have thought being stuck with a gorgeous man would be a plus. But now, instead of being a bonus, Grayson's looks were a huge negative. Thank God he had such a gruff personality, or she'd really be in trouble.

In any case, she decided as she forced herself to turn away from the window, she was determined to be positive from here on out. No more self-pity. No more wallowing in how bad her decisions had been over the past year or so, especially those that had involved Victor. She was going to charge full speed into the fresh start she'd decided on yesterday.

Starving again, when she walked into the kitchen and didn't see any evidence that Grayson had eaten yet, she decided to make them both breakfast. When the bacon was nearly crisp and the eggs were almost ready to slide out of the frying pan, she opened the front door and yelled, "Breakfast!" the same way she had her whole childhood when it was time for her brothers and sister to come to the table.

With eight kids, everyone in her family had had a chore. She'd been in charge of cooking breakfast, getting everyone to the table and cleaning up the kitchen afterward. That skill set had come in handy many, many times as an adult. Not only for overnight guests, but also when out on the road with a troupe of dancers. She refused to let anyone who danced for her starve themselves when she needed them at their very best, and she had wooed more than one figure-conscious performer with her signature blueberry and lemon pancakes.

She was just pouring freshly squeezed orange juice into glasses when Grayson walked in. He was sweaty and had wood chips stuck in his hair and on his clothes, but at least he'd put his shirt on, thank God. She didn't think she could handle another close-up shot of all that male perfection—not before getting some sustenance in her to build up some resistance, anyway.

He didn't say anything—not "good morning" or "thanks for breakfast"—just sat down and started to eat. With a roll of her eyes, she followed suit.

Last night their silent meal had been perfectly fine with her. She'd been tired and in no mood to chat. But she'd go crazy having silent meals forever. Clearly, if she wanted to start a new mealtime trend, she was going to have to make the first move.

"I'd love to know more about your farm."

He ignored her and kept eating, but Lori had grown up with six older brothers. She wasn't the least bit daunted by being ignored.

"What do you specialize in?"

He took a long slug of orange juice before answering her. "I run a CSA."

"I was reading an article about Community Supported Agriculture on the airplane yesterday." He gave her another look that had her realizing she'd accidentally said too much. "A couple of my siblings are members of CSAs. So people come here once a week to pick up their fruits and veggies?"

"No one comes here."

Wow, that sounded a little ominous. *No one comes here.* Jeez, he acted like they were in some Gothic novel. She worked to shake off a little shiver at the darkness in his tone. Certain that it had come out more strongly than he had to mean it, she asked, "Then how does everyone get their food?"

By now he was looking more than a little irritated with her endless questions, but if she was going to work with him she'd have to understand how his business operated.

"Eric picks up the boxes. People go to his farm once a week to pick up their food."

"But in the article I read," Lori said with honest confusion, "it sounded like the farmers sell directly from their own farms, and most of them even have barn stores where people can drop in throughout the week if they need something extra."

"That's not how I do things."

But Lori was already two steps ahead as an exciting idea hit her. No doubt Grayson was simply too busy running the farm and producing the food for his CSA to find those extra hours for the weekly community pickups. But she could change all of that for him.

"Now that I'm here, I could run the pickup days so you don't have to have your friend do it on his farm." She instantly loved the idea of it, getting to meet everyone in town. It was how her life and house had always been—an open door for friends and family. Maybe she'd been wrong about life on a farm being so isolating. "I could even open a farm store for you!"

Grayson's eyes were cold as he pinned her with them. "I said, that's not how I do things."

This time his words were loud enough—and hard enough—for her not to miss them, or their intent. He wasn't doing things this way because he was too busy. He'd set it up specifically so that he wouldn't have to deal with anyone else.

"Do you have agoraphobia?" The words popped out of her mouth before she could shove them back inside.

"No." He shoved away from the kitchen table, his plate in his hands. "I just don't like people."

She was torn between wincing and laughing. What kind of person didn't like people? She just couldn't understand it. Which was why, even though every inch of his body language was telling her to back off, she had to ask, "Why?"

She asked too many questions, damn it. Worse than that, though, was that despite himself, Grayson wanted to ask her just as many. Where had she come from? What did she do for a living when she wasn't trying to masquerade as a farmhand? And how the hell was she able to make the best damned breakfast he'd ever eaten…so good that he'd almost embarrassed himself when he'd started eating it?

"Do you want to hear about my last farmhand?"

She looked a little wary at the unexpected question. "Something tells me this is a trick question. But if you're finally feeling all chatty, go ahead."

No question about it, she wasn't just pretty, she was smart, too. And sassy as hell, despite the pithy one-word answers he'd growled at her throughout breakfast.

"He was twenty-two, young enough and strong enough to work circles around me. He couldn't cook, but he could chop wood, herd cows, shear sheep, bale hay, harvest the crops and do construction. But his best quality was that he didn't speak. At all. He just grunted when he was hungry or needed help with something."

Lori blinked up at him with wide eyes, at least a thousand times too pretty for his peace of mind this morning. He hadn't been able to sleep just a wall away from her and had finally given up and gone outside to chop firewood.

Good. Maybe he'd finally gotten through to her. If she wanted to stick around for much longer, she needed to zip it.

"Wow," she said in a tone that had him being the wary one this time, "I don't think you've said that many words in total to me since yesterday."

He turned and started to wash his plate off with hard strokes of the sponge over the porcelain, a string of curse words playing out in his head. He'd been trying to make a point—quite a clear point, he thought. He wasn't interested in conversation, just in getting the work done.

"Hey, that's my job." She shoved in beside him at the sink. "Scoot."

He could wash his own dishes, damn it, but when he felt her hip bump against his to gently push him out of the way, he dropped his plate so fast to put distance between them that he practically shattered it on the bottom of the sink.

Just touching her hand last night when she'd cut her finger had been too much. Knowing anything at all about the feel of her hips—that they were toned, yet with a woman's softness—was miles beyond anything his self-control could deal with.

"Let me make sure I understood what you just said," she offered as she started deftly washing off the plates, her hands looking too elegant to be so efficient. "You don't like to talk to or interact with people. And I love both those things, which you find annoying." She shot him a glance. "Do I have that right so far?" When he just stood there and stared at her, she said, "Do you also agree that it's doubtful that either of us is going to change anytime soon?" At his continued silence, she said, "No, don't bother using up one of your precious words. I already know the answers."

This was it. This was where she was finally going to accept that she needed to leave so he could get a real farmhand. Grayson was sure the relief was going to come any second now. After all, hadn't that been what he'd been wishing for since the first moment he'd set eyes on her—that she would just go?

He had to work like hell to ignore the voice in his head that told him he'd been wishing for a hell of a lot more than that…and that most of his wishes had Lori naked and reaching for him.

"It seems to me," she said in a considering tone as she turned off the faucet and began wiping the plates dry with a clean dish towel, "that we'll just have to agree to disagree." The sunny smile she followed that inane statement with nearly knocked his feet out from under him, giving her enough time to quickly segue into, "So now that I'm almost done washing up, what do you want me to work on first?"

He'd never been a big talker, but that wasn't why he didn't answer right away. He couldn't believe anyone could be this stubborn. *Delusional* was another good word for it.

Why wasn't she packing up her things and leaving already? Under any other circumstances, he would have done it for her, but the memory of the way she'd cried in her bed last night was still too fresh in his head.

Somehow he needed to find something for her to do that she couldn't screw up. Even better, something that would convince her she was not meant for the farming life. Toilet brushes and chickens hadn't daunted her... so what would?

His lips almost moved up into a smile as he hit on it. "Pigs."

She couldn't hide her immediate look of horror. "You have pigs?"

He couldn't believe how difficult it was to keep the grin off his face. There hadn't been much cause for smiling these past few years, not until an irritatingly beautiful stranger had shown up and declared herself his new farmhand. Fortunately, he would have bet his farm that she was going to hate dealing with the pigs, with all their mud and mess—and their surprising intelligence.

"They need fresh water and feed."

"That doesn't sound so hard."

It wasn't, unless the pigs were feeling frisky and the mud was fresh. Maybe it wasn't fair to have her work in their outdoor enclosure rather than the indoor pig house with the cement floor, but after the rain they'd had a couple of days ago it *did* need to be cleaned up. "That's why I'm letting you do it," he pointed out.

"Didn't I prove to you that I could handle yesterday's chores *and* that I can cook?"

"You cook and clean well," he agreed, "but I need more than a maid."

She gritted her teeth as she leaned in across the kitchen island, her hands flat on the wood surface as she snarled, "I can't *wait* to feed and water your pigs."

Never in his life had he met a woman like her, one who didn't back down from a challenge or from being purposely insulted. She stomped out to the porch and was already heading for the pigpen when he finally saw the shoes she was wearing.

"Those are the shoes you're going to wear to muck out the pig stalls?"

Her eyes closed for a split second at the word *muck,* but then she was pushing her shoulders back and saying, "When I'm done with my work for the day, I'll head into town to pick up some more appropriate shoes."

If he had his way, when she was done with her work for the day, she'd head into town...and keep going.

"Wait," she said suddenly as she looked down the drive, "where's my car?"

"It wouldn't start this morning. I had it towed to the shop. They'll bring it back later this week."

"So—" she finally looked daunted by something "—I'm stuck here with you now?"

Did she have to remind him? "Just until Sam fixes your radiator and whatever else you busted on my fence post." He led her over to the pigs, pointing out their feed and showing her where the hose was. "Whatever you do, make sure you latch the gate all the way, or the pigs will destroy my crops."

He gave her some simple instructions on how to muck out the pigs, then left her in her fancy jeans and inappropriate shoes to deal with the dirtiest animals on earth.

Seven

After growing up with six brothers, Lori knew her way around mud and dirt, and she wasn't particularly squeamish about it. Still, as she surveyed the pigs from outside the fence, she had to admit that she'd never seen a mess quite like the one in the pigpen.

She knew Grayson had chosen this task to see whether she'd get all girlie about it and quit, and now a part of her wondered if he had already been out here this morning watering everything down so that the pigpen would be extra wet and squishy. But at breakfast he'd been covered in wood chips, not mud, so she knew that was just her lingering frustration with his little sermon on silence at breakfast.

Grunting. That's what his last farmhand had done rather than speak. And Grayson had *liked* it that way.

Frankly, she was glad that she could get down and dirty with the pigs this morning, if for no other reason than to let off a little steam. She'd always worked out her frustrations by dancing before. Today, she'd just have to work them out with some stinky, snorting pigs instead.

She opened the gate and took a careful step inside. Of course her ballet slipper sank nearly all the way into the mud. After carefully latching the gate, she turned back to the crew of pigs facing her, a half dozen or so in the large pen. They were actually pretty cute, but bigger than she'd realized. Fortunately, they didn't look the least bit threatening. Maybe a little curious about who the stranger was, however.

She figured she'd get them their water and feed and then when they were busy chowing down she'd work on mucking out their stalls. Moving slowly through the mud, she was halfway across the pen when she stepped in a particularly slippery spot and her feet almost slipped out from under her.

Years of needing to stay on her feet no matter what had her quickly righting herself and widening her stance to make sure she wouldn't fall again. She was just about to start heading forward when she looked up and saw one of the pigs making a beeline toward her, much more quickly than she could have ever believed possible for such a stocky animal. Its little hooves were powering through the mud and its curly tail was wagging.

The next thing she knew it was pushing between her legs and lifting her up off the ground. "Hey!" she exclaimed as the pig kept on moving through the mud with her stuck to its broad back. "What are you doing?"

But she already knew, didn't she? The pig was having a *fabulous* time carrying her off through the pen... with all of its friends watching with eager eyes, probably vying for who would be next to mess with the total greenhorn.

And then, just as quickly as she'd been hoisted off the ground and onto the pig's broad back, she was unceremoniously dumped on her rear in the mud with a hard splat.

She sat in the mud for several moments as she worked to get her breath back from where the ground—and the very mischievous pig—had knocked it out of her. Only, when she looked down at herself completely covered with mud, and thought about just how ridiculous she must have looked riding bareback on a pig, instead of getting upset she started to laugh.

Who knew working on a farm could be so crazy? So full of mishaps? Or that a bunch of stinky, unruly pigs would be the ones to get her laughing again? It reminded her of when she and her brother Gabe and twin sister, Sophie, would go out and make mud pies in the backyard after a storm when they were kids.

The sad truth was that Lori hadn't felt like a kid in a very long time. Not until today, when the pigs had made any chance at being anything but a messy, muddy buddy of theirs an impossibility.

Of course, getting down to the pigs' level only made her more interesting to them, especially to one of the babies who had started snuffling around at her face.

"Hey, cutie," she told him, "maybe when you're a little bigger you could sweep me off my feet, too." She stroked his snout. "I *have* always loved a guy in pink with a little facial hair."

She could have sworn he gave her a grin as she

slipped and slid while getting back up on her feet. And as she went about her duties while singing a pop song that the pigs seemed to like despite her horribly out-of-tune voice, she made sure to keep her legs close together to stave off any more impromptu pig-riding trips around the pen.

Grayson could easily have spent the rest of the day focused on the new roof he was putting on the cottage, but he needed to check up on Lori. Not, he told himself, because he'd missed seeing her since breakfast, but because letting her work on his farm was like keeping a box of fireworks next to a roaring fire—you never knew when one little spark was going to light off the whole damned thing.

That was why he'd told her to work in the pigpen. How much damage could she possibly do there?

As he approached the pigpen from a distance, he couldn't miss the fact that she was covered in mud. Even though he figured that should have been the last straw for her, he could hear her singing in a god-awful voice as she petted one of the pigs, her little bottom wiggling back and forth as she all but danced around in the mud.

He'd never met anyone like her before in his life—a city girl who would sing and dance in the mud with the pigs, rather than bailing at the idea of the hard, dirty work. With every passing second that she remained on his farm, he could feel her not just getting under his skin, but going even deeper. Just as she had the previous night when he'd heard her crying in bed.

God, he hoped she didn't cry again tonight. Because

if she did, he wasn't sure he was strong enough to keep from going to her and pulling her into his arms and kissing away those tears.

Grayson was about a hundred feet away from the pigpen when he saw something big and pink out of the corner of his eye down by his strawberry patch.

Oh, no, had she left the gate open? One instruction—to make sure it latched securely—was the only thing she needed to follow. But had she done that?

He ran over to the big sow, hollering at her to get out of his strawberries, but the pig was too busy mowing down the neat and flourishing rows of fruit to look up in his direction. It was as if a rototiller had been driven over his strawberry plants, the very ones he'd been planning to load into boxes this week for his customers. It was a sweaty and difficult job corralling the sow, but ten minutes later he had her back where she belonged.

Lori was working with the hose, spraying down the pens, and clearly didn't hear much above the sound of the water and her singing until he'd pushed the sow back into the pen.

When she finally caught sight of him, she was so surprised that she blasted him with the freezing-cold water straight in the chest. The clear fury in his gaze had her quickly trying to turn it off, but her hands were muddy enough that it took her more than a few tries to finally get it. By then, Grayson wasn't only pissed as hell, he was soaked, too.

"Sorry about that! You surprised me." She looked down at herself, her clothes and skin liberally covered with mud. "If you want to turn the hose on me to make us even, that probably wouldn't be a bad idea."

She reached out to hand him the hose and he batted it out of her hand so that it landed in the mud with a splat.

"I knew you were trouble when you drove like a maniac up my driveway." He pointed to his obliterated strawberry crop. "I told you to shut the goddamned gate. Look at what happened because you can't be trusted to do even one little thing right." Somewhere in the back of his mind he could hear how harsh he was being, but Lori didn't even flinch.

Instead, she came right back at him with, "I did shut it!" She moved across the muddy pen with surprising grace and reached behind him to shut the gate again with a frown. "I did it just like this."

She slipped just enough in the mud for her hip to push the gate, and as she reached out to steady herself the latch began to wobble. She pushed a little harder and it came completely loose so that the gate popped open.

"See?" She turned to him, her beautiful face full of righteous indignation. "I told you I closed it."

Feeling like a total ass, he waited for her to demand an apology from him. But she didn't, which only made things worse. Probably because she didn't think he was capable of making one.

And she was right. He couldn't seem to find the words he should be saying to her. Instead, he told her, "I need something from the hardware store. Go wash up and I'll take you into town to pick up some boots."

"New shoes?"

Her eyes were wide with surprise, and when he nodded she smiled up at him. Even covered nearly head to toe in mud, she was still the most beautiful woman he'd ever been near.

Her smile grew even bigger as she told him, "You're forgiven."

And that was when Grayson realized he was sunk.

Because if he wasn't really, really careful, Lori Sullivan was just going to keep stealing his heart one sentence, one meal, one smile, at a time.

"There's an outdoor shower on the other side of the barn. Go use it."

With that he turned his focus to fixing the gate of the pigpen…and not on what Lori must look like naked and soapy in the outdoor shower on the other side of the barn.

Eight

It was amazing what a hot shower and some soap could do for a person. Lori felt like a new woman in clean skinny black pants and a red shirt. Knowing they were actually going into town, she'd pulled her makeup bag out and swiped on some mascara, blush and lip gloss. The only clean shoes she had left were heels, so she picked a red-and-black pair with three-inch heels, slung her purse over her arm and headed back out to the porch to see if Grayson was ready to go.

He took one look at her and his scowl deepened. She would have scowled back, but she guessed it would irritate him more if she smiled instead.

She might have forgiven him for being a total jerk out there with the pigs, but it still smarted that he'd immediately jumped to conclusions and treated her as if she were a few brain cells short of a full set and couldn't even manage her way around the simplest thing. She'd gone to dance school in California, but she'd turned down several Ivy League schools to do it.

Without saying a word to her, he headed for his truck. She shot an evil grin at his broad back. The trip to the General Store from his farm took about fifteen minutes, and she figured a quarter hour was easily long enough to get a little revenge for the way he'd acted in the pigpen.

As they headed down his long drive, she let herself study his profile. His cowboy hat was pulled down over his slightly long, dark hair, and with the dark stubble already growing back in across his tanned jaw he looked more gorgeous than ever.

Not to mention extremely unhappy to be stuck with her as his passenger.

Facing him rather than the beautiful view of the sweeping green fields outside, she asked, "Were you related to the people you bought the farm from?"

His jaw tightened, but he must have realized he was well and truly trapped with her in his truck because he said, "No."

"Did you own a different farm somewhere else before you got this one?"

"No."

She was tempted to pull a piece of paper and pen out of her bag to keep track of how many words he answered with during the next fifteen minutes. So far, she'd have a grand total of two.

"But you grew up in Pescadero, right?"

"No."

Didn't he realize he was only making her more curious with his purposely terse—and very mysterious—answers?

"Where did you grow up, then?"

He scowled. "It's a good four miles to either my farm or the General Store from here." He looked at her shoes. "Gonna make your feet pretty damned sore to have to walk all that way in those ridiculous shoes if I dump you out right here."

She shrugged as if the thought didn't bother her in the least. "Someone's bound to pick me up and give me a ride."

"Lori."

Her name was little more than an irritated growl from his throat. One that got her way too hot, considering that Grayson was the last guy on earth she should be interested in. He was so grumpy, and bossy, and domineering…and super, crazy, wicked hot.

Her ex had always been so full of sweet, sexy words. He had known how to say exactly the right thing at exactly the right time, but all those words had turned out to be nothing but lies. Whereas when rough, gruff Grayson growled at her, she could imagine only too easily how it would sound if he also growled her name when they were making love and he was moving his big, strong hands over every inch of her naked skin.

Fortunately, she was smarter now. And completely off men. Which was why she would turn her libido off and very carefully stay on task. There was still the important matter of getting her revenge for the pigpen incident, after all.

And since she knew exactly how much Grayson hated the sound of her voice—and that sharing personal details clearly felt to him like being gutted with a knife—the best thing she could possibly do was keep on asking him questions.

"You were about to tell me where you grew up," she said, pleased to see a muscle now jumping in his jaw.

"New York."

"What part?"

"The city."

Okay, now they were getting somewhere with his new, fancy *two*-word answers. "I love New York City. I almost went to Columbia," she told him, "but in the end I couldn't imagine being that far away from my family." And dance training had taken precedence over everything else. Maybe, she wondered now that she was giving up her dance career, it might have been a good idea to get a broader education. Although the truth was that no matter what her future held, she wouldn't have given up all those years of dancing from morning until late into the night for anything.

Grayson had pulled up at a stop sign and was staring at her, his dark, haunted eyes full of surprise. "Columbia is my alma mater."

"You went to Columbia?" Realizing how her question sounded, she said, "Not that I don't think it takes a lot of brains to run a big farm like yours. I'm sure it does. I've just never met anyone who graduated from an Ivy League and became a farmer. What was your degree in?"

"Finance."

Both of her eyebrows went up. "So if you have a degree in finance from one of the best universities in the country and only bought your farm three years ago, what were you doing before that?"

By now she honestly wasn't trying to irritate him— she was simply curious about *him*.

"I get it," he said, instead of answering her last question. "You're not happy with the way I dealt with the pig getting out, so you're going to torture me with endless questions."

"My ears are still ringing from your yelling."

"Would it make you happier if I apologized?"

She crossed her arms over her chest and raised an eyebrow. "You? Apologize?" She made a clear sound of disbelief. "I'm pretty sure I'm going to see one of your pigs fly first."

He stopped at another stop sign and turned his too-beautiful face to hers. "I'm sorry. I was an ass. It won't happen again."

"I was with you all the way up until the 'won't happen again' part. You and I both know it will." She couldn't hold back her grin. "Probably inside of the next ten minutes. Especially since I do a pretty good job of living up to the nickname my family gave me as a little girl."

"Nickname?"

She was so pleased by his unexpected interest in her that she turned the full wattage of her grin on him. "Naughty."

Despite the fact that his irritated expression remained in place, she could have sworn his lips were twitching as he put his foot down on the gas pedal.

How fun would it be to actually see him smile? Lori

knew she shouldn't want it as badly as she did. Alas, she had never been very good at being prudent.

Not when impulsive had always been so much more fun.

After Grayson headed toward the hardware section, Lori found the cutest cowboy hat ever. She immediately plopped it onto her head to buy along with new boots, then waved at her teenage friend behind the deli counter.

His face immediately turned red, just as it had the first time she'd talked to him, and his voice broke as he said, "Hello."

She was just about to go over and do a little flirting with him when she realized her bag was buzzing. She pulled her phone out with far more caution than she usually did. Normally, her cell was like a fifth appendage. But she wasn't ready to talk to anyone yet, and if anything other than her sister Sophie's face had appeared on the screen, Lori would have dropped it right back into her bag unanswered.

"Hey, Soph," she said as she put it to her ear, "how are the cutest little babies in the world doing?"

"They're fine," Sophie said, which was strange, because normally, asking her about her kids meant getting a good ten minutes of details that Lori was certain only a mother herself could possibly care about. "I got a call from a friend in Chicago who went to see your show. She said you weren't there. What happened, Lor? And where the heck are you?"

Lori hated that she'd worried her sister. She hadn't figured anyone would know she had left the show early, had hoped that she'd be able to disappear for a little while. But she should have guessed that someone in her huge family would know someone in Chicago and that word would get out before she was ready for it.

Lori had always been ready for anything, eager to grab every ounce of joy from life with both hands, both arms and both legs. When, she suddenly wondered, had she stopped being ready and eager?

Especially, she thought as she caught sight of Grayson through the slats of the tall shelves on the other side of the General Store, for a man who turned her inside out with nothing more than a dark look, or a very few words. The couple of times he'd actually touched her were still imprinted on her skin as though he'd branded her instead.

"I'm okay," she said first.

"Thank God," Sophie said, and then, "Are you still in Chicago?"

"No." This small farm town she'd chosen to visit on a whim couldn't be farther from the skyscrapers and busy traffic in the Windy City. "I'm actually back in California."

"You are? Why didn't you call to let us know you were home?"

"I needed some time to think."

"Lori." Her name on her twin's lips was infused with such unconditional love that Lori nearly teared up in the middle of the store. "Tell me what happened. It was Victor, wasn't it?"

"That's over now." Lori's voice was hard.

"You've said that before, too many times. Do you really mean it this time?"

"Forever, Soph. I'll never, ever go back to him. I promise you, I won't."

Her sister's exhale of relief was loud and long. "How about I leave the babies with Jake tonight and you and I can go catch a double feature somewhere with extra-buttery popcorn and every box of candy in the place?"

She loved her sister so much, and it was so tempting to head back to San Francisco to let Sophie take care of her. But Lori had something to prove to herself first before she could go back to her real life.

And she hadn't yet proved it, hadn't even come close to turning the darkness that had settled inside her these past months back to bright, vibrant color.

"I love you, Soph," she said first, because it was the most important thing of all. Now and forever. But she also had to say, "But I can't come home. Not yet."

"At least tell me where you are," Sophie insisted.

"I'm working on a farm."

Lori could easily picture her sister's stunned expression as she repeated, "A farm?"

"With pigs and chickens and crops. I'm buying a pair of cowboy boots right now."

"How could you have possibly ended up on a farm?"

"You know how these things go," Lori said with a grin.

"There isn't another guy involved, is there?"

"No," Lori said, even though being around Grayson kept making her insides go all hot and fluttery. Even when he was being all grumpy and cranky. Especially then, if she was being completely honest with herself. He was just so different from any man she'd ever known. He didn't waste one single second on trying to be charming or complimenting her so that he could get something from her. "I swear I just need to shake things up for a bit." And, boy, had she ever done that, if the past twenty-four hours were any indication.

But her explanations clearly weren't doing it for her sister, who was making little worried sounds into the phone. "Lor, this is crazy, even for you. If you won't talk to me about what's going on, you should at least call Mom."

Panic skittered up Lori's spine. If Mary Sullivan wrapped her warm arms around her daughter the way she had for as long as Lori could remember, she'd fall into a million pieces.

"Does Mom know I'm back?"

"No, not yet, but—"

Lori quickly cut her sister off. "When you and Jake had your one-night stand after Chase's wedding and you got pregnant with the twins, I didn't run off to blab to Mom. I kept your secret as long as you needed me to keep it. Now it's your turn to keep mine."

Her twin was silent for a long while. Too long for Lori's peace of mind. Finally Sophie said, "I don't like this. Especially when I've already been keeping secret everything that's happened with Victor for almost two years."

"Please, Soph," Lori begged, "I just need a little while longer."

"Okay," her sister agreed, "but you've got to make me a promise back."

"What is it?" Lori asked warily.

"If you start to feel like you're really in trouble, promise you'll call me and let me come take you home."

"I promise."

"And—"

"Wait," Lori said, cutting her off, "you already got your promise."

"Well, I need one more," Sophie said, just as stubborn as she was, twins both inside and out. "You've got to promise me you'll come to Sunday lunch with everyone in a week and a half."

Lori clenched the phone. "Soph, I—"

"You had already planned to take a short trip back from Chicago for the weekend to see everyone," Sophie reminded her. "Promise me, Lori, or the deal's off."

God, she hated being forced against the wall by anyone or anything. And maybe if it were anyone but her sister doing it to her, she would have fought her on it. But how could she when she knew she'd be saying the exact same thing to Sophie if their situations were reversed, simply because she loved her?

"Fine," she grudgingly agreed. "I'll make sure I don't miss our big family lunch in a week and a half." Knowing it was long past time to get her bloodhound of a sister off her case, Lori quickly asked, "Have you heard anything from Megan and Gabe?"

"Megan hasn't admitted to being pregnant. Yet," Sophie told her, "but when I met her for lunch, she got a little green when the guy next to us had the egg salad. Gabe is going to be such a great dad, isn't he?"

"Our brother is going to be an amazing father," Lori agreed. Gabe was a firefighter who had met his future wife and eight-year-old stepdaughter when he saved them from a horrible apartment fire a year ago. "Just like you're a totally amazing mom. Summer is going to be so excited when they finally 'fess up and tell her she's going to be a big sister. And Jackie and Smith will have another cousin to play with." Suddenly, Lori saw Grayson coming toward her. "I've got to go."

"Back to the farm?" Sophie asked with more than a little incredulity.

"Yes," Lori confirmed again. "Back to the farm."

"You'd better call me every day with an update on how you're doing," her sister warned her, "because I'm going to worry every second until I hear from you again. And if I don't know you're okay, I'm going to have to come after you, whether you want me there on that farm or not."

Everyone thought Sophie was so quiet, so sedate, but Lori knew better than anyone, apart from Sophie's husband, just what a powerful force her sister could be. Especially if she thought someone she loved was in trouble.

"Kiss the twins' cute little faces for me and tell them Aunt Lori misses them and is going to play tickle monster with them soon."

She hung up her phone and slid it back into her bag just as Grayson rounded the corner and came into full view again. She picked up a pair of red-and-black boots.

"What do you think of these? Aren't they cute?"

Instead of answering, he just stared at her, that muscle in his jaw jumping as he took in her new hat. On a deep glower, his gaze finally dropped to the boots she was holding up.

"They'll do the job," he said with no appreciation whatsoever for the absolutely gorgeous flame design running up both sides of the cowboy boots. "I'll be waiting for you in the truck."

So much for the momentary truce. Just as she'd predicted, it hadn't lasted long.

Grayson clenched his teeth even tighter as Lori walked outside wearing her new boots and hat. God, she was cute…and so damned sexy. He'd had a perpetual hard-on since the second she stepped out of her car that first day in her ridiculously revealing outfit and heels.

It didn't help that he was still seeing red at the way she'd told him she would have climbed into a stranger's car if he'd made good on his threat to drop her off on the road for talking too much. He couldn't believe she would be that stupid, even if he'd been the one to make the equally stupid threat.

On top of everything else, it was hard to push down thirty-plus years of good manners and not get out from behind the wheel to open the door for her and help her up into the passenger seat. But he was very much afraid that if he did, he would rip the new hat from her head and chuck it into the street, because the last thing he needed was for her to become even more irresistible. Unfortunately, the way she looked in the cowboy boots and hat were threatening to rip what was left of his self-control to tatters.

Especially after he'd overheard her side of a conversation with a person he'd quickly guessed had to be her sister. Lori, he figured, had no idea just how well sound echoed throughout the General Store. Particularly when he was—stupidly—hanging on her every word.

Clearly, her sister was worried about her. And while Lori hadn't given too much away, she had made it clear that she was on his farm to get a break from her real life...and she had promised to return to it in a "little while."

The knowledge should have filled him with joy.

But it hadn't.

For three years, solitude had been his companion and he'd convinced himself that all he'd ever need again were the blue sky, a thousand acres of pasture and the crashing waves of the ocean. Until, from completely out of the blue, Lori Sullivan had barged into his life... and promptly blown his carefully emotionless world to shreds.

All of the facts—the truths that he couldn't ignore—made him angry. With her. With himself. And especially with the whole damned world for dropping someone so irritating and irresistible and impossible to ignore at his feet.

As soon as the passenger door clicked shut and she'd buckled her seat belt, he started the engine. She had a small bag on her lap and, a moment later, she pulled something out of it and held it out to him. "Want one?"

She was holding out something long and sticky and

covered in sugar. It was fluorescent green and wasn't even close to being edible.

"No."

"Your loss." She shoved it into her mouth instead and started chewing the candy.

And that was the problem. He knew she was right. Because when she did finally decide to leave, it really was going to be his loss.

Somehow he needed to hold his focus on the farm, on the never-ending work that came with owning a thousand acres and more than a hundred animals. "Have you ever worked with crops before?" he asked her.

Around a mouthful of gummy candy, she said, "I used to help my mom with her veggies when I was a little girl. She said I had a green thumb. Why? Is planting seeds next on my list?"

"No," he told her. "Weeding is."

He figured she'd groan at hearing that news. Instead, just as she kept doing over and over, she surprised him by saying, "Oh, good. I enjoyed helping her plant things, and seeing them grow was cool, but I always liked ripping things out even more."

He could see the wide grin on her face in his peripheral vision. That was as close as he could come to looking at her without allowing his control to be completely destroyed.

"It's like the difference between a pirouette and a grand jeté. Both are fun, but sometimes you just prefer one over the other. Right now, I've got more of an appetite for destruction."

He'd spent enough years going to the ballet in his

previous life to know what she was talking about. He shot a look at her gorgeous legs. Even in her dark jeans, her lithe strength was obvious, and the beautiful way she moved had caught his eye from the first.

Was that her story? Was she a dancer? And if she was, then what the hell was she doing on his farm pretending to be a farmhand when she should be up on a stage somewhere?

Thank God he pulled into his drive before he could do something stupid, like ask her any of those questions. Her questions during the ride over had been bad enough.

From here on out, he vowed to keep them loaded up with so much work that neither of them would have time to worry about anything else, starting with the weeds in his asparagus patch for her and the new roof on his cottage for him.

Nine

Damn it, Grayson thought the next morning as he rubbed down his horse after a particularly grueling ride, he'd all but worked the two of them into the ground the day before, but it hadn't made a bit of difference.

He still wanted Lori more than he'd ever wanted anything in his life. So much that even though she'd made him another fabulous dinner and then breakfast, both times he'd told her he couldn't stop working long enough to eat with her and that he'd grab the leftovers when he could.

And later, when she'd said that she was worried about the cat not eating much, after he'd told her Mo was lucky to still be here at all, she'd glared at him and turned on her heel without another word.

"Grayson?" Lori poked her head into the stables. She'd been fearless everywhere else on his farm, but she never ventured too close to his horses. "You just got a call from Eric. He said he's going to need to come an hour early tonight to pick up the boxes of food. What do you need me to do to help with that?"

Grayson barely bit back a curse. So much for avoiding Lori today. In order to get all of the food together in time, the two of them would have to work together. And work well.

"I need you to go into the storeroom and pull out the cartons so that we can fill them. Lay them out across the tables inside the barn. You'll have to stack them two-deep."

"How many should I pull out?"

"I've got two hundred and fifteen subscribers, but we'll make an extra dozen." People sometimes needed an additional box or two, plus he liked Eric to do a few free drop-offs at the end of every pickup day with whatever was left.

"Got it." She turned immediately to take care of the work that needed to be done, but it wasn't until she was gone that he realized something had been different.

She hadn't smiled. Or done or said anything to get a rise out of him. She'd simply given him the message, then asked him what needed to be done. It was exactly what he'd told her he wanted from her. And yet, it felt wrong.

He tried to push the crazy thought out of his head, but by the time he joined her in the barn and saw the incredibly fast progress she'd made—along with the slightly dimmer light in her eyes—he couldn't help but feel like a total ass for not only being so hard on her, but also for going out of his way to avoid her.

Was she upset about having to eat alone? Was she

thinking he was an ogre about the cat? Or did it have nothing to do with him at all and she simply missed her family...or whoever else she had run from to come to his farm?

The thought of Lori with another man was like a hard punch straight to the gut. He couldn't let himself have her, but Lord, he couldn't stand the thought of anyone else touching her, either. Not when, despite her resilience, he couldn't help but see the sweet vulnerability in her eyes when she was exhausted enough to accidentally let down her guard.

She quickly picked up on his plan for that week's box and they worked silently together to pick the remaining strawberries, artichokes, asparagus, peas and squash. After a short while, Lori started to arrange each of the boxes in a way that Grayson had to admit was far more pleasing to the eye than the way he normally laid out everything for his customers. He could only imagine how happy everyone would be when they picked up their produce this week. They would likely be even more inspired to go home and start cooking up and eating the bounty with their families.

Because of Lori.

When he was done picking the fresh fruit and veggies for the week, he moved to the other side of the table to help her put together the rest of the boxes and said, "These are looking great."

He'd been hoping for a smile, or maybe if he was really lucky, some laughter. That was what he'd expected her response to be. Anything but a head that stayed down as she simply nodded and kept filling boxes.

"Lori—"

Shit, he didn't even know what he wanted to say to her, just that it had to be something. Anything to bring back the smile he was getting way too used to seeing… and the motormouth that had started to sound better than any symphony he'd ever heard.

Her hands immediately stilled, and when she finally looked up at him, he hated the shadows in her eyes.

"What is it, Grayson?"

Four crisp words were all he warranted now. "I wanted to say—" When he paused to try to get a grip, he saw the hope light up in her eyes.

"Go ahead," she said with a soft curving of her lips that held him entranced. "I'm listening."

But everything he wanted to say, everything he needed to tell her, got stuck in his throat. And in the end, all that came out of his mouth was, "If you're tired, I can finish up."

Just as quickly as she'd opened herself back up to him, she shut down, looking at the artichoke in her hand rather than up at him.

"I'm not tired." She took off her cowboy hat then, and hung it from a nail on the wall.

Her taking off the hat felt like an omen, a bad one. Where he'd wanted to yank it off and toss it into the street the day before, now he wanted to pick it up and jam it back down onto her head.

But before he could say or do anything more, he heard the crunch of tires over the gravel on the drive. Eric walked into the barn a minute later. "Hey, Grayson, sorry about the schedule change today." When he saw Lori, the usually taciturn young farmer broke out into a huge grin. "You must be Lori."

She grinned at Eric in exactly the way she hadn't been smiling at *him* as they shook hands. "It's so nice to meet you, Eric. And thanks for your suggestions about what else to try feeding Sweetpea. I'm going to try the liver tonight. I'll let you know how it goes."

What the hell? First she was lighting up for Eric and then it turned out that they'd already swapped cat-feeding tips with each other? Had she also told Eric what an ass her boss had been since the second she'd signed on as his farmhand?

"Wow," Eric commented when he looked at the boxes of produce, "these look great this week." His smile was all for Lori. "Must have needed a woman's touch."

Without a word to either of them, Grayson started carrying the boxes over to Eric's truck. Lori and Eric chatted like old friends the entire time, with Eric happily answering each of Lori's rapid-fire questions. "So how do the pickups work? Is there a check-off list? Do you know everyone? Are they all locals or do they come from other towns? Do people bring their kids and pets and hang out or are they just in and out?"

Telling himself this was the perfect way to get her out of his hair, Grayson cut off Eric halfway into his lengthy explanation of how the evening's pickup would work. "Go and see for yourself."

He didn't have to offer twice, as Eric and Lori immediately grinned at each other and said, "Great!" at the same time.

Grayson's hands would have fisted had he not been

carrying three heavy boxes stacked on top of one another. Eric and Lori were perfect together. Both of them had a ready smile. Both of them could talk your ear off for hours. They even looked good together, Eric blond and muscular next to Lori's dark-haired grace.

"Oh, I almost forgot," Eric said to Grayson when he finally managed to yank his gaze away from Lori. "A journalist called right before I came over here. He's doing a story on the popularity of CSAs, but when I told him that I'm just the pickup guy he asked if you could give him a call back." Eric reached into the front pocket of his jeans. "I've got his number here."

"I don't need the number."

Lori frowned at him as Eric asked, "You sure? He sounded like a nice guy, even told me that he'd heard about your CSA from several people who said you're running the best one in the area."

"I'm not interested in press, thanks." Grayson couldn't stand the thought of anyone poking into his past, not when he could guess how fast the story would turn from one about his farm and CSA into a "tragic" story of love and loss. He had never spoken to anyone about his story, and he never planned to. Putting the final boxes into Eric's truck, he said, "Looks like you're all set to go."

"I'll make sure to bring Lori back safe and sound in a couple of hours."

Grayson barely kept himself from growling that Eric had better do just that or he'd make sure he paid.

Lori was just leaving the barn when she suddenly turned around and grabbed the cowboy hat off the nail.

When she plopped it back on her head, Eric grinned at her and said, "Great hat."

"Thank you." Her smile at his compliment was so bright it could have lit up the entire town.

And as Grayson watched them get into Eric's truck and then drive away, he wondered what in the hell he was doing sending her off alone with Eric. It wasn't that he thought the other man would do anything to hurt her or frighten her. On the contrary, Eric was a good-looking young guy who was reliable and responsible. He didn't have any issues, didn't have any reasons not to make a play for Lori and hope that she played, too.

The two hours that Grayson spent hammering away on the new cottage roof, so hard and fast that his shoulder ached, didn't bring him any closer to erasing the memory of the way Lori had smiled at Eric.

When he finally heard the truck come back up the drive, he was hard-pressed not to yank her out of it and claim her as his once and for all with a kiss that would have both of them forgetting anything but how good they could be together.

Of course, Eric came around and helped her out of his truck like a gentleman. She gave him a hug goodbye and then stood in the driveway and waved as he drove away. Her smile was still intact as she said, "That was so much fun!"

Grayson's heart swelled in his chest at seeing her so happy, even if he hadn't been the one to make her that way. But when she finally looked up and realized he was standing by the side of the barn watching her, her smile fell away.

"I can't believe you don't do the pickup here," she said, evidently no longer giving him the silent treatment. "Your customers are the neatest people and they're so grateful for the food you grow for them. Don't you want the satisfaction of seeing how happy they are—or at least give them a chance to say thank you?"

She'd only been back for sixty seconds and already she was laying into him. How could he have been upset about her earlier moratorium on chatting?

Knowing she was going to keep glaring at him until he answered, he told her, "I'm too busy."

She made a sound of disbelief. A loud one. "You can't spare two hours once a week to actually interact with your customers and community? Eric told me you give away free food to people who can't afford to subscribe to your CSA every single week." She shook her head. "I don't understand you at all, Grayson. Not even a little bit." With that, she headed inside the house and slammed the door.

The sick truth was that he didn't understand himself, either, didn't know how he could be feeling what he was feeling for her so quickly. She'd only been with him for a few days, and she had pushed every one of his buttons repeatedly—and likely on purpose—more than half of that time.

As exasperating as she could be, he was torn between wanting to strangle her and wanting to kiss her. Quite frankly, he wasn't sure which was going to happen first. Although when he finally walked back into the house and found Lori curled up on the couch sneezing her head off with Mo on her lap as she tried to coax her to "just take one more teeny-tiny bite of the super-yummy liver," anyone with half a brain would have placed their bets on kissing.

Which was why he immediately grabbed his keys from the kitchen counter and headed straight for the local bar to watch a game he wasn't interested in and eat a burger he didn't want, making sure not to return until he could be sure Lori was asleep.

It was long past midnight when he finally headed up his driveway, and when he saw that her bedroom light was still on, he was suddenly hit with the crazy urge to rewind the past six hours—hell, the past several days—so that he could get things right with her this time.

But as soon as he got out of his truck, she turned off her bedroom light.

Ten

Grayson had obviously had breakfast by the time Lori woke up—a little late, due to the fact that she'd been waiting up to make sure he got home safe and sound after the way he'd barged out of the house the night before. She ate quickly, then went outside to feed the chickens and collect their eggs. When she was done, she headed into the pigpen.

"Hey, Chase," she said to one of her favorite pigs. "Beautiful day, isn't it?"

The pigs acted almost like puppies as they snuffled at her new boots and came for pats on the head. There were seven of them, so she'd decided to name them after her brothers and sister. And since Grayson was off somewhere doing secret farmer things that she'd likely have to pry out of him with a crowbar if she was interested enough, she talked to them the way she would have talked with her siblings.

"Pretty amazing how beautiful it is when the sun sets here, isn't it?" she told the pig she'd named after her photographer brother. "Probably wish your hooves weren't so dirty so you could pick up a camera and capture it, don't you?" She could have sworn the pig nodded.

She was refilling the water troughs as the fastest pig raced over for a drink, reminding her of her car-racing brother, Zach. "There was the most beautiful classic Ford truck on Main Street yesterday. Wouldn't it be great to go zipping down the farm road in the middle of the night, under a full moon, pedal to the metal?" Just as her brother Zach would have, the pig ignored her and kept on drinking.

She grinned as she picked up the bag of feed and the oldest pig of the bunch kept a watchful eye on her, letting the younger ones feed first. "You're definitely Marcus," she said, her heart tugging hard as she thought about how much her oldest brother, who owned a winery in Napa Valley, would love the rolling hills of Pescadero. "Maybe you should give some thought to convincing Grayson to put in some grapes out here, too." The pig simply kept a calm watch over the rest of his motley crew.

Talking to the pigs like this didn't make her miss her family any less, but it kept her smiling. And she knew that was the most important thing right now. Especially when the only real person she had to talk to was little better than a living, working ghost.

She didn't know how he did it—how he managed to be so big and yet so silent, so domineering and yet invisible, all at the same time. In some ways, Grayson reminded her of her twin sister, Sophie. Soph could slip in and out of a room and notice absolutely everything in it without people being any the wiser.

Lori had always loved helping Marcus out with his vineyard in Napa but, even so, she was still surprised by how much she liked working on a farm—with the exception of cleaning bathrooms, of course. She'd enjoyed using the riding lawn mower that morning, and had loved the thrill of having all that power between her legs. She also really liked having her hands in the rich soil as she weeded the garden, and the pigs and chickens had become like a second family to her.

She had just finished mucking out the mama pig's stall and was giving her boots a gentle hose-down when Grayson suddenly walked out of the stables. "I just heard from the neighbor to the west of here that one of my fences is down and the cows are grazing on his land. We need to get over there immediately to fix it. I've saddled Rosie for you."

Lori knew she could be stubborn and full of pride. Impulsive, too. But she wasn't stupid. Which was why she had no problem at all admitting, "I don't know how to ride a horse. Can't we get out to the fence another way?"

"Not without the sound of the motor driving even more cows into the neighbor's field."

She took a deep breath. "Okay, then, why don't you give me a quick riding lesson?"

"We don't have time for a lesson."

He looked as frustrated as she felt. She knew they were nothing more than employer and farmhand but, oh, how she wished he'd talk to her, look at her, for some other reason than because of a fence or a dirty house that needed cleaning or because she'd just screwed something up.

She wished even more that she could just stop wishing already.

Finally, he informed her, "You're going to have to ride with me." He looked none too happy about it.

"You've got to be kidding," she said, not happy about it, either. But her body instantly heated up at the idea. At the same time she knew that his avoiding her had been a good idea...and that riding double on a horse was an equally bad one.

She couldn't get on a horse with Grayson; there was no way she could be that close to all his marvelously big, hard muscles. Especially when he was looking even more brooding, mysterious and super-crazy-sexy today in his jeans and work shirt and cowboy hat and boots.

"More of my cows could get out if we delay much longer and it looks like there's a storm coming in. Go put on a coat."

As he went back into the stable to bring his horse outside, she looked up at the puffy white clouds in the bright blue sky. There was a light breeze, but the sun was warm and she didn't believe there was even the slightest chance of a storm in the near future. No, she suspected he was simply trying to make her cover up so that he could pretend she wasn't a woman while they bumped and slid and rocked against each other in the saddle.

He gave her one of his finely tuned irritated looks

when he returned and saw that she was still just wearing her thin T-shirt. She shot him a look right back.

"Come here and I'll hoist you up."

Hating the way he talked about her as if she were a sack of grain, she said, "I can get up on the horse myself, thank you."

But, boy, did it seem like a long way up, and when she stalled a minute too long a sound of deep frustration came from Grayson. The next thing she knew his arms went around her waist and he all but tossed her up on the horse's back. She grabbed the saddle horn and hung on for dear life, but he was seated behind her a moment later, his strong legs and hard chest holding her firmly in place.

When he kicked the horse into a trot, it wasn't the sudden movement that stole all the breath from Lori's lungs, it was Grayson's warmth, his strength, his deliciously male scent…and the swift rush of desire that she didn't have the slightest prayer of ignoring.

Lord, why did the cows have to bust through the fence today? And why hadn't he taken an extra couple of minutes to figure out something else—*anything* else—so that he wouldn't be up here in a hell of his own making with the sexiest damned cowgirl who had ever graced the earth?

Grayson had never been so hard in all his life, and he had a bad feeling he hadn't been thinking clearly when he'd decided Lori would have to ride with him.

"Wow, is all of this really yours?" He couldn't miss the wonder in her voice as she added, "It's so beautiful—do you ever feel like you're living in a painting? And, oh, look at that!" She gasped with pleasure as she pointed at the ocean. "No wonder you decided to move here from New York."

For the past few years his land had been a refuge. It had been a way to leave the rest of the world behind. But he had never let himself truly take in the beauty. Not until he couldn't help but see it through the wonder in Lori's eyes.

"You're very lucky," she said as they rode closer to the broken fence, close enough to hear the waves crashing on the shore below. "Very, very lucky."

She was right, he was, but not because he owned such amazing property.

No, today his luck meant getting to hold a beautiful woman who saw wonder in everything. Luck meant having her in his arms a little while longer under the pretext of needing to keep her steady on his horse.

Because even though it was the last thing he should be doing, in this one rare moment where they weren't arguing, or glaring, or being frustrated with each other, Grayson couldn't find a way to stop himself from drinking in every precious second with Lori.

Two hours later...

Lori tried not to shiver, but it was getting so cold. Where had the wind come from so quickly? When they'd left Grayson's farmhouse, the sky had been blue and cloudless, the air perfectly still. She hated that he'd been right when he'd told her a storm was coming in and she should put on a jacket.

If only she didn't feel as if she needed to do the opposite of everything he said. It was just that if she didn't, he'd think he was winning.

And she couldn't let him win. She couldn't let any man win ever again.

Which was why it was so important that she stay on top of things with Grayson. Especially when it came to blocking the attraction between them that simmered beneath the surface of every look, every word, every accidental touch.

She didn't even *like* him. Not very much, anyway. So she refused to want him. Period. No ifs, ands or buts. She was not interested in sleeping with Grayson. Definitely not.

Only, despite how much she was willing herself to remain warm in the cold breeze, she couldn't keep a hard shiver from running through every last inch of her. She sighed as she picked up the pliers, the cool handles feeling like blocks of ice in her already chilled hands.

The problem, she thought with another deep sigh, was that deciding not to feel something was very different from actually *not* feeling it. And just as she was unable to stop her shivers from taking her over head to toe, she was very much afraid that she wasn't going to be able to keep her attraction to Grayson at bay for very much longer, either.

Fortunately, she knew that as long as she never acted on it, he certainly wouldn't. Talk about a completely unbendable, rigid guy. It was his way or the highway.

And her way was definitely not a direction he had any intention of following.

He couldn't have said even a hundred words to her today, and they'd been working outside with each other for hours. She'd never said so little to anyone in all her life…or been quite so powerfully aware of someone else. Once he'd gotten her going on the fence and could be reasonably well assured that she wasn't going to completely screw up her part of it, he'd left her to her own thoughts, only stopping by every half hour or so to look over her shoulder at her workmanship.

Amazingly, despite the fact that she didn't have anything else to focus on but the patterns of the twisting wires in her hands, thoughts of Victor hadn't assaulted her, hadn't crept in to take over every last open space inside of her and turn light to dark. Maybe, she thought yet again, she was right to have come here to a farm miles from anyone she knew, from anything she'd ever experienced and far away from the man who had hurt her deeply.

If it hurt her female pride a little bit that Grayson was as far from falling for her as any man had ever been, well, she didn't care. She didn't want a man in her life, anyway. Her whole life seemed like it had been one seduction after another. Not only as a dancer and choreographer trying to get jobs, but also as a woman trying to get men to notice her.

Her mother had raised her to be more than that, but growing up in a family of such dynamic, smart siblings, Lori had needed to carve out her own niche early on.

Naughty was what her brother Chase had christened

her so many years ago, and she'd worked hard to fit that description every day since. Her hair, her makeup, her clothes, had always been wild and sexy. She wasn't someone who ever left the house looking anything but fantastic, even if it was to go get milk or pick up the paper. When people looked at her, she made sure it was worth their while. And they *always* looked.

Out here on Grayson's farm was the first time in her adult life that she'd ever forgone a blow dryer or let her skin be bared to the sun. No mascara, no blush, no lipstick. She was living in jeans and T-shirts. The only part of her old life that she was not going to let go of was the lace and silk lingerie she wore beneath her clothes.

The problem was that putting both dance and seduction aside left her feeling as if she was trying to hold on to air as it flitted through her fingers. Dancing and love had always gone together for Lori, from her first crush as a little girl on the teenage boy in her ballet class who could lift her so high, so effortlessly. All her adult life she'd fallen for other dancers and choreographers as she'd twirled and swayed in their arms on worn wooden studio floors and stages.

Only, when her mistakes with Victor had made her stop believing in love, she'd also lost her love for dancing. And she had no idea how to recapture either of those loves.

She'd never been helpless before, and she refused to feel helpless now as she stood up to stretch her back and look out over the hills that rolled all the way to the ocean. She was struck with wonder yet again at the beauty of the land, the quiet, the ever-changing colors of the landscape. Even the clouds, which were dark now and which covered the whole expanse of previously blue sky, had a stunning beauty all their own.

Suddenly, a crack of lightning split the sky and Lori turned her face up to the darkening clouds just as they opened. It shouldn't make any sense that she should find such joy in the freezing pellets of rain that pummeled her—anyone with a lick of sense would be rushing to take cover from the harsh elements—but she couldn't have held back her laughter for the world.

Lori opened her arms and leaned back to take it all in, to let the force of the storm barrel into her, her sudden laughter joining in with the thunder and lightning.

The rain was astonishingly cold on her bare skin as it quickly soaked through her T-shirt and jeans, but she swore she could feel it washing her clean, pouring over her arms where Victor had once touched her, drenching lips that Victor had once kissed. She'd thought she'd been so free, so wild, her whole life, but every time she went back to Victor after he'd hurt her, walls had started to grow around her heart, building up an inch at a time until they'd held her trapped inside.

Now, with each boom of thunder, with each bolt of lightning, those walls began to crumble.

Only Grayson's curse could have been louder than either her laughter or the storm. Lori was still smiling when she looked over at him, still lost in the wildness that surrounded them both. Besides, she was getting used to seeing that scowl on his face whenever he looked at her. She was even starting to think it was a little bit cute, truth be told, as though he were just a little boy who wasn't getting exactly what he wanted right when he wanted it.

Belatedly, she realized he already had his tools, and hers, put away in the saddlebags, and seconds later was swinging onto the horse's back. From up on the horse, he reached down for her.

Suddenly, she could see him as he would have been hundreds of years ago, a warrior up on his horse, big and strong. A man a woman could count on to protect her, no matter what.

But her romantic visions were yanked away a second later when he reached down and scooped her up into his arms so quickly that she didn't even have a chance to fight him. He grabbed her, brought her chest to his and, with nothing but one arm, he settled her on his lap, her legs straddled over his…and then he was riding away with her.

It shouldn't be sexy or romantic, damn it, and she shouldn't be getting turned on by having to hold on to his big muscles, or by the way the seam of her jeans rubbed up against his in just the right way, right where she'd been overheated since the first time she'd laid eyes on his too-beautiful face and his too-perfect body.

No, instead of being turned on by his barbaric behavior, she needed to be rightfully outraged by the way he'd yanked her up onto the horse again. Only, just as she was about to open her mouth to give him a piece of her mind over the sound of the rain crashing down on them, another crack of lightning flashed—close enough that they could actually see the bolt slam into a tree less

than a quarter of a mile away. Thunder rolled in immediately afterward.

The horse reared, and as they started sliding in the
saddle Lori automatically tightened her grip on Grayson, holding on to him for dear life with her arms and
legs. He cursed again as he worked to keep them steady,
his grip tightening around her waist so that she wouldn't
slide off.

"We're not going to be able to get back to the house,"
he yelled over the rain as he quickly changed direction,
heading down closer to the ocean rather than back toward the farmhouse. "I've got to get Diablo out of the
storm."

Of course, all he could think about was getting his
horse to safety. He clearly loved his horse, and planned
on keeping him forever. Whereas Lori knew she had
been nothing but a total pain in his rear, and he couldn't
wait to get rid of her.

Still, he was so warm despite the cold wind and rain
that she couldn't help but bury her face in the crook of
his neck and breathe him in. No man had ever smelled
as good as he did, like soap and sweat that came from
working hard, like fresh grass, and rich soil, and clean,
sweet rain.

When a thick drop of rain ran down from his chin
into the hollow of his neck, how could she do anything
else but lick out against it so that she could finally drink
him in the way she'd been secretly wanting to all along?

Another shiver went through her as her tongue met
his skin and she finally found out just how good he
tasted. Only, this time it had nothing to do with being

cold…and everything to do with the desperate wanting she'd sworn she wouldn't let herself feel.

When she'd come to Pescadero she thought she was dead inside, but Grayson had made her feel again, right away, despite knowing better. And now, the even bigger problem was that Lori had no idea how to keep some walls up while others fell. All she could do was let them all break to pieces, one by one, and pray that her heart would be strong enough to withstand being out there in the open again.

Of course, it wasn't her heart she was thinking with as she went to take another taste. She had never been ashamed of her natural sexuality, and didn't know how to start tamping it down now. Not when she was achingly hungry for Grayson's touch, for the wonder of being his other half as they came together.

Lori had always been in tune with her body, had always automatically translated everything she felt, everything she saw, into dance. Until things with Victor had gotten so bad that she'd all but forgotten how to read or speak that language.

But now, as she held on to Grayson's hard muscles, as she felt the pounding of the hooves moving through her while his horse galloped through the wet fields, as she gazed out through the rain to the raging ocean at the bottom of the cliffs, she finally saw things through the eyes of a dancer again.

The rain had become sparkles of light pouring down from the ceiling of an auditorium over dancers dressed in the blues of the sky and the green of the grass and the reds and oranges and yellows of the flowers. Giving in to the storm, they danced, wild and beautiful. She could see a lone male dancer moving through them, solid despite the power of the storm as he reached for one of the female dancers, who was a colorful wildflower just breaking loose to go flying away, away, away.

The picture of the dance Lori was painting in her mind's eye was so clear that she knew the male would cradle the female against him, hold her steady…then finally let her loose to fly again when she was stronger, and the beautifully wild storm had abated enough that it was safe for her to be set free.

And just like the wildflower in her vision, as the wind whipped through her hair and the rain pelted down on her limbs while Grayson held her steady and safe on top of the fast-moving horse, Lori felt as if Grayson had just given her back the freedom she'd been afraid was lost when she'd left Chicago.

Lost in her visions, Lori was surprised to realize the horse had stopped galloping and Grayson was on the ground. She immediately felt chilled without his arms around her. Fortunately, she didn't have long to wait for him to touch her again, because his large hands were on her waist and he was lifting her off the horse's back to the ground.

For a moment everything got mixed up in her head between the man she'd been living with for nearly a week and the man from the dance in her visions. When her feet hit the ground again and she blinked up at him in the rain, the world stopped spinning as she stared into his eyes.

His gaze was dark and mysterious, just like always.

Instead of stepping away from him she reached up to stroke his face. She had to feel beneath her fingertips what she'd just tasted moments ago.

She watched as fire leaped in his eyes, felt the vibration of his groan, felt the heat and purity of his desire for her move through him and into her as he turned his cheek slightly to press into her hand. But, too soon, he wrenched himself away from her.

"Get inside the cabin while I take care of the horse."

His words were loud enough to be heard over the storm. They were hard, too. As hard as anything he'd ever said to her, and even though she thought she'd been doing a good job of blocking his grunts and growls, this one sentence pierced her. Enough that she wanted nothing more than to get away from him for a few minutes to try to regain her bearings.

And to stop seeing him as she had in her vision of the storm-turned-dance—as strong, as gentle, as nurturing.

She'd been stupid too many times before with men, had let her body and heart take her down a path that she should have run from instead. She wouldn't do it again.

Especially not with Grayson.

Eleven

Grayson took Diablo's saddle off and brushed him down, then gathered up wood from the pile in the rack under the roof overhang and carried the heavy load inside.

And all the while he refused to let himself remember how Lori's tongue had felt against his skin.

Or the way her lithe curves had fit against his while her toned legs were wrapped around his waist and her strong arms were locked around his neck.

Nor would he let himself remember that she'd looked like a beautiful witch who couldn't have been more pleased by the storm she'd brewed up.

And while he was at it, he would also force himself to forget how beautiful the sound of her laughter had been…and that even in the middle of the rain, that sound had warmed him better than the sun ever had.

It was the first time he'd seen her laugh like that, with her whole body, her entire heart and soul behind the happy sound. When she'd opened up her arms to the storm and tilted up her face to let the rain wash over her, she not only looked like she belonged on his land, she looked so beautiful that he'd felt as if something inside of him had been struck by lightning.

He yanked open the door to the old log cabin, harder than he should have considering the age of the hinges. Early settlers had come here and laid down stakes and dreams in the West. Harsh weather often tore through this part of the coast, but right in this spot, the mountains and trees gave enough shelter from the worst of the rain and the wind. From the porch, there was nothing but open land and ocean as far as the eye could see.

Grayson had never come here with anyone else, had kept it as his own private space all these years. He had never even been tempted to bring anyone else here with him.

Lori Sullivan was the last person he wanted in his sacred space. She was too loud. She moved too fast. She *needed* too much.

Grayson gave endlessly to his animals. To his land. But never again did he intend to give any part of his soul to a woman.

Inside the cabin, he couldn't find her at first, not until he realized she was kneeling in front of the fireplace, lighting matches that were blowing out immediately. There was a pile of wasted matches on the ground in front of her.

Damn it, he asked himself in a silent but furious voice, *why the hell did his senses come alive every single time he looked at her?*

The anger that came from having to acknowledge

he'd never felt quite so alive in all his life than he did when he was with her had him biting out, "I'll get the fire going."

He knew better by now than to think she'd listen to his orders, and she didn't disappoint. She didn't look up at him from the floor, either, as she muttered, "I know how to start a fire," then lit another match.

He dropped the wood in a pile beside the fireplace and yanked the box of matches from her. "You're going to waste them all."

Only, just as he said it, the fire she'd laid in the stone fireplace finally took. He waited for her look of victory, but she didn't give him one; she didn't look at him at all as she stood up and moved away from him.

Guilt twisted in his gut at the way he'd ordered her to get inside earlier. But didn't she see that she simply should have held on so that she didn't fall off the horse, rather than moving in his arms like a woman did when she wanted a man or, worse still, slicking her tongue over his skin? And making him want her with a fierce fury that stunned him.

She was pushing him all the way to the edge…the very last place he'd sworn ever to go again.

Of course, just because he'd hurt her feelings didn't mean she could keep her mouth shut for more than five seconds. Even while they were out working on the fence, she'd been humming show tunes in an off-key voice the entire time.

"I've read so many books about this exact thing happening in England," she muttered, "when the hero and heroine get caught in a storm and have to take shelter in an old cottage. You'd be a duke and I'd be a virgin who's afraid to be alone with you in case you lose control and can't stop yourself from taking my innocence." She made a noise that was somewhere between a snort and irritated laughter as she shook out her wet hair and leaned in closer to the fire. "Of course, you're no duke, and I'm definitely not a virgin. The books made it all seem so romantic, but clearly they forgot to mention that being wet and freezing cold isn't romantic at all."

He refused to acknowledge the clenching of his chest at the way she'd said she was "definitely not a virgin." Picturing other men touching Lori, making love to Lori, shouldn't matter to him, so he forced himself to ignore his senseless possessiveness where she was concerned.

But he couldn't ignore the way she had her arms wrapped around herself and how hard she was shivering. "Take your clothes off."

She turned to him with a bemused expression. "Excuse me?"

Finally realizing how it had sounded, he said, "You're going to get chilled if you keep your wet clothes on."

"Why, Grayson," she drawled, "I didn't know you cared."

Hell, but she grated on him. And turned him on more and more with every one of her sassy responses.

"You're going to be even more useless on the farm if you get sick."

Before she turned away from him, he saw something move through her eyes, another flash of hurt that had him feeling even more like a guilty ass. Especially when she hadn't done a half-bad job on the fence this afternoon.

He walked to the window and looked out at the rain pelting his land. Just as he'd never intended to share this cabin with anyone, he hadn't planned on sharing his land, either. But now he could see Lori everywhere he looked, could sense her footprints, her touch, in so many things that had been all his up until now.

For days the two of them had been acting like kids out on the playground, with him pulling her pigtails while she threw rocks at him. Someone had to be the bigger person. He knew it needed to be him.

"You did a go—"

The words died on his lips as he turned and saw Lori standing in only her underwear, her jeans and socks and boots in a wet heap at her bare feet as she pulled her wet T-shirt up over her head. The muscles of her taut abdomen rippled slightly under her creamy skin, and her breasts threatened to spill out from over the top of her lacy bra.

The first second she'd gotten out of her car after crashing into his fence post, he'd thought she was gorgeous. But Jesus, looking at her in her underwear, he was on the verge of having a heart attack. Especially when the fabric barely covering her was so wet and see-through it was almost sexier than if she'd been wearing nothing at all.

When Lori had pulled her shirt all the way off and dropped it to the floor, she lifted her chin as she stared back at him. "Is this how you wanted me?" She gestured to her bra and panties. "Or maybe you meant that I should take *everything* off?"

She was a foot shorter than he, but as she stared him down inside the cabin, he forgot how small she was. He forgot that she was deliberately trying to rile him up, forgot everything but how damned much he wanted her.

Grayson didn't want to want her.

Hell, he didn't want to want anyone or anything the way he wanted her.

His lack of control made him angry at her.

But it made him even angrier at himself.

Wanting her like this felt like weakness. A terrible weakness that had been eating away at him one second, one minute, one hour, at a time over the past few days, ever since she'd invaded his space, his farm. His life.

Somehow he'd let himself get caught in a vicious circle of wanting, and then denying. Wanting, then denying.

And yet, even as he was telling himself there was right and wrong, black and white, the echo of her taunt rang out in the log cabin. As the rain poured down outside the windows and the fire leaped to life in the stone fireplace, everything that had ever made sense to Grayson could go straight to hell for all he cared.

He was within touching distance a moment later. He had his hands on her and pulled her nearly naked body tightly against his in the span of another.

And in the end, all that was left was his primal need to have Lori…the need to make her his.

His mouth came down on hers just as hers lifted

to his and that first taste of her was sweet, so much sweeter than anything he'd ever known, that he had to plunge deeper, had to take more from her than a first kiss should have allowed.

Grayson was in the prime of his life, strong from the intensely physical work he did every day on his land. But being this close to Lori, having her wet hair in his hands, her lips, her tongue, against his, was making his heart pound so hard that he wondered if he was anywhere near strong enough to live through it.

He couldn't get enough of her mouth, couldn't seem to learn the contours, the flavors, of her fast enough. With his tongue, his lips, he traced hers again and again, loving the way she gasped with pleasure when he teased the corners where her lips met, when he sucked her tongue into his mouth and especially when he scored her full lower lip with the edges of his teeth. And then, she was doing the same to him, kissing him in a way no woman had ever kissed him before, with such passion and desire and focus that he didn't have a prayer of continuing to lead their wild dance.

No, all he could do was partner her in movements that should have been familiar, but felt fresh and new and oh so sweet.

She'd tasted his neck on the horse with the tip of her tongue, but now he was the one bending her back so that she arched into his arms and he could run kisses from her gorgeous mouth down to her chin and over the edge to the underside of her jaw. She shivered in his arms and her nipples pressed hard through the white silk of her bra against his chest as he ran his tongue all the way down the line of her neck, until it dipped into the hollow of her collarbone.

His name fell from her lips as he let his mouth roam over the swell of her breasts above the silk and lace.

This was so much more than he'd ever thought to have of her, and it should have been enough. But, damn it, it wasn't. Not even close. Not even when he sucked one taut peak between his lips and laved her nipple through the silk. And when he reached back to undo her bra and finally bared her breasts to his hands and mouth and gaze, that wasn't enough, either.

Still holding her arched back against him with one hand, with the other he cupped her and brought her to his mouth again and again, first one breast and then the other. Sweet Lord, he couldn't remember ever touching such softness or witnessing such beauty. Lori was so responsive, a woman made for loving.

The shaky grasp he had on his sanity stretched thin, then broke entirely as he reached down for her panties and pulled the last of the silk from her body.

Being in his arms, being touched by Grayson, was nothing like any lovemaking she'd ever experienced before. Yes, Lori knew how to make sure she came while in bed with a man, whether he was focused on her pleasure or not, but with Grayson she knew she wouldn't need to do one damn thing to make sure she was satisfied.

He was still wearing his wet flannel shirt and thick jeans, and the contrast of the rough fabric against her bare skin as she writhed against him only inflamed her more. But then he was putting his hands on her waist and holding her back from his body. She didn't know why, couldn't get her brain to process a single reason he might not want to keep touching her, until she felt the heat of his gaze all across the surface of her skin and suddenly understood.

No one had ever looked at her like this, as though she was a gift he'd never expected to find waiting for him...looking as if he couldn't think of one thing he'd done to deserve it.

Needing to touch him, she tried to move back into his arms, but he held her where she was.

"I'm not done looking yet," he growled.

Even in lovemaking he was bossy, and that realization should have made her pull away, should have reminded her that they were no good together. Instead, it made her want him with a fierceness that stunned her.

For Lori, life had always been a journey of jumping from one high peak to another, with the occasional dip into a shallow valley. At least, until everything had come to a head after Victor had chipped away at her piece by piece over the past year and a half. She'd gotten lost in a hole so dark and deep she hadn't been able to see a way out.

And yet, despite her experience with such extremes, she'd never felt such a powerful craving for anyone, or anything, in her life. Doubts, concerns, worries—none of them had a chance against this craving, against the hunger that was eating her up moment by moment.

Oh, yes, she loved the way Grayson looked at her, but she needed to have his hands, his mouth, on her, too. And thank God, a few moments later, he was moving his hands up from her waist to cup her breasts with such reverence that the gentle heat of his touch stole what was left of her breath away.

"I can't believe you're here. That you're real. That you're really this beautiful."

His murmured words had her heart beating even faster against his thumbs. Lori knew she was pretty, and wasn't at all ashamed to have used her looks to her advantage for most of her life. It was natural that as a dancer she should emphasize her best features, along with her most fluid lines, for the benefit of the audience. But with Grayson touching her, she wasn't capable of doing anything at all but looking down at his deeply tanned skin against hers.

He was right—the way the two of them fit together was so beautiful, one large, the other smaller, both full of a desire that was stronger even than the thunder and lightning raging outside the log cabin.

He ran his hands down past her ribs, over her flat belly, his fingers playing over her hip bones, until he was cupping her hips in his hands and dragging her back against him to take her mouth again. She sank into his kiss, into the hands cupping her so firmly, so warmly, so sweetly, as they massaged her gently from her bottom to the muscles of her back and shoulders, sore from both the ride on the horse and the hard work she'd put in fixing the fence.

One of his hands moved back to brush against her cheek before plunging into her hair, already drying from the heat of the fire behind them. With his other hand, he stroked down the hourglass of her curves, from the swell of her breast to the indentation of her waist, back out to the flare of her hips.

"Grayson."

She'd sworn never to beg him for anything. She would earn, with hard work, every day on his farm and every night in the bedroom he'd given her. And yet, begging him to touch her, to take her all the way over the edge he'd already brought her to, was as natural as breathing. As natural as the path of his hand from her hips to her stomach.

She was trembling now with need for him, but when he slowly slid his hand down lower, and then lower still between her thighs, she wasn't the only one who couldn't find steady ground.

"So hot." He groaned the words into her neck, where he'd buried his face. "And so goddamned wet. God, I can't believe how ready you are for me."

He slipped one finger, then two, into her, and she couldn't think, could barely remember to breathe.

All she could do was feel.

The heat of him. The sensuous sweet slide of his fingers in and out of her. The press of his thumb over her clitoris.

The storm came to a head outside with thunder and lightning crashing down on the cabin just as the storm inside her broke. She rocked into his hand and he crushed his mouth to hers again to drink from her cries of pleasure.

He couldn't stop kissing her, couldn't stop reveling in the slick softness between her legs. God, he wanted to taste her, wanted to drop to his knees and kiss every inch of her beautiful body. And then, after he made her come again against his tongue, he wanted to pull her down to the floor with him, her gorgeous legs wrapped around his hips as he took her fast and furiously.

The storm that was raging outside had raged just as powerfully inside him—until the moment he realized he didn't have protection on him, damn it.

Why would he? He didn't need condoms to head out into the field to work with his horses and cows, to fix fences, to rotate his crops.

But even as practicalities stopped him cold, he knew they weren't the real reason he wasn't going to pull Lori down onto the crude wood floor and take her. And it wasn't because he didn't want her. Lord, he couldn't ever remember wanting to make love to a woman more, had never needed to know this badly what it would feel like to sink into her.

All these years in California he'd made sure to keep to himself, to feed a community without ever connecting with anyone beyond the food he grew for them. He couldn't allow himself to fall in love again, refused to let anyone touch his heart, his soul, when he knew he needed to keep them both locked up and punished for the way his wife had died.

But even as Grayson reminded himself of all the reasons he couldn't permit himself to feel anything for Lori, he couldn't stop thinking about the moment she had finally stilled in his arms after her climax.

He'd felt every inch of her softness in his arms…and every bit of her vulnerability.

She acted so tough, put on that sassy act at every turn. But he'd seen the flashes of pain in her when she didn't think he was looking, simply because he couldn't look away. It was why he'd let her stay when he thought she'd be next to useless as a farmhand.

Because he'd recognized in her the need to heal that had been in himself three years ago when he'd found the farm.

And yet, even though he'd lived with her for nearly a week, and even though she'd just come apart in his arms and it had been one of the most beautiful things he'd ever experienced in thirty-five years, he still didn't know a damn thing about why she was on the farm.

Or what she was hiding from.

Grayson knew what he needed to do. He needed to push her away; needed to lash out hard enough that she couldn't possibly stay; needed to find a way to live with himself for adding more pain to her eyes, more tears on her pillow. He needed a way to forget that he had begun to respect her for turning out to be much stronger than he'd initially given her credit for, filled with a determination that couldn't help but impress him.

And, most of all, he needed to remember that the last time he'd let himself fall for a woman, he'd ended up losing her.

Grayson couldn't repeat that. Ever.

Lori's fingers were moving to his belt buckle when he removed his hands from her and forced himself to take a step back as he said, "This never should have happened."

Twelve

Five words were all it took for Lori to feel as if she'd just stepped out into the cold, hard rain, a complete one-eighty from the bliss Grayson had just given her, immediately making everything that had warmed freeze up again.

She knew he was right, that they shouldn't be doing this, but it didn't stop his abrupt rejection from hurting. Hurting like crazy, actually, as though his words had run a sharp grater across her already raw insides.

Lori bent down to reach for her clothes, but they were so wet she could barely peel them apart, let alone shove them on so that she could get away from a man she didn't understand. A man she shouldn't want to understand when he pulled her into him one second, and shoved her away the next.

She'd been there. She'd done that.

Never again—wasn't that what she'd vowed?

Oh, how she'd loved being naked in Grayson's arms, but now that he'd pushed her away, she hated her nakedness. She felt powerless, as if he could see all the way through her when he'd put every single one of his guards back up.

A sob rose as she tried to get her stupid clothes to come unstuck from each other, and she wasn't quick enough at swallowing it down. It didn't help when Grayson handed her a blanket from the couch.

"Wrap this around yourself."

Why did he have to choose that moment to be kind? If he'd been gruff like he usually was, she could have stopped any tears from falling...but now all she could do was take the blanket from him and turn away to move closer to the fire as she wrapped it around herself, hoping he hadn't seen them. Her years of dance training were what made it possible for her to hold herself proud and straight even as another tear fell.

"Lori—"

She could hear the regret in the way he said her name and she hated it. Hated that he felt sorry for her for wanting him the way she did.

"Don't." The word came out sharply. "We don't need to talk about what happened. We can just chalk it up to an accident."

She assumed he was silent because he agreed with her. But she could feel his gaze on her, feel the heat of it burning even hotter than the fire.

Lori Sullivan had always known exactly what she wanted, and she'd trusted herself to follow her heart every day of her life. But now that she'd had to face up to the mistakes she'd made in trusting her ex when she definitely shouldn't have, she hated that she couldn't trust what she felt with Grayson, either.

She stared into the fire and watched the flames leap in no pattern whatsoever. But she'd followed the same pattern her entire adult life: she'd fallen for men who promised everything, then after she'd given herself to them, no holds barred, each and every one of them had taken their promises back.

She told herself it shouldn't matter that Grayson had just hurt her, too.

But it did.

He moved to her side, but instead of looking at the fire, he stared directly at her profile. "It wasn't an accident."

She was shocked enough that she turned her tear-streaked face to him forgetting to wipe it clean first.

A surprising tenderness—along with obvious regret—flashed in his eyes at the sight of her tears, and she might have been able to write it off as just another accident on his part if he hadn't followed it up by brushing one thumb across her cheek to wipe the wetness away.

"No," she finally agreed, "it wasn't." But that didn't change anything. "So," she said in an effort to change the subject as she turned her face away to swipe at her damp cheeks with the back of her hand, "do you have any board games in here that we could play while we wait out the storm?"

"Why are you here, Lori?"

What was he doing? Why wasn't he letting them

move into shallow waters again? Didn't he realize how much easier it would be?

Lucky for him that she was a master at acting as if everything was okay even when it wasn't.

Lori started to move away from him as she asked, "Or maybe a deck of cards?"

But he was quicker than she was, and his hand came around her wrist before she could get far enough away from him to take a full breath. "I want to know why you came here with the want ad in your fist when you'd clearly never set foot on a farm a day in your life."

She couldn't think straight when he was touching her. All she could do was crave the feeling of those rough, calloused fingers moving across her breasts again, over her hips, between her legs. Her breath was already coming faster when he dropped her wrist as though she'd turned into one of the flames in the fireplace.

"I told you already. It looked like fun."

"Bullshit."

When his gaze didn't waver from her face, she felt herself begin to crumble. "The past few weeks…" God, was her voice really breaking? She took a deep breath that shook far more than she wanted it to. She hated feeling sorry for herself so much that she forced the corners of her lips up into what she hoped looked at least a little like a smile. "They weren't good."

He didn't smile back. "Why?"

"Seriously?" The anger she felt wasn't entirely directed at Grayson. Yes, he'd hurt her by pushing her away a few minutes ago, but it was Victor she was thinking of as she said, "You've made me come and now you suddenly think I owe you my life story?"

He ran one hand through his wet hair, looking as though he was at war with himself. Well, she knew exactly how that felt. Finally, he said, "I know this isn't your world, Lori. What is?"

He was right—endless pastures and cows and pigs weren't any part of her world. And yet, she was falling for it all the same.

Just as she was falling for him.

"I'm a dancer."

Grayson's dark gaze ran the length of her covered in her blanket, then back up to her face. "Of course you are. I had already guessed it from the way you move."

She should have been surprised to hear him admit that he'd watched her move, that he'd paid any attention to her at all.

But she wasn't.

"Why aren't you dancing?"

She turned away from him then, and this time he let her go. It hurt to think of dancing. Of *not* dancing. Her whole life, dance had been her cornerstone. The one thing she could count on.

Lost.

She was utterly lost without dance at her center. If she could have done anything else, she wouldn't have walked away from it. But her lifelong, soul-deep love for dancing had left her without a word of warning. Leaving a big, black hole inside of her that she couldn't figure out how to fill.

"I don't want to dance anymore."

"You lie as badly as you drive."

God, he was like a dog with a bone, and she spun around to face him. "Why do you care if I'm telling the truth about wanting to dance again, or not? You don't want me on your farm. You don't want to have sex with me. Nothing would make you happier than my packing up my things after the storm breaks and getting the hell out of your hair."

He didn't contradict her. She didn't expect him to. Rejoicing was closer to what he'd do the day she threw her suitcase into the trunk of her rental car and drove down his long driveway back to the city.

"You can't leave Mo." She couldn't read his expression as he said, "Not yet."

"Sweetpea?" She was trying to figure out where that had come from. "Why are you talking about your cat?"

"You've made her depend on you. You feed her from your hand, for God's sake."

It was a ridiculous reason for her to stay, especially when he could easily feed his cat by hand if she left.

Was it his way of saying he wanted her to stay? She tucked the blanket more tightly around her and picked up her wet clothes, hanging them over the back of a chair near the fire. Whatever his reason, between the gentleness of his touch on her cheek as he'd wiped away her tears and his obvious concern for his cat, she suddenly felt safe enough to finally tell him a little bit of what had happened to her in Chicago.

"I was in a relationship for the past couple of years. A rotten one that everyone I knew kept telling me to get out of, but I didn't listen until I found him in bed with a dancer I had personally hired." She sighed at her own stupidity. "Well, it's over now, and I needed a break from everything. From dancing. From my life." She couldn't stop herself from adding, "And especially from men." Because how could she have known that when she grabbed the want ad at the General Store she was going to be applying to work for a modern-day cowboy who ran a fabulous CSA and could have made serious dough modeling for a high-end underwear ad?

Grayson didn't reply for a long while, and when she finally looked at him, she expected to see disinterest. Or pity, maybe.

But not disdain. And disgust.

"Why are you looking at me like that?"

"You broke up with your boyfriend? That's what sent you running away from your real life? That's why you stopped dancing?"

Whoa. What was going on here?

And why did having him look at her like that hurt so badly? Even worse now that she'd—stupidly—let him touch her.

"He told me he loved me, he said he couldn't live without me, but I found out he was only using me to dance his way up the ladder. I also found out, too late, that he stole jobs that should have been mine, and did whatever he could to undermine the ones he couldn't get. He told lies to my face, then lied about me behind my back." It exhausted her to say it all out loud. And made her furious all over again. "How can I keep dancing when I can't even remember why I love it?"

She hated what a fool she'd been, that she'd been so

blind to what was happening when everyone else had seen it. How desperately she'd wanted to be loved, so desperate that she hadn't put a stop to Victor's emotional abuse until it had sucked the will to dance—and to love—from her.

But she could see that nothing she said made any difference to Grayson. "You think I'm a big crybaby, don't you? That I'm just here to hide from everything and lick my wounds?" She took a step toward him and poked him in the chest. "So what if I am? What makes you the judge and jury for what counts as real pain?"

He grabbed her hand hard enough that she would have cried out if the fury on his face hadn't stolen her breath away before she could make a sound.

"My wife died in a car crash. Three years ago. It was our tenth wedding anniversary."

"Grayson."

He let her hand go and cursed. "The storm is letting up. We need to get back to the farm to make sure the rest of the animals are okay."

Her own pain instantly forgotten in the wake of Grayson's confession, Lori desperately wanted to go to him. She wanted to put her arms around him and console him for the pain he'd suffered. And, most of all, she wanted him to trust her enough to bare his soul to her and let her help him finally heal.

"I'm sorry," she told him over the sound of the crackling fire. "So sorry for what you've been through. And for what I just said."

His face was granite when he turned back to her. "It was three years ago. I'm over it now." His lie was a thousand times worse than hers had been—thinking that being a farmhand would be fun. "I'll go get the horse ready to take us back."

He was gone before she could reach for him, before she could say anything else. But so much was clear now. The way he'd pushed her away at every turn. The solitude he'd chosen despite the great community that surrounded him.

He was right, his pain was so much worse than hers—and yet, whether he wanted to see it or not, they were kindred spirits despite themselves. Because she'd made the very same vow not to love again or risk another painful loss.

But that didn't mean she couldn't find a way to help him....

Thirteen

Lori understood what Grayson wanted her to do. He wanted her to leave him alone. He wanted to pretend that he'd never told her anything about his past.

She hadn't seen him since the previous day when he'd taken her to his log cabin in the storm. She hadn't been sure what to expect when they'd finally arrived back at the farmhouse. Would he come in to go to bed, or would he simply sleep somewhere else instead so that he wouldn't have to talk to her?

But even though she understood what he wanted from her, she just didn't see how it could be healthy for him to keep all his pain inside—especially for so long. She'd been thinking for the past twenty-four hours that, maybe if he finally let some of it out, he could start moving forward again. Not necessarily off the farm— she could see how much he truly loved his home here and his way of life with the animals and his CSA. But she hadn't seen him interact with anyone other than herself and Eric.

These should be the best years of Grayson's life. He should be making the most of them. Things didn't add up at first—why would a gorgeous, thriving man in the prime of his life choose to live in the middle of nowhere with only animals for company? But it all made so much more sense now.

But just because it made sense didn't mean it was right.

Lori was a much better farmhand now than she'd been at first, but she still knew she hadn't been much help to him so far. Maybe if she could help him with his grief, then coming here would have been worth it.

And she would know she'd done at least one truly worthwhile thing in her life.

Filled with purpose, as soon as she'd finished her most important chores and the sun was just starting to set as a bright red-and-orange ball falling over the rolling green hills, she went to look for him. It didn't take her long to find him in the stables.

He didn't look up when she walked in, but she could see his shoulders tense slightly. It was tempting to turn around and walk out again, to hide from a conversation that she knew wasn't going to be at all easy. But she owed him this—the chance to finally unburden himself of the weight he'd been carrying around for so long.

Only, she couldn't quite figure out where to start, so she moved closer to admire the horse he was grooming. "You really do have the most beautiful horses." He didn't say anything, but she hadn't expected him to. Not yet, anyway. "How long have you been riding?"

Of course, instead of answering her simple question, he stayed right where he was behind the horse's flanks. "Do you need something, Lori? Is the farmhouse on fire? Or have you 'accidentally' let a fox into the henhouse?"

His sarcasm stung, but she refused to let him push her away that easily. Not when she guessed that was how he'd dealt with the world ever since his wife died, just by pushing and pushing and pushing until no one dared come close anymore.

Feeling much bolder around his horse since she'd survived the ride the day before, she gently ran her hand down the soft hair on his muzzle and took strength from the big brown eyes staring back at her. Funny, she'd never realized just how much she loved animals until this past week. If only she didn't travel so much, she would want at least one dog and a cat at home.

Although, if she wasn't going to dance again...

Wait, she hadn't come into the stable today to work out her own mess of a life. She was here to help Grayson. To get him to see that he could trust her enough to finally open up.

She moved around the side of the horse so that she could see Grayson's face. "My father died when I was two. He was forty-eight and my mother was left with all eight of us to raise. I would climb into her bed to cuddle with her some nights and her pillow would be all wet and she would just hold me until we both fell asleep." She could guess without Grayson's telling her that he hadn't had anyone to hold after his wife died. Or if he had, he'd turned away from them before they could get too close. "I know how hard it is to lose someone—"

"You don't know a damn thing about how hard it is!"

His outburst was so loud the previously calm horse spooked and began to rear up. Grayson yanked Lori out of the stall before a hoof could connect with her head.

His expression was so fierce, his grip on her arm so hard, that she had to steel herself not to shrink back from him. He needed her, she knew he did.

Surely it was why he'd worked so hard to keep her at arm's length.

"I know you must still be in terrible pain over what happened. Have you talked to anyone about your wife? Have you tried to work through any of your grief? Because if you haven't, then maybe if you talked to me about it, I could help you—"

"Help?" He spit the word out as he released his grip on her so quickly she almost spun into the opposite stall. "*Helping* is all you've been trying to do since you got here. *Trying* so damned hard."

"I *have* been trying, Grayson, and I've been doing a pretty good job with everything," she interjected. "But I think the reason I ended up here, on your farm, wasn't because I needed to learn to be a farmhand. Maybe—" She forced herself to continue despite the fury on his face. "Maybe I had to come here because you needed me."

He laughed, but instead of joy, the sound was harsh and brittle, as far from true laughter as anything she'd ever heard.

"All you've done since you showed up is ruin things. Break things. Push your way in where you shouldn't be." His eyes were black as night, hard as coal. "All you've done is go where you're *not* wanted."

Holy crap, he was mean. Even meaner than her ex had been when she'd finally told him what she thought of him and his dancing and his endless career-climbing. Even meaner than he'd been when she'd accidentally let the pig she'd nicknamed Sophie decimate his strawberries.

But when pushed hard enough she could be mean, too, cruel enough to remind him, "You wanted me plenty last night."

"Then that makes both of us idiots." His glare was hot enough to spark a fire in the loose hay they were standing on. He raked his eyes down the length of her body and she actually felt dirty by the time he looked back up at her face. "You could take off every scrap of clothes right here, right now, and I wouldn't be stupid enough to make that mistake again."

No, damn it, she wouldn't let another man tell her she wasn't good enough. She wouldn't let anyone else chip away at her until her insides curled up into a tight little ball of misery.

"Don't worry," she told him in an equally hard tone, "I won't make the mistake of trying to help you again, either. If you want to wither away in your grief and let it eat up your entire life and your future, go right ahead. I thought you were worth helping, that maybe there was a real human being—a man with a beating heart—beneath all the fury and nastiness. But now you've helped me see that you aren't worth anything at all."

She turned to walk out on him, but before she could leave him to stew in his own misery until kingdom come, he said, "Instead of pestering me with your questions, you should be asking yourself what the hell you're doing hiding on my farm. Because we both know this isn't where you belong, *Naughty*."

God, it hurt to hear him say that, and then to fling the family nickname at her, one she now knew she never should have shared with him, as if every last part of her was tainted. Unlovable.

Because if she didn't belong here with the animals and the land and the bright blue sky—and if she no longer belonged in the dance world—then where did she belong?

Lori knew she just needed to keep putting one foot in front of the other, to keep on walking out of the barn and out of his life. But even as she tried to get away, he kept coming at her with more words aimed where they could do as much damage as possible.

"How would you like it if I turned my focus to fixing you, because it was easier than fixing myself?"

His accusation stopped her cold, even when she knew she should be running from him as fast as she could, before he could do deeper damage than he'd already done. He'd hurt her yesterday with his complete dismissal of her feelings in the cottage during the storm. Badly. And he'd made her doubt her own feelings, made her ask herself if she was really nothing more than the self-absorbed person he'd made her out to be.

"Do you know what I saw that day when you drove into my fence and sent my chickens running down the road?" He didn't wait for her to answer, didn't stop to notice that she was crumbling apart one word at a time. Or if he did see it, he clearly didn't care just how badly he was hurting her. "I saw a scared little girl who's had everything she ever wanted, everything she's ever needed, handed to her on a platter. And then, when she hit one little bump in the road, she was so spoiled that the only option she saw was to give up." He put his hands on her shoulders and spun her around to face him. "If you're a dancer, then you should be dancing, damn it."

She couldn't stop the tears from falling down her cheeks, and not just because he was gripping her shoulders nearly hard enough to leave bruises. "I'm not a dancer anymore."

He stared at her for a long moment, the sparks of heat and anger and a still-undeniable connection going off between them, before he dropped his hands from her shoulders. "No, you obviously never were a real dancer if you're able to give up this easily."

She didn't have to stay here and listen to his insults. She could go work on someone else's farm. She could clean someone else's toilets until they sparkled and keep their chickens and pigs fed and weed their rows of vegetables. Not, of course, that she needed the money, considering she had plenty socked away from some of her higher-profile gigs. It was just that she couldn't imagine not having something to do. Being left alone with her thoughts all day long would be terrible. Even cleaning bathrooms would be better than that.

Without saying another word, she made a beeline for the farmhouse, kicking her dirty shoes off on the porch before going inside. Just because she wouldn't be cleaning Grayson's house anymore didn't mean she needed to make it harder for the poor person he tricked into replacing her.

Just as she walked into her bedroom and yanked her suitcase out from under the bed, she heard a sound that had her chest clenching tight. She ran out to the living room, where Sweetpea was coughing and shivering on top of her blanket.

No, not now. She couldn't deal with this, too, not when her heart was already torn to pieces.

Lori scooped the cat up into her arms, pressing her lips to the soft, hairless spot between her ears. "Poor baby," she said as she rocked her in her arms. "Poor, poor baby. You feel rotten, don't you?" She kissed her again. "It's been that kind of day for me, too."

Grayson walked in, but she was so concerned about the cat that had been her one true friend for the past week that his presence barely registered. While Grayson had been God-knew-where avoiding her the past few days, Lori had spent many hours with Sweetpea warm and purring on her lap, stroking the cat's bony back as she tried to get her to eat the food and drink the milk she brought her every few hours. She'd been about to leave to save what was left of her heart, but now she knew that, no matter how much it hurt to be near Grayson, she needed to stay for the one true friend she'd made on his farm.

"Don't worry, Sweetpea," she told her furry friend. "I'm not going to leave. Not as long as you need me."

When Grayson stepped into the house and saw Lori with his cat in her arms and heard her make the promise to stay no matter what, the relief that flooded him was so strong it nearly buckled his knees.

Before the storm, before they'd ended up in the cabin, he'd wanted her. But now that he'd touched her, tasted her, he realized that earlier wanting amounted to little more than the buzzing of a fly around his ears. He'd known that he'd pay for those moments of weakness in the cabin, and boy, was he. Because how could he possibly ever regret knowing how soft, how sweet, Lori had felt in his arms, how beautifully sweet the sound of her moans, her gasps of pleasure, had been as she came?

And how could he ever forgive himself for the way he'd just lashed out at her, when he knew all she was trying to do was help him? Especially when she'd told him that she'd come to his farm to take a break not only from dancing, but also from men.

He knew he couldn't be what she needed, but he shouldn't have to hurt her to prove that.

"Lori," he said in a low voice as he approached her, "I promised I wouldn't do that to you again. I broke my promise." He felt like he was swallowing fire as he said, "I'm sorry."

God, he would have given up every one of his thousand acres just to see her smile up at him, just to hear her say, "You're forgiven," again like she had the day he'd lost it over the pigs and then offered to take her to buy cowboy boots.

Of course, he knew that wasn't going to happen, not when he'd crossed over the line—way the hell over it—with her just now.

"We both know you meant every word you said to me," she replied in an even voice, though her eyes flashed with fire. "And I meant every word I said to you. But don't worry." She stroked a gentle hand over Mo's patchy fur and the cat gave a soft purr of joy at being showered with such pure, sweet love. "As soon as Sweetpea doesn't need me anymore, I'll be out of your hair." Lori sneezed before adding, "And until then, we can just stay out of each other's way as much as possible."

She turned her full attention back to the cat then, and he knew he'd been dismissed. So completely that he might never have been there at all.

Leave. He should leave, go to his room, take a shower and hit the sack to make up for all the sleep he hadn't been able to get with Lori only a wall away at night—visions of her naked and beautiful beneath her sheets running through his head on repeat until sunrise.

But he knew she had to be hungry after the long day she'd put in, so instead of leaving, he started to pull together dinner. Thirty minutes later, after having listened to Lori sneeze practically the entire time, he had two plates of spaghetti ready for both of them.

"Dinner's ready," he told her.

"I'm not hungry."

"I know how hard you've worked today," he said in

a soft voice. "And I've seen you eat. You've got to be starved." He put the plate down on the coffee table in front of her. "Please eat dinner, Lori."

She looked from the plate to him, her brow furrowed with confusion. For another moment, he thought she'd refuse his peace offering, but then she said, "I really don't understand you, Grayson."

He wanted to tell her she understood him better than anyone else ever had, that everything she'd said to him had been right.

He wanted to tell her how wrong he'd been for lashing out at her when it wasn't her fault that his wife had died.

He wanted to confess that he didn't know how to get over his guilt for the way his marriage had crumbled and turned into tragedy.

He wanted to make up to her every harsh thing he'd said and done.

He wanted to hear the beautiful sound of her laughter and know that he'd pleased her, rather than constantly being the source of her tears.

But three years of near-constant silence made the words stutter to a halt inside his head before they could reach his lips. Instead, Grayson brought his plate over from the kitchen, sat down in the living room and ate in silence with Lori and his cat.

Fourteen

"Do you have anything nice to wear?"

Lori was in the barn the next day getting another bag of feed for the chickens when Grayson walked in and asked the totally random question. She hadn't been able to forget the unexpectedly deep look of longing in his eyes as he'd come into the living room the previous evening to apologize. But neither could she forget the way they'd blown up at each other in the barn. So, instead of telling him that, yes, she had several really pretty dresses in her suitcase, she gestured at her mud-spattered jeans and T-shirt.

"What could possibly be nicer than this?"

That muscle in his jaw started moving. He needed to stop clenching it so hard or he was going to end up with terrible headaches. Not that she was going to make the mistake of telling him that. No, from here on out she'd keep her mouth shut and her opinions to herself. That was what they both wanted, after all.

She knew she could leave his farm at any moment but

somehow, now, that wasn't an option. Sweetpea needed her, of course, but on top of that, Lori still didn't have anything to go back to…and she couldn't bear to face her family and friends the way she was right now.

They all thought she was invincible.

It was one thing for Grayson to be disappointed in her. It was another entirely for the people who loved her to feel that way.

Grayson swept his dark gaze over her again before saying, "If you show up with me at the barn dance looking like that, people are going to talk."

The word *dance* grabbed her gut and twisted it. Hard enough that she lost her breath and her balance for a minute, and she had to reach out to grab a beam to steady herself.

"Why would you want me to go anywhere with you? I thought we had agreed to keep to ourselves from here on out."

He shrugged. "I've been alone on this farm long enough that people are starting to think I'm fair game. If you're with me, they'll stop thinking that."

"People? Fair game?" She finally realized what he was talking about. "You mean women?"

"Yes." He gritted out the word between teeth that were clenched tighter than she thought possible.

"So, if you go to this barn—" she didn't even want to say the word "—*thing* without me, you'll be subjected to pretty little ladies throwing themselves at you left and right?"

"Be ready at six," he said without bothering to answer her snarky question.

He was already walking away when she said, "Why should I?"

She wasn't sure she liked the look in his eyes when he turned to face her. "I've let you hide out here on my farm all week, that's why."

She could no longer argue with him about the hiding out part, but she could take issue with the fact that he was acting like she'd been a freeloader. And she was sick to death of men who thought they could take her accomplishments down a peg. "I've been working hard, not just lying on the grass in a bikini asking you to crank up the blender for my next drink refill." She could only imagine the fit Grayson would have pitched if she'd done that. "I know I screwed up some things at first, but I've been doing a great job since then."

He moved closer, close enough that her heartbeat kicked into overdrive. "If you're that afraid to go to the dance, just tell me and I'll let you off the hook."

The challenge in his words reverberated through every last cell in her body despite how softly he'd uttered them. And this time she was the one gritting her teeth so hard she nearly cracked her molars.

"I'll be ready at six."

Fury had Lori weeding like a fiend for the rest of the afternoon, but she didn't get any satisfaction out of the work she'd accomplished. Not when she was too busy planning how to make Grayson regret he'd ever made that challenge to her.

Oh, she'd dance all right. With every man in town but him. And she'd make sure that he was the perfect target for every single woman within a hundred miles of Pescadero.

At five o'clock she locked herself in the bathroom with her war chest. For nearly her whole life, she'd depended on the contents of this bag—makeup, lotions, nail polish, blow dryer, curling iron—in the same way that she'd needed food and sleep. But for one whole week she hadn't so much as unzipped the bag. It was at once comforting and familiar...and strange. She loved the way she felt when she looked good, yet there had been surprising freedom in not caring one way or the other.

She took out everything and laid it along the small counter. She grinned at the way her girlie things immediately took over every possible surface in his bathroom, and how irritated Grayson would be if she left it all for him after she was gone.

With that happily evil thought cheering her, she stripped off her grimy clothes and stepped into the shower. The hot spray felt great on her overworked muscles, the water turning from brown to clear as she soaped up and washed the dirt from her skin, from her hair, from beneath her fingernails. She took extra care to shave her legs from ankle to hip, slicking lotion over her entire body before she got out of the shower.

She had no intention of letting any man benefit from the softness of her skin tonight, but Grayson didn't need to know that.

It was as natural as breathing for her to do her hair and makeup and to paint her nails. Maybe, she found herself thinking, that was what she'd do now that her

YOUR PARTICIPATION IS REQUESTED!

Dear Reader,

Since you are a lover of our books – we would like to get to know you!

Inside you will find a short Reader's Survey. Sharing your answers with us will help our editorial staff understand who you are and what activities you enjoy.

To thank you for your participation, we would like to send you 2 books and 2 gifts – **ABSOLUTELY FREE!**

Enjoy your gifts with our appreciation,

Pam Powers

SEE INSIDE FOR READER'S SURVEY

For Your Reading Pleasure...

We'll send you 2 books and 2 gifts
ABSOLUTELY FREE
just for completing our Reader's Survey!

YOUR READER'S SURVEY
"THANK YOU" FREE GIFTS INCLUDE:
- ▶ 2 FREE books
- ▶ 2 lovely surprise gifts

PLEASE FILL IN THE CIRCLES COMPLETELY TO RESPOND

1) What type of fiction books do you enjoy reading? (Check all that apply)
- ○ Suspense/Thrillers ○ Action/Adventure ○ Modern-day Romances
- ○ Historical Romance ○ Humour ○ Paranormal Romance

2) What attracted you most to the last fiction book you purchased on impulse?
- ○ The Title ○ The Cover ○ The Author ○ The Story

3) What is usually the greatest influencer when you <u>plan</u> to buy a book?
- ○ Advertising ○ Referral ○ Book Review

4) How often do you access the internet?
- ○ Daily ○ Weekly ○ Monthly ○ Rarely or never.

5) How many NEW paperback fiction novels have you purchased in the past 3 months?
- ○ 0 - 2 ○ 3 - 6 ○ 7 or more

YES! I have completed the Reader's Survey. Please send me the 2 FREE books and 2 FREE gifts (gifts are worth about $10) for which I qualify. I understand that I am under no obligation to purchase any books, as explained on the back of this card.

194/394 MDL GEXA

FIRST NAME | LAST NAME

ADDRESS

APT.# | CITY

STATE/PROV. | ZIP/POSTAL CODE

ROM-514-SUR13

♦ **HARLEQUIN**™ READER SERVICE — **Here's How It Works:**

Accepting your 2 free Romance books and 2 free gifts (gifts valued at approximately $10.00) places you under no obligation to buy anything. You may keep the books and gifts and return the shipping statement marked "cancel." If you do not cancel, about a month later we'll send you 4 additional books and bill you just $6.24 each in the U.S. or $6.74 each in Canada. That is a savings of at least 22% off the cover price. It's quite a bargain! Shipping and handling is just 50¢ per book in the U.S. and 75¢ per book in Canada.* You may cancel at any time, but if you choose to continue, every month we'll send you 4 more books, which you may either purchase at the discount price or return to us and cancel your subscription. *Terms and prices subject to change without notice. Prices do not include applicable taxes. Sales tax applicable in N.Y. Canadian residents will be charged applicable taxes. Offer not valid in Quebec. Books received may not be as shown. All orders subject to credit approval. Credit or debit balances in a customer's account(s) may be offset by any other outstanding balance owed by or to the customer. Please allow 4 to 6 weeks for delivery. Offer available while quantities last.

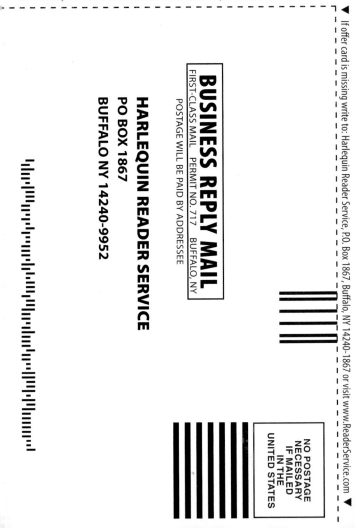

If offer card is missing write to: Harlequin Reader Service, P.O. Box 1867, Buffalo, NY 14240-1867 or visit www.ReaderService.com ▲

BUSINESS REPLY MAIL
FIRST-CLASS MAIL   PERMIT NO. 717   BUFFALO, NY

POSTAGE WILL BE PAID BY ADDRESSEE

HARLEQUIN READER SERVICE
PO BOX 1867
BUFFALO NY 14240-9952

NO POSTAGE
NECESSARY
IF MAILED
IN THE
UNITED STATES

dancing career was over. She could open up a small salon somewhere far away from here and help other women feel better about themselves. It wasn't what she had dreamed of doing her whole life, but it would be better than nothing.

When she was finished primping, she wrapped herself in a towel and left the bathroom. Grayson wasn't even in the house, as far as she could tell. It figured that he wanted her to put all sorts of effort into looking good, but he'd probably just put on a new pair of jeans and clean pair of boots and be ready inside of thirty seconds.

She'd left her luggage open on her bed and now she pulled out a red dress made up entirely of satin and sequins. The straps were thin and it was almost completely backless, ending just above the curve of her hips. She'd danced in outfits with far less material than this dress, but she could easily guess that it would be the most inappropriate outfit *ever* for a barn dance.

Yes, she decided as she slipped it on, that was what made it so perfect. As were the four-inch spike heels she slipped on next. Where most women could barely have walked in them, Lori could dance all night without any problems at all.

And she would, damn it, just to spite Grayson.

Grayson looked at his watch: 6:15 p.m. Lori was late, which came as no surprise given that she'd been locked in her bedroom for over an hour now.

Just the idea of the barn dance had him feeling out of sorts, but he knew he had to do it for her. Because he owed Lori something more than an apology for the way he'd behaved. For the things he'd said.

But when she finally stepped out of the bedroom, all thoughts of apologies scattered.

"What the hell are you wearing?"

He hadn't seen a dress like that in years—bloodred satin and sequins that perfectly showcased the curves he hadn't been able to get out of his head. The skirt was higher in the front than it was in the back and swished around her ridiculously gorgeous legs as she moved toward him in heels so high she actually came up past his chin now.

Holy hell, his heart was either going to explode from racing so fast, or just stop beating altogether. That was how badly he wanted to rip the dress from her and drag her back into the bedroom and make love to her until both of them forgot that it was a mistake.

Acting as if he wasn't about to burst a blood vessel just from being near her, she gave him a pretty little smile and twirled. "Just a little something I had in my bag." Her smile still glittered, even brighter than the sequins, despite never quite reaching her eyes. "I take it you don't like it."

Fuck. Why did he keep hurting her? It wasn't Lori's fault that his wife had died.

And it wasn't Lori's fault that he couldn't stop wanting the beautiful, sassy farmhand he'd never meant to hire.

He knew he needed to apologize again and was just about to say the words, but as she went toward the front door and he finally saw the back of her dress—or rather, the back of the dress that should have been there, instead of the most gorgeous, creamy skin he'd ever seen—he couldn't think straight, couldn't stop himself from grabbing her arm.

"You are not wearing that dress tonight."

Her eyes lit with fury as she whirled around to face him. "Watch me."

She tried to yank her arm from his grip, but being this close to her made his head spin too fast for him to let her go...or to stop himself from dragging her against him and taking her mouth with his.

Grayson had wanted to kiss her at least a thousand times since the afternoon in the log cabin, when she'd been pure heat and sensual woman in his arms. He hadn't been able to recover from that, not even by reminding himself of all the reasons he needed to stay away from her.

He needed this kiss so badly that he barely registered how stiff she was in his arms, until she wasn't anymore and the hands that had been pushing him away were trying to pull him in closer instead.

God, she was soft.

And so damned sweet he could barely believe it.

Soon he had her backed up against the door. In the log cabin, he'd been desperate to touch her, to find out if she felt as good against him as she looked. But now that he knew exactly what waited for him beneath the thin fabric of her dress—skin so warm and pretty that he'd be stunned every time his mouth or hands made contact with it—it only made him crazier for her. And then there were the little sounds she'd make as he rained kisses over her—little gasps, soft moans, that would take hold of his sanity and yank it completely away.

Only this time, instead of him being the one to put the brakes on when he was on the verge of heading for the point of no return, Lori was the one dragging her mouth from his.

"How can you kiss me like this," she asked him in a voice that shook slightly, "when you won't even talk to me about what happened to you?"

She didn't say, *"Stop."* She didn't tell him, *"We shouldn't do this."* Just, *"You won't even talk to me about what happened to you."*

But it was enough. Because she was right—he had no business kissing her like that, or even thinking of going further, when he could still barely think about his past, let alone share the details of it with someone else. With her.

She was still trying to catch her breath, her breasts rising up in the slinky dress as she gasped for air. "I wasn't trying to make you hurt worse by asking you questions about your past, Grayson. That's the last thing I would ever want to do and I'm so sorry if anything I said in the stables hurt you. I swear I was only trying to help."

God, he'd nearly yanked her dress up to her waist and taken her against the front door, and she was the one apologizing.

"I know," he said. And he did. Because for all of Lori's faults—and he felt as if he'd gotten to discover each and every one of them over the past week—she was a good person. Maybe if they'd met in a different time, years ago, when he was still in the city...

No. He couldn't go there, couldn't wish that things had been different. Because if he was going to turn back time, wasn't there only one thing he would ever be allowed to wish for? His wife, alive and healthy? And if Leslie were still alive, then Lori Sullivan would have no part of his life at all.

His gut twisted twice as hard at that thought.

Grayson already knew that there was no way to win, that the grip his past had on him was too strong to ever get away from. Because while he simply couldn't imagine his world anymore without Lori in it, he also couldn't move beyond the loss he'd suffered before her.

"I'm still so damned sorry for grabbing you the way I did in the stables, and I never should have pushed you up against the door just now." It took every ounce of self-control he had left to step away from her. "I understand if you don't want to go to the barn dance with me now, Lori."

He felt awkward and too formal, as though he couldn't get anything right with her. He didn't deserve to have her on his arm, didn't deserve any more of her smiles, or the sound of her laughter as it floated through the air.

Lori stared at him as if she'd never seen him before. "Are you actually asking me what I want to do?"

He ran a hand through his hair. "You don't have to do anything you don't want to do, Lori. You know that."

Her smile came so suddenly he actually felt the wind knocked out of him at the beautiful force of it.

"Of course I know that, but it's so fun to see if I can make you lose it," she teased, and amazingly his gut untwisted a little. "Plus, it keeps Sweetpea entertained when you stomp around and smoke starts coming out of your ears—doesn't it, baby?" she said to the cat, who was watching the two of them from the bed of pillows and blankets Lori had made for her on the floor beside a heating vent.

"Don't let her pull you into this discussion, Mo," he warned the cat.

Lori laughed out aloud, a sweet waterfall of joy that untwisted his gut even farther. "Aha! You finally talked to her like she's a person." She clapped her hands. "Just because of that, I'll go with you to the barn thing."

She wasn't pushing him anymore on his wife's crash, so he wouldn't push her on the fact that she couldn't even say the word *dance*.

But he wanted to. And that was what worried him most—even more than the desire over which he had no control whatsoever. It was why he was taking her to the barn dance, after all—because he'd heard her on the phone with her sister and knew how badly she missed dancing, how important it really was to her.

For three years he'd been so careful to keep himself from getting close to anyone, but Lori had barged into his life and refused to take no for an answer when he'd told her he didn't have time to train a farmhand who had no experience and was worse than useless.

Somehow she'd gotten under his skin.

And he didn't know how to get her out again.

He was frowning when the soft, oh-so-sweet touch

of her hand on his jaw finally made him stop and look down at her beautiful face again. "I've thought a lot about what you said to me in the stables," she said in a soft voice. "It turns out you were right about it being easier for me to focus on helping you rather than looking at my own life."

"Don't." He covered her hand with his. "Please don't let me off the hook like that. I fucked up, Lori. And you shouldn't forgive me."

The last thing he expected her to do was smile up at him. "You just said it yourself—you can't keep me from doing whatever I want." She lightly stroked his cheek. "And I want to forgive you. But only for what happened in the stables. Because what just happened here against the door…" Her eyes flashed with heat. "Well, I can't think of any part of your kisses that you have to be sorry about."

With that, she turned and walked out the door toward his truck. Still reeling from everything that had just been said between them, it was a hell of a job for Grayson to try to keep his eyes from wandering to her hips as he followed her, especially when he had a bad feeling that she wasn't wearing anything at all beneath the formfitting dress.

Sweet Lord, what he'd give to touch her naked skin again, to press not only his hands, but also his mouth, to her. To all of her.

Before she could reach for the door handle of his truck, he opened it for her, then offered a hand to help her up. She looked surprised, but she placed her hand in his.

He forgot to let go as he looked down at her finger-nails. "You've put on nail polish." And she smelled like vanilla and spice, so sweet and sultry that he was barely able to tamp down the overpowering urge to bury his face in the curve of her neck and breathe her in.

"Mascara, too," she said as she fluttered her eye-lashes at him. "I didn't want people to think you couldn't do any better than a girl who didn't know how to take care of herself."

God, he was so mesmerized by the flick of her tongue against her glossy upper lip that he could barely remember why he'd taken her hand. Finally, he real-ized they were standing beside his truck and the door was open.

"Can you climb in okay with those heels on?"

She shot him a sassy look. A look that owned every last letter of her naughty nickname.

"I can do absolutely *anything* in these heels."

As he closed her door and walked around the back of the truck, he had to adjust himself in his jeans to try to hide his hard-on. The vision of making love to Lori while she was wearing nothing but those red spike heels wouldn't go away as they drove from his farm to his neighbor's property fifteen minutes away.

Grayson parked in a dark corner behind a large grouping of shrubs at the very edge of the parking area. When Lori got out of his truck, it was so dark that she asked, "Are you sure there's a party here tonight?" Before he could answer, she walked around the thick shrubs and finally saw the brightly lit barn, and the colored lanterns that were placed along the path from the parking area.

"Look at all these lights and the lanterns and the decorations! I swear, it looks like the moon has been hung above the barn just for tonight. Why didn't you tell me it would be like this?"

Because he'd never appreciated any of it until right this very second when he could see it through her eyes—eyes that saw the beauty in absolutely everything. But instead of telling her that, he simply held out a hand. "Sounds like the band is already playing. Ready to head in?"

She looked uncertain for a moment before nodding. When she put her hand in his, he realized that holding her that way was so right, as though she really was his girl and he was taking her out for a night of dancing, country style.

Fifteen

Lori loved how it felt to hold Grayson's hand. He wasn't giving her his trust, wasn't baring his soul to her or letting her try to help him, but even though holding hands was something small, it wasn't nothing.

Yes, she knew it would be smarter to keep her walls up around him. Especially since he'd already proven he knew how to cut her to the quick—all it took was a few well-placed words and a disgusted expression to rip her heart to shreds.

But now that she had some insight into what he'd suffered, how could she just turn away from him?

Just then, she stumbled over a rock in the dark and Grayson caught her in his arms. And when she looked into the barn over his shoulder, she realized everyone was gawking at them.

"I don't think you'll have any problem convincing the neighbors that you're off the market," she murmured as she drew back from him.

"Good," was all he said as he escorted her inside the barn.

The barn was just as beautifully lit inside as it was outside. In a glance she took in the hay bales lining the large space, the country band playing up on the stage at the far end of the building, the dance floor that had been cleared in front of them and the drink and food stations positioned all throughout the rest of the barn.

She was the only person in satin and heels, although there were plenty of sequins on display, so at least she'd gotten one thing right. She'd intended to make Grayson look ridiculous…only now she was the one who had to get through the night looking as if she should be at the Oscars rather than at a community barn dance. Whereas Grayson looked exactly right in his dark jeans, denim shirt, cowboy boots and hat.

"Grayson, glad you could make it." A man in Wranglers and a big black cowboy hat that matched his shiny black boots patted Grayson on the shoulder hard enough that she could feel it vibrate through her.

"Place looks great, Joe," Grayson responded. "I'd like you to meet Lori."

The man tipped his hat to her. "Pretty girls are always welcome in my barn." He winked at her. "Just don't tell my wife I said that."

"What are you not supposed to tell me?" asked an attractive middle-aged woman with honey-blond hair wearing a jean skirt that fell to her knees and a leather vest over a fitted white shirt. She smiled at Grayson, but her eyes chilled a bit as she took in Lori's outfit.

"That I've never been to a barn dance before," Lori said with a smile that she hoped didn't betray how out of place she felt. She hadn't met this woman at the CSA pickup, but everyone else had been so nice there she had no reason to think this woman wouldn't be nice, too. "Everything looks amazing."

"Thank you," the other woman said with perfect politeness before turning back to Grayson and saying, "I'm so pleased you finally decided to come to one of our dances. You'll have to tell me what changed your mind."

Lori looked at Grayson in surprise. He'd never been to one of these before? He'd made it sound as if they hadn't had a choice about coming here tonight. What reason could he have had to force her to come with him?

But before he could answer the woman's question, more people started coming up to talk to him. He was, she realized, a very popular man. And yet, they hadn't had a single visitor on the farm in the week she'd been working for him. It was almost as if everyone was scared of ruining the perfect wall of solitude he'd built up around himself over the past three years.

A short while later, a little girl with pigtails skirted through the adults' legs to touch her dress, but just as Lori was about to bend down to say hello, the frosty woman pulled her away.

I'm not here to cause any trouble, Lori wanted to tell her. *All I want to do is help Grayson, I swear.*

The band began to play a song by one of her favorite bands, and from her vantage point around the men with whom Grayson was talking about tractors she could see the people on the dance floor trying to do a line dance. She craned her neck to see better, but her view was impeded.

She felt Grayson's thumb brush lightly across her palm as he said, "You want to dance."

He said it as if he didn't know that she wasn't interested in dancing ever again, as if she hadn't already told him that dancing meant nothing to her anymore.

"No," she said firmly, even though she was getting that little itch in the soles of her feet that always happened when just the right song was playing. "It's just that if, instead of doing a brush kick on the two, they pivoted—"

She realized, too late, that he was giving her a funny look, and clamped her lips shut.

"Sounds like you know this dance pretty well," he pointed out.

She would have tried to play off her reaction to the line dancing, if right then Joe's frosty wife hadn't said, "Funny, you don't look like the line-dancing type."

Lori had never been known for her patience. And it had been one heck of a week. Between having to finally face up to the fact that her ex was a total douche bag, and then dealing with the trials of not only learning to work Grayson's farm, but also trying to push away her intense attraction to him, she was left holding on to an extremely short string.

"I was the choreographer for Lost Highway's video." She paused a beat to appreciate the shock registering on the woman's face. "This is *my* line dance."

The next thing she knew, Grayson was giving her a gentle shove in the direction of the dance floor and she was standing in front of the group of line dancers. Quickly picking out a couple of teenagers who had good timing, she explained who she was and what she'd like them to try to do with her. Scanning her dress and heels, the teens both looked at her as if she was crazy, but when she started dancing, doing the moves as easily in her heels and fancy dress as she would have in boots and denim, their mouths dropped open.

As she ran through the moves of the line dance, a fancy stranger in the midst of a very tight-knit community, she realized she was the only one moving on the dance floor. Everyone had stopped to gape at her... except a really cute little girl Lori recognized from the CSA pickup who didn't seem to realize that anything strange was happening at all. With the music pumping through her veins, not the least bit daunted, Lori grabbed a teenage boy's arm so that he could twirl her around in a modified do-si-do. By the time she let him go, the teen was grinning and jumping in beside her, picking up each move she'd just done perfectly.

Soon the two of them were joined by half a dozen more and, as the band launched back into the song from the beginning, it seemed as if every person in the barn was claiming a spot on the dance floor. They were all ready to kick up their heels and laugh with the person twirling in their arms.

Grayson stood against the wall and watched as Lori worked her way through the dancers to help get them back on track and to call out the moves when things got a little hairy.

My God, she could dance. He'd never seen anyone move like her, not even in his old life, when he'd had the chance to mix with professional dancers from time to time.

Her dress was clinging slightly to her skin now as the barn heated up from all of the dancers, and her long, dark hair was starting to curl against the damp nape of her neck. Watching the way she moved so effortlessly in the heels and beautiful dress gave him a clear view into the world she'd come from. One that he guessed was very similar to the one in which he had lived in New York City.

And yet, she'd been just as comfortable in jeans and a T-shirt, and even though she muttered about going into the pigpen, he knew she secretly loved mucking around like a little kid let loose in a mud puddle after a storm.

Grayson honestly couldn't choose which version he liked better—the made-up Lori was just another side of her, something he hadn't been prepared for. All he knew was that she was beautiful…and that, somehow, despite everything he'd done to try to stop it from happening, she'd managed to steal his heart, one sassy smile at a time.

Sixteen

Applause rang out in the barn at the end of the line dance that had gone on for a good fifteen minutes straight. Lori loved how the little kids didn't think twice about wrapping their arms around her waist to hug her.

"You're so pretty, ma'am. What's your name?"

Lori smiled down at the little girl with the big brown eyes and bright pink cheeks, the same one who had wanted to touch her dress earlier. She couldn't have been more than four years old, but she'd been out there dancing up a storm, following the moves even better than most of the bigger kids and adults.

"Lori. What's yours?"

"LuLu." She barely paused for breath before saying, "You'll be here for the next barn dance to teach us some more, won't you, Ms. Lori?"

Lori felt a lump descend into the bottom of her stomach. Could she stay here forever? Could she hide out beneath the beautiful blue sky and have dirt under her fingernails every day? Could she dream about more of Grayson's kisses?

Still feeling the rush of the dance floor beneath her feet, the thrill of moving her body to the music, instead of answering the little girl's question, Lori smiled down at her and asked, "Do you want to fly?"

The girl's pigtails bounced as she nodded. "Oh, yes!"

Lori held out her hands and when the little girl took them she winked and said, "Hold on tight." And then she started swinging them both around in a circle, a perfect pirouette with a giggling partner's sweaty little hands grasped tightly in hers. Again and again they spun until she thought the little girl must be getting dizzy, and finally put her down.

"Mama, Mama, did you see me?" the girl said to her mother as soon as her little cowboy boots hit the floor. "I was flying."

LuLu's mother no longer looked frosty as she stroked her daughter's cheek. "Like a beautiful bird, baby." As she hoisted her daughter up into her arms, the woman finally smiled at Lori. "You're a wonderful dancer. Thank you for teaching all of us how to do the line dance tonight."

Couples quickly paired up all around Lori as she stood and watched the mother and daughter walk away with a longing that frankly stunned her. When she'd been line dancing, she'd felt like she belonged, that she wasn't just some city girl playing around on a farm.

But now that aloneness came back to hit her smack-dab in the center of her chest with a hard thud.

The lump in her throat grew bigger as she caught sight of Eric grinning at her from across the barn. She smiled back, and when he started to move toward her with the clear intention of asking her to dance, she fought to keep her smile in place. Eric was sweet. He was good-looking. He was a gentleman. He was everything she should want, especially in the wake of the snake her ex had turned out to be.

But, stupid her, who did she wish was coming for her on the dance floor instead? Grayson, who was more deeply wounded than any man she'd ever met before.

When Eric was less than a dozen feet away and she was just about to make herself move toward him, a large hand suddenly took hers and she was spun into a hard chest.

The very hard chest she'd been so foolishly dreaming of.

Lori was so stunned—and so pleased to be close to Grayson again as he led her in a country waltz— that she simply laid her head against his shoulder and moved with him.

Just one dance. That was all it was.

One perfect, beautiful, impossibly romantic dance with a man who made her heart pound like crazy and her brain turn to mush.

There were a million reasons why she shouldn't be here in his arms, moving to the music. And yet she was so dazed by the sure way he led her across the floor, so wrapped up in the dance, in the feel of his body against hers, his muscles contracting against her, that there was no room for thinking, no space to do anything but be putty in his talented hands.

Second by second he'd taken over more of her thoughts, her dreams, until she had begun to forget what her life had been like before he was in it. All she knew now was that it couldn't have been as full of sparks, emotion…or desire.

Even the waltz, a dance she'd done a thousand times before, both onstage and off, had never been this wonderful. This special.

When the song finally came to an end, Grayson drew her tightly into his arms and held her there for a long moment. The band had started to play yet another waltz but she knew she couldn't survive another dance with him.

Not if she wanted even one small piece of her heart to remain intact when she finally left his farm to go back to her real life.

She tried to move away, but he wouldn't let go of her hand. "You've been dancing for a while now with no break. You need lemonade."

He didn't ask her if she wanted one, just took her to the table on the side of the room where the two teenagers she'd been line dancing with were busy flirting. He got her a cup and he was right—she was thirsty, so she drank it.

Lori told herself she shouldn't feel so weird around him now. Not when it had just been one little dance. But, oh, what a dance it had been. And when she closed her eyes, she'd be returning to it in her daydreams for a very long time.

Trying desperately to act as if it was no big deal, she said, "You're a good dancer." Knowing that compliment was far too grudging for just how talented he was on his feet, she amended it to say, "Actually, you're a fantastic dancer."

The last thing she expected him to do was say, "Thank you," then reach out to brush a strand of hair from her cheek and push it behind her ear.

She shivered at his touch. Didn't he know just how dangerous this territory was that he was heading into with her? First the dance, and now a touch so gentle, so sweet, that it tore at her already weak heart. She knew how to deal with rough, rude Grayson. But this? She had no idea what to do now…especially not when she coupled his sudden tenderness with the way he'd touched her—as if she was precious.

"Where—" she began, but the way he was gazing down at her with such dark eyes had her losing her train of thought. Oh, God, this was such a bad idea. She needed to keep on track. He was her boss. She was his farmhand. He was country. She was city. When they weren't kissing, they were both driving each other crazy. "Where did you learn to dance like that?"

"Years of ballroom dancing lessons."

For a moment she thought he was kidding, but then she remembered what he'd told her about where he'd come from. It was just that he was such a part of the land, such a cowboy at heart, had such a love for the farm, that she kept forgetting about his previous life in New York City.

What he'd created all by himself out here in the wilds of Pescadero was truly amazing. Maybe at first she hadn't appreciated just how much hard work went into taking care of his animals, his crops, his crew, the customers who depended on the food he grew for them, but after a week of working with him, she did now.

"Dance with me again, Lori."

She should say no. All she needed to do was put her lips into the right position and breathe out the word. Lord knew she'd had enough practice saying the word, not only as a child, but also during the past week. She'd used the word on Grayson whenever he'd been acting unreasonable and she knew she'd been a brat—all for the sheer pleasure of annoying him.

But now, when it felt as if her entire future, along with the safety of her heart, rested on a little two-letter word, she just couldn't say it. She couldn't get her feet to walk her out of the barn so that she could leave Grayson and his cowboy hat and boots and pigs and Sweetpea-the-cat behind.

And maybe, she found herself thinking as the waltz continued, he had some sort of previously agreed-upon arrangement going with the band, because when he drew her back into his arms in front of the lemonade table and the wide-eyed teenagers, she couldn't seem to catch her breath.

Being with Grayson was so simple and yet so complicated all at the same time. He made her want to stomp and yell…but he'd also just given dancing back to her when she'd thought that dream, that love, might be gone forever.

Apart from her twin sister, she'd never met anyone whom she hated and loved in the same breath.

Love.

Oh, God, she was falling in love with him.

No! She couldn't.

Not him.

Not here.

And not when she knew he was not only still grieving his loss, but also that he might very well choose to grieve forever.

All the strength Lori hadn't been able to find a few moments earlier flooded her as panic took hold. She was out of his arms like a shot, moving so quickly toward the big, open barn doors that she skidded in her heels and barely caught herself on the wall before she went down on her butt in front of everyone. Kicking off her heels and leaving them on the barn floor, she didn't notice whether anyone was watching her flee, couldn't feel anything but the pressure of that love she could no longer deny coming down over her chest to wrap tightly around her heart.

No. No. No.

What was wrong with her? Why couldn't she love someone who would love her back? Why couldn't she have what her brothers and twin had? Why couldn't she find a lover, a friend, someone who would always have her back, someone who would give up absolutely everything for her…and someone for whom she would give up absolutely everything? Why couldn't she be one half of two people who didn't need anything but each other?

That was all she wanted. It was all she'd ever wanted.

Instead, she was wild.

She didn't think before acting.

She talked too much.

And she fell too fast.

Lori was running away from the barn dance, sprinting for home, when it hit her midstride that what had started to feel like her home wasn't hers at all.

It was Grayson's. Everything was his. This land. The animals.

Oh, God, even her heart was his.

And still she ran, barely feeling the dirt, the grass, the sticks, beneath her bare feet. The firm muscles in her legs, the power of her lungs, had always made her strong. But Grayson, she found out a breath later when his arms came around her and he lifted her off the ground and against his chest, was at least as strong.

"You can't run from me," he told her in the middle of the field beneath a dark purple sky as he held on to her.

Lori had always given herself entirely over to love. She'd believed it would make everything okay, make everything work out in the end. But it didn't. It hadn't. And she knew she shouldn't be stupid enough to make that mistake again.

"Yes, I can," she said as she fought his hold, trying to get back on solid ground where she only had herself to rely on, where she could do whatever it took to keep herself safe.

"Not tonight, Lori." His lungs were pumping just as hard as hers were from the run and from the struggle to keep her with him. "I know you're not going to stay, but please don't run from me tonight." She made the mistake of looking up into his eyes. "Please," he begged again, "just give me tonight."

Maybe it was the fact that, for the second time in one night, he'd actually asked for something rather than just demanding it from her. Maybe it was the way he was looking at her, as if he'd be lost without her. Maybe it was the fact that their dances together had solidified something that couldn't possibly be put into words: a connection between two people who were, whether they wanted to be or not, a perfect fit. At least for a little while—while their lives collided.

Maybe it was simply that falling in love wasn't something Lori would ever be able to turn away from, regardless of just how much pain she knew would be coming down the pike. And maybe, just maybe, as long as she never actually confessed to him how she felt, that would make it okay to give in to what she felt for Grayson for one night, beneath the moon, with the smell of wild grass and the ocean all around them....

Seventeen

Grayson had never wanted anyone the way he wanted Lori, but it wasn't just physical anymore, even though her beauty while she'd led the entire community in her line-dancing choreography had simply stunned him all over again, as though he was seeing her for the very first time.

He wanted to hear her laugh.

He wanted to feel her breathing softly as she fell asleep against him, her head on his shoulder.

And he wanted to see her spin a little dark-haired girl around and around in circles, a girl who looked like both of them, a spitfire who would yell, "No," at them just as loudly as she would declare her love before falling asleep in the home they'd made for her and her brothers and sisters.

They were all crazy dreams—especially the last one. Dreams that would never be anything more than pure fantasy…but he already knew those fantasies were what would keep him going long after she left. He also knew that keeping her hidden away on his farm for more than a stolen week or two would unfairly deprive the world of her truly special gifts.

Lori made everything finally seem real, and she gave meaning to what had only seemed like routine before. It was why he was afraid to put her down, to let her toes touch the ground again. If she changed her mind about tonight, then all the brilliant colors she'd painted for him since she'd blown into his life like a hurricane would turn back to gray.

Even after watching her dance, he'd been trying to keep his distance, had been telling himself he needed to do whatever it took to resist her. But then, from across the barn Eric had come for her, to dance with her, to hold her in his arms…and Grayson had simply broken. He'd had to pull her into his arms, had to give in to how good he knew it would be to waltz with her, to put his arms around her and feel her lay her cheek against his shoulder.

He knew exactly why Lori had run from the barn dance—he wasn't the only one who had tripped and fallen into the last person on earth he should ever want to hold on to. But all the good reasons to stay away from her were lost in the visions of her laughing with men and women who never usually took to outsiders, the way every little boy and girl in the barn had fallen head over heels in love with her as she danced with them.

How could they not fall for her?

"I need to love you," he said against her hair, still holding her so tightly, even after she'd promised not to run from him tonight.

Of course, she surprised him all over again when she wrapped her legs around his waist and held as tightly to him as he was holding her.

"Love me, Grayson."

As he finally captured her lips, he realized she kissed the way she danced, without holding anything back. He wanted to lay her down in the grass, wanted to love her beneath the moon and the stars. But he couldn't stand the thought of her soft skin being scratched by sticks or rocks, so even as he kissed her, he was walking back toward his truck with Lori wrapped around him.

"Riding you is so much more fun than riding a horse," she said, laughing against his mouth.

The sound of her joy was so sweet that he couldn't keep moving forward, couldn't do anything but stand in the grass and wildflowers and kiss her.

"I put clean sheets on your bed today," she informed him with a naughty little smile when he finally pulled back from her sweet lips, her gorgeous face lit by the moonlight. "Let's go mess them up." And then she was unwrapping her legs from around his waist, saying, "Race you to the truck," and running off through the field.

Her long dark hair was flying out behind her as he chased her again, her limbs strong and fast as the satin of her dress tangled up in her beautiful legs, her laughter filling his heart until he was sure it was going to overflow. He reached out for her hand just as she reached back for him, and their fingers threaded together as he pulled her back into him for one more hot kiss.

He opened the passenger door of his truck for her,

and this time when he helped her up, he let his hands roam across her perfect ass, which she wiggled into his palms.

"You know," she said as he slid in behind the wheel seconds later, "I've never made love in a truck before."

God, he thought as the blood rushed hotter, faster, through his veins, it was tempting. So tempting to stay right here in this dark and deserted corner where he'd parked, and drag her onto his lap, even though he had been fantasizing all week long about making love to her in his bed.

Grayson had spent the past three years controlling everything. His farm. His animals. His emotions. His needs. But now, in the span of a few seconds, it was all slipping out of his grasp.

Because the mere thought of taking Lori in his truck was so potent that he couldn't do a damned thing to stop the Neanderthal lurking inside him from emerging to take. To claim. To possess.

By the time he had his hands on her and was dragging her onto his lap, hers were already on him, moving up his chest. *"Grayson."* She breathed his name into the crook of his neck, the same place she'd licked on the ride during the storm a couple of days ago.

Though he was on the verge of ripping off her dress when she twined her arms around his neck and he pulled her closer with desire raging heated and wild all around them, for the moment, just holding her tight was not only enough…it was more than he'd ever thought to have.

* * *

I love you.

Lori knew she could never say the words aloud. Not only was Grayson not even close to being in an emotional position to give his love to her, but he wouldn't be able to accept her love, either.

She'd never loved anyone because of what she could get back from them. And as she pressed her cheek against Grayson's and felt his breath move with hers, slower now as they shared a perfect moment of closeness, she was shocked to realize that she'd never felt anything this strong, this deep and true, for any other man.

Because what she felt for the man holding her so tightly—as though he was worried she'd disappear if he didn't make absolutely certain to keep her there with him—was richer, and so much sweeter, than anything she'd ever felt before.

She wanted to heal Grayson, wanted to give him her heart, her love, until they finally overshadowed tragedy and pain.

She wanted to make love with him for hours and hours, and she knew from his kisses alone that she'd never get her fill of being intimate with him.

She wanted to be his partner and have him trust that she would be there for him in a way that no one else had ever been.

And, oh, how she wanted to see him smile. One perfect smile. One full-bodied laugh. And then she'd know that she'd given him something important, something real, something that mattered.

When he started to rain kisses down over her cheek, and then her chin and neck, she used her dancer's flexibility to arch way back so that he could have unfettered access to even more of her.

"Damn you for being so tempting," he growled with a nip at the upper swell of her breast. "Fifteen minutes, that was all we needed to get back to my farm. Fifteen goddamned minutes. Is that too much to ask? Is that too long for you to stop being so irresistible?"

Her heart swelled a little more at every irritated word that fell from his yummy lips. "Mmm," she said when she could finally find her breath again, "I was wondering where Mr. Crankypants went."

"I wanted to take my time with you tonight," he grumbled against her skin as he ran little biting kisses over her shoulder until she was shuddering with need. "But you're tempting me into taking you right here, right now."

Maybe it shouldn't have turned her on, the way he managed to be irritated with her even when they were making out, and yet it did. So, so much. Grayson had made her feel alive even when she believed she was dead to everything she'd once cared about.

She loved the idea of their being in his bed together, of all the wild and wicked ways they could love each other. But as his hands gripped her hips to pull her more tightly into him while he licked up the curve of her neck and sent thrill bumps running over every inch of her, wasn't it somehow more fitting that they'd end up all over each other in the cab of his truck?

Their relationship had never followed the rules, not

from the start when she'd crashed into his fence post and he'd done everything to get her to leave but pick her up and toss her off his property. And even then, she'd seen something in his eyes that told her he wanted her, despite all the reasons he shouldn't. Not only a desire for her that matched hers for him, but a soul-deep longing that she also understood. All too well, even when those longings shouldn't make any sense.

Good thing she'd never cared much whether things made sense. No, she'd always simply followed her heart instead.

Amazingly, her heart had led her here. To Grayson's farm.

And into his arms.

"I did promise to be the best darn farmhand you've ever had," she reminded him in a husky voice that said as much about how badly she wanted him as any words she spoke. "I'll bet you never had one who could do this."

With one quick shimmy, she let the slim straps holding her dress drop over her shoulders, the bodice slipping down, as well, revealing her breasts.

"Lori."

She thought she'd be prepared for his reaction this time. After all, he'd seen her breasts in the cabin during the storm, had tongued and teased them until she'd catapulted all the way over the edge of pleasure. But the way his eyes darkened and desire completely took him over as he gazed at her naked flesh…

No, she'd never get used to being stared at with such overwhelming hunger.

"How am I doing so far?" She reached out to brush her fingertips over the square line of his jaw. When he didn't answer, and just kept staring at the rapidly tightening tips of her breasts until anticipation had her nearly wild with needing his hands and mouth on her, she teased, "Would you say this is *fine?*" She purposely used the not-quite-compliment he'd given her so many times before now.

"Nothing has ever been better than this, Lori. Not one goddamned thing."

Grayson shifted lower on his seat and covered one aching nipple with his mouth, then the other, then both at the same time as he cupped them in his large, strong hands. She arched into his sweet caresses, and groaned aloud when he raked his teeth over her.

He was so big and hard and wonderfully male between her thighs, and as she rocked into him, she was already so close that even with her dress and panties still on, her arousal had grown big enough that all it would take was one more tug of his mouth over her and she'd be—

"Oh, God..."

Grayson was right there with her in an instant, one of his big hands sliding beneath her dress, up her bare leg and thigh and inside her damp panties to help intensify the already shockingly sweet climax. With his thumb on her clitoris and two of his fingers slipping in and out of her, her initial orgasm gave way to another, even bigger one.

As she spiraled off and off and off, she cupped his face in her hands and kissed him with every ounce of passion she possessed. He kissed her back just as desperately as he continued to stroke between her thighs, both of their mouths rough and hungry.

When her inner muscles had mostly stopped pulsing in the aftermath of her double climax, she realized just how out of breath she was, that she was panting as hard as if she'd just done all thirty-two of the *Black Swan's* fouettés.

"My God, you overwhelm me," he said, burying his face against her breastbone as he slowly slipped his hand from between her legs to pull her tightly against him again.

She felt him work to regain his control so that they would actually make it out of his truck and into his bed their first time. But Lori knew she couldn't wait for that anymore, that this was exactly how things were supposed to happen, with both of them too overwhelmed to think straight.

Sex with Grayson in his truck was wild. Crazy.

And oh so perfect.

"You overwhelm me, too," she said as she stroked his soft, dark hair. When he tilted his face up to meet her gaze, she whispered, "Overwhelm me some more," then rocked her pelvis into the thick bulge behind the zipper of his dark jeans.

On a growl of pleasure, he pushed just as hard into her, both of their bodies young and strong and so hungry for each other that even the confines of his truck and their clothes could barely get in their way now.

"Please, Grayson," she begged. "Take me. All of me."

As wild as their night had been so far, at her breathless urging, Grayson finally let go of the hold he'd been keeping on his control, and the next thing she knew, he was moving them so that she was flat on her back on the bench seat and he was taking her pretty dress in his fists and ripping it in two. She gasped not from fear, but from excitement, as he reached for her thong next and shredded it to pieces with little more than one hard tug.

All week they'd been vying with each other to see who was stronger, tougher, who could hold out longer, but tonight they were equal partners in everything: passion, desire, need. She reached for his shirt and tore it open.

She couldn't wait to get her hands on his bare chest, and had daydreamed about it so many times that she couldn't believe it hadn't happened yet. And, oh, that first touch of hard, tanned muscles was so good.

"You're the one who can't possibly be real," she said as he levered himself up over her so that she could run her hands over his gorgeously muscled shoulders and chest, and then the deep indentations of his abdominal muscles.

"You make me forget," he said in a raw voice. "Everything but how much I want you."

"You don't have to remember tonight," she told him, both of them panting from the force of their desire. "All you have to do is make love to me the way I've wanted you to from the first moment I saw you."

He followed her plea with a searing kiss that made her head spin even more than it already was. And his hands, his mouth, were roaming over every last inch of her naked body. She couldn't possibly keep up as he tasted her breasts in one moment, then nipped at her hip bone the next. His hands sometimes led, other times followed, the devastating path of his lips and tongue and teeth over her overheated skin.

She'd already come twice, but when he curled his hand around her ankle and lifted her leg so that her foot was resting on the dashboard, then stared down at her with the hottest, hungriest expression she'd ever seen, she nearly climaxed again without any further contact at all.

"Swear to God," he said as he reached out to stroke the slick flesh between her legs, "I've never seen anything prettier than you in all my life." He moved down from the seat to kneel on the floor of the truck before adding, "And I'll bet you taste even better."

She gasped in pleasure when his tongue found her. He'd splayed his hands on her inner thighs to open her up even farther to him, and when she looked down and saw his tanned fingers on her pale skin, his tongue moving over her, and his eyes lifted to her face so that he could watch her reaction, she tumbled abruptly into yet another sinfully perfect climax.

Slowly, he kissed his way up her body as he climbed back over her. "You were just as sweet as I thought you'd be," he said right before he covered her mouth with his.

She was working on his belt buckle when he grabbed her wrists. "I need you," she pleaded as she fought to break free of his hold. "I can't wait another second to have you."

"I don't have any protection. We have to go back to my house." He was already moving away from her to let her up as he said it, and she barely bit back a groan of frustration.

So close. She'd been *so close* to finally having him, and now because neither of them had thought to bring a condom to the barn dance, she was stuck having to shift back into her seat and put on the long-sleeved shirt he handed her over her naked body for a far-too-long fifteen-minute drive home.

Lori knew she should be thankful that he'd remained lucid enough to stop before they had unprotected sex. Especially after what had happened to Sophie on the night she'd had a one-night stand and become pregnant *despite* using a condom.

But right now, with need roiling around inside her, Lori didn't feel grateful at all.

On the contrary, what she felt was a clawing need to claim—and be claimed by—Grayson, once and for all.

Only, once she finally got his shirt on and was sitting in her seat, instead of starting the engine and burning rubber so that they could continue where they'd left off, he just sat there and glared at her. Three back-to-back orgasms with no big finale in sight made her ornery as she glared back.

"What's your problem now?"

"I'm waiting for you to put your goddamned seat belt on."

She started at his tone, and the hardness of his gaze that had been so full of hunger just seconds before, and was opening her mouth on a sarcastic retort when she remembered what she couldn't believe she'd almost forgotten: he'd lost his wife in a car crash. No wonder he was so adamant about her putting her seat belt on, even in the wake of what they'd just been doing with each other.

With trembling hands, she snapped her seat belt into place, at which point Grayson pushed the gas pedal down hard enough that gravel sprayed out from his tires.

Minutes felt more like hours as Grayson forced himself to take the dark farm roads just barely above the speed limit. And then—*finally!*—he was pulling into his drive.

Lori was about to jump out onto the gravel when he caught her in his arms. "You left your shoes at the dance."

"You had no problem with me walking around in bare feet on the gravel before," she reminded him.

He nuzzled her cheek and breathed in her sweet, wild, oh-so-feminine scent. "That was before I liked you." Grayson was stepping on his porch and was about to kiss her again when he realized she was pushing at his chest.

"I think all the excitement has made my ears go wonky," she declared. "What did you just say?"

God, he could hardly think at all with her soft and warm in his arms, his long-sleeved shirt falling open over her beautiful breasts. He kicked his front door open and tried to remember, but all he could come up with was, "I don't want you tearing up your feet on the gravel."

"No," she said, "after that."

He'd had so many fantasies of Lori naked and begging for him to take her here in his bedroom that as he carried her into it, her question was instantly forgotten. He laid her down on the covers, pulled the shirt he'd given her to wear in the truck all the way open and slid it from her body.

Sweet Lord, he wanted to start all over from the beginning, wanted to make her come another three times with his hands, his mouth.

Just as he was lowering his mouth to her breasts, she said, "Did you mean it?"

Reluctantly moving his mouth away from her chest, he cupped her breasts in his hands and teased the nipples with his thumb and forefinger instead until they were sharply aroused points. "Did I mean what?"

Now she was the one losing hold of their conversation. "That—" She arched deeper into his hands. "You—"

He took advantage of her confusion to lick across one tip and then the other, loving the way she gasped with pleasure as he tasted her. He was just sliding one hand down her flat stomach to the bare, slick flesh between her legs when she finally got all the words out.

"You said you *liked* me, Grayson."

Again, it took him longer than it should have for her words to actually make it all the way through to his brain. Especially when he had his hand cupped over her sex and he could feel how wet, how ready, she was for him.

But when he lifted his gaze to hers, and he saw the surprising vulnerability in them, he finally understood what she was asking: Was he just making love to her tonight because he wanted her body?

Or had they, against all odds, developed a deeper connection than that?

Grayson knew he shouldn't have let her stay on his farm all week, and that he definitely shouldn't be taking her to his bed now. He also knew that he should be working overtime to keep tonight to nothing but sex.

But knowing all those things hadn't made a damn bit of difference so far, had they?

"I do like you, Lori," he admitted in a low voice. "More than I should."

"I like you, too," she whispered as she reached out to gently touch his face. "More than you know."

Her eyes were full of such sweet emotion that his heart shuddered in his chest.

For three years he'd sworn to himself that nothing—and no one—would ever touch him again. But he'd never counted on Lori Sullivan blowing past every wall, every fortress, in less than one week.

And it scared the hell out of him.

Eighteen

Grayson knew what he needed to do. He needed to stop them from going any further, just as he had in the cottage. He needed to turn his back not only on desire, but on affection, as well. Because while he hadn't been a monk these past three years, there hadn't been any risk at all of emotional connection with the women he'd slept with.

But with Lori, *everything* was at risk.

"Grayson."

His name on her lips had him refocusing on her, and when he did, he was surprised to find her smiling as she gazed back at him. He could still see desire in her beautiful eyes, but more than that, he realized there was understanding.

Understanding he'd done nothing whatsoever to deserve.

"One night. That's all you have to give me." She leaned in close, as if to tell him a secret. "And I won't tell anyone that you like me, if you don't tell anyone that I like you, too."

With that, she drew him back down over her so that she could give him one hot, sweet little kiss after another, each one of them made to confuse and inflame and drive his demons back down. Soon they were tangled up in each other again, his hands greedily filling themselves with her sleek curves, her sighs of pleasure sounding out against his mouth as he stroked over her breasts, her hips.

Grayson wanted nothing more than to hear, to feel, her come apart again in his arms, but before he could take her over yet another peak with his hands and mouth, she moved so quickly, and with such remarkable strength, that the next thing he knew, he was lying on his back with Lori straddling him.

"Next time I come," she informed him in a no-nonsense voice, "you're going to be inside me. Or else."

Hell, those beautifully filthy words coming out of her pretty mouth were almost enough to finish things off for him right then and there, but of course she had to make things even more touch-and-go by reaching for his belt buckle and brushing her fingertips over his raging hard-on.

"There's nothing you like more than torturing me, is there?" he asked as he shoved her hands aside to yank his jeans and boxers off himself.

"Actually," she said as she stared at his erection with wide eyes, "there's one thing I think I'm going to like a whole lot more than that."

Before he could prepare for it, she reached out and

wrapped her hand around him. His loud groan reverberated off his bedroom walls.

"Lori—"

"You had your fun with me, now I'm going to have mine with you."

Naughty didn't even come close to the way she looked as she licked her lips greedily and moved her hand down, then back up the length of him. And maybe he would have gritted his teeth and let her have her fun awhile longer if she hadn't shifted just then so that the tips of her long, dark hair tickled his chest and he could feel her warm breath coming down over him.

"Time for you to come again, farm girl," he said as he yanked her back up his body. "So if you want to make good on your threat, you'd better grab one of the condoms out of my bedside table."

"God, you're bossy," she said, but she'd never looked happier about his bossiness than she did when she leaned over to pull out the box of condoms. "You've never opened the box." She frowned as she caught sight of the date stamped on it. "These expire next month. When's the last time you had sex?"

"It should have been twenty minutes ago in my truck," he growled as he grabbed the box out of her hands and ripped it open, sending condoms flying everywhere. Grabbing the nearest one, he had it on in seconds. "Now be quiet, and get over here."

She was half laughing, half scowling as he lifted her back over his hips, but as soon as he began to slide inside, her eyes fluttered closed and she gave a low moan of pleasure.

He held tight to her hips so she wouldn't move too fast—at least, not this first time, when he wanted to memorize every single sensation. How warm and wet and ready she was. How she fit him as though she'd been made for him.

"Please," she begged him, his strong, dancing farm girl entirely lost to sensation. To need. "Please. Please. *Please.*"

Needing her just as much as she needed him, Grayson reached up to thread his fingers into her hair and pull her mouth down to his at the same moment that he flipped them over so that her back was pressed flat against his sheets. With one hard stroke, he thrust all the way inside, and as her inner muscles clenched tight around him, he completely forgot every one of his vows about holding back.

All that mattered—as he pulled her tightly to him and she held him just as close while they drove each other even higher and farther—was loving Lori.

And letting her love him, too.

Grayson was crushing her, but Lori didn't care if her lungs collapsed from trying to breathe with two hundred pounds of pure muscle pressing her deep into the mattress.

She'd never felt so good in all her life.

From almost-truck-sex to completely messing up his sheets, Grayson had totally rocked her sensual world to pieces. Here she'd thought she was a connoisseur of sex, but none of her previous lovers had made her come so fast, so hard or so repeatedly. Heck, just lying here beneath him, she was practically on the verge again.

Only, making love with Grayson had been about so much more than just physical pleasure. For the very first time in her life, she actually felt whole; as if she'd needed to date and mess up with other men and relationships all these years just so that she could finally come around to this farm in the middle of nowhere and find the one man who truly mattered.

As they lay together, he continued to stroke her hip with one hand, her hair with the other. In his arms, she felt sated and adored and protected, and could have stayed like that forever.

Of course, considering she and Grayson had almost never seen eye to eye on anything, she wasn't too surprised that he had other ideas—ones that included pulling her up from the bed.

"Is it time to mess up my sheets now?" she asked hopefully.

"Nope," he said as he dragged her into his bathroom, turned on the warm spray of the shower and pushed her under it. "It's time to clean up instead."

She still wasn't happy about having to be upright again, but at least she was getting a really nice eyeful of his naked body—not to mention an erection that wouldn't quit. After he went to pick up one of the unused condoms that had fallen onto the floor, she reached for him with both hands.

He took them, but didn't move into her arms. "I don't know if I can control myself with you. You're too beautiful."

Her ex's sweet words had been little more than lies to get what he wanted. But Grayson never said anything but the truth. Knowing he truly thought she was beautiful meant everything to her.

"Well, I *know* I can't control myself with you." She tugged at his hands. "Now come here and let's both lose control again."

Before she could even blink, Grayson had the condom on, then was lifting her up so that her back was pressed up against the tiled shower wall and her legs were around his waist.

"I wanted to seduce you this time, damn it," he said in a grumbly voice against her earlobe that sent shivers up her skin. "Slowly." He bit down on the soft flesh, then added, "Gently."

"Later," she said as she tightened her legs around his waist so that she could keep her hands free to run down over his shoulders and magnificently muscled back. "Right now *this* is what I want. *You're* what I want."

She lowered herself onto him just as he plunged up into her. Wet skin slid against wet skin, hands grasped, moans sounded, as he angled his hips up perfectly to send her spiraling off yet one more time into such incredible pleasure she wondered if she was strong enough to survive it. Especially when he found his own pleasure and sent her rocketing off even higher with every rough, deep stroke of his body inside hers.

A few minutes later, Grayson moved her away from the shower wall and she unwrapped her legs from his waist, but even as the water grew colder they continued to kiss, going from hungry to sweet, then back again.

After he'd toweled off both of them, carried her back to his bed and drawn the sheets up over her as she yawned, she was snuggling into him spoon-style when she felt the evidence of his ongoing arousal pressing thick and hard into her hips.

"I've always really loved sex," she teased him over her shoulder, "but you're insatiable. Tell me again, when's the last time you got some?"

"It's not just the sex, Lori," he said in a voice that held both desire and sleepiness—and maybe even a little momentary contentment, she hoped. "It's *you*."

Less than a heartbeat later, she was rolling over for the slow, sweet lovemaking they hadn't been able to get to in the shower. As they kissed and ran their hands over each other, as he wrapped his arms around her and she wrapped her legs around him, as he slid into her on a groan and she sighed with pleasure while lifting her hips into his to take him deeper still, Lori couldn't remember ever feeling so safe. So incredibly good.

Grayson gathered her even closer to bury his face in the damp crook of her neck, and after the force of his climax triggered yet one more beautiful release for her, too, he rolled her over so that her head lay on his chest and her legs were entwined with his.

The last thing she was aware of before she fell asleep was the soft press of his mouth against her forehead as he kissed her good-night.

Nineteen

It was the first time in three years that Grayson had slept past sunrise.

Sunlight was streaming in his bedroom window as Lori slept in the circle of his arms. Actually, it was more that she was sprawled completely over him so that he was both her mattress and pillow. But even though he'd always preferred to have plenty of space to himself in bed, he found he didn't mind the way she'd unconsciously claimed his entire bed—and his body—as her own.

Lori Sullivan wasn't just Naughty, she was a force of nature.

He'd tried like hell to push her away a dozen times this past week, but she was still here. Even last night, when he'd asked her for so much more than he deserved, she'd not only given it to him without reserve, she'd made love to him with a wide-open heart, too.

"You're an awesome bed," she said as she slowly flexed and stretched her limbs one at a time over him, which brought every inch of his body completely awake. "I make a pretty good blanket, don't I?"

He loved the way she woke up with a smile. "Not just good. Amazing."

"I know I am," she said with a teasing grin as she rested her chin on her hand and gazed down at him from where she was perched over his chest. "Now tell me, is it my sparkling personality, my wicked hot moves in the sack or my deft hand with pig feed that's got you in raptures this morning?"

He knew he should just grin back and let her continue teasing him. But he hadn't awakened with a woman in his bed in three years—especially not one this beautiful, this giving—and he couldn't think of one thing he'd done to deserve it now.

"How can you forgive me again and again for what I've said to you? For the way I've acted?" In his experience, forgiveness was the hardest thing of all.

Her hand immediately moved to stroke his cheek, her eyes softening as she looked down at him. "My brothers and sister and I fought a lot when we were kids. Most of them were stupid fights about dolls or the last brownie or who won the race. But sometimes, we went too far and really hurt one another. Not just with bruises and black eyes, but with words that we didn't know how to take back." She smiled, thinking about her family. "When my mother'd had enough, she'd take us by the scruff of our necks like we were unruly cats, and then she'd lock us in a room together."

His eyebrows went up. "Wasn't she worried you'd keep pounding each other?"

"Oh, we definitely did that. But even that got old after a while. Eventually we would both realize we were stuck in a room with the one person we *hated*." She laughed out loud at the memory of those lock-ins. "With eight kids to keep in line, my mother had to have plenty of tricks up her sleeve. And her genius was in knowing that no matter what we said or did, no matter how deep the arrows had gone, nothing had actually changed. We still loved one another and always would. It was just that, for a little while there, it was easier to lash out and be nasty than it was to actually work through whatever was really making us feel bad. By the time she came to let us out, we were usually too busy playing some silly game we'd made up to want to leave the room. And we'd forgiven each other without ever needing to say the words, because we'd never meant to hurt each other in the first place."

She grinned at him, the sunlight streaming in over her head giving her a temporary halo. "Just in case you haven't already figured it out, my mother is amazing."

"No wonder."

She cocked her head. "No wonder what?"

"No wonder...*you*."

"That's another reason I forgive you," she said as she lifted his hand to her lips and pressed a kiss to it. "No one has ever said anything so sweet to me before." She gave him another soft kiss. "You didn't mean to hurt me with anything you said or did, Grayson. You didn't even know me when I came here. You were just doing whatever you needed to do to keep me from finding out too much, or from having to revisit the pain from your past." She wiggled her eyebrows as she added, "But if you think it would still do both of us good for you to lock yourself in a room with me—naked, of course— there's a little game I just thought of that we could play."

It was a big deal for Lori to wake up in Grayson's bed. She'd always been sexy and fun and had believed it was up to her to keep her lovers "on their toes" so that they'd stay interested in being with her. But after she'd fallen asleep in his bed—on top of him, no less— instead of keeping things light and easy this morning, he'd gone deep right away. Now, with her teasing comments about playing a game together, she thought she was giving him another chance at an out he surely had to want, from emotional back to sexy. And when he got up off the bed and locked the door, all of the sensitive spots on her body immediately heated up.

But instead of getting back into bed with her, he knelt beside it. "That day in the cabin when you told me why you were here, I not only didn't listen, I did something terrible by turning around the fact that your family has always been there for you. I made that sound like a weakness." She could read the regret on his beautiful face as clearly as she could hear it in every word. "You told me that you'd been in a relationship for the past two years, and that the guy was scum, right?"

"Total scum. But I kept thinking he'd change, that one of those times when he swore he loved me, he'd actually mean it. Long after my sister begged me to dump him, I finally realized he never would. Then, I found him in bed with the lead dancer in the show we were putting on in Chicago." The pain of realizing what a fool she'd been came over her again as she said, "He didn't even respect me enough to cheat on me with a stranger. It was like he did it that way on purpose to rub it in my face, to prove to me just how much power he had over not only me, but the entire cast and show, too." Grayson's expression was fierce, his hands tight fists beside her on the bed as she laid hers over them. "But I knew I had just as much power. The power to leave. The power to start over. And the power to make him mean as little to me as I did to him."

"It sounds to me like you made the mistake of forgiving him one too many times, too."

"No," she said in a firm voice, "you and Victor are nothing like each other, so you can give up trying to make the situations seem the same. And even if it's stupid and gets me in trouble sometimes, I won't apologize for not being cynical and hard and holding a grudge."

"Never apologize to anyone for who you are, Lori."

"What about when I break something? Or if I accidentally let another pig out? Or," she said as her lips curved upward at the corners, "what if it turns out that I used the wrong paint on the back side of the barn by accident?"

His eyes narrowed at her little admission before he broke out into laughter. It was a sound so sweet that she could hardly believe she was finally hearing it. Maybe the rest of the world wouldn't think that making Grayson laugh was as big an accomplishment as performing in the shows and on the stages she'd been gunning for her whole career...but Lori knew it was at least a thousand times more important.

Because it meant that she'd helped him, at least a little bit, to reclaim a part of his soul.

"Well, maybe that might warrant an apology," he teased, before claiming her mouth as he climbed back onto the bed. "Or at least keeping the door locked until you make it up to me."

"Mmm," she murmured against his lips, "maybe you should convince me not to make the same mistake again."

She felt the proof of how much he liked that idea as she rubbed over him, and was glad that she could take them both to a fun, playful place for a little while, at least. Grayson had lived too seriously for too long, and even though she knew there was more he wanted to say to her this morning—things he'd kept inside for far too long—she also recognized from her years of dance training when it was time to take a little break to relax or laugh or just wiggle around and be silly before putting in more hard work.

Fortunately for Grayson, she was a master of silly. And of laughter. Not to mention, she thought with a grin as she quickly got up and repositioned herself so that she was lying facedown across his lap, a master of fun, dirty sex.

His pupils were dilated and his breath was coming faster by the time she looked up at him, bit her lip and whispered, "I'm ready to be convinced now," in a breathy voice. She wiggled her behind for effect, but instead of playfully spanking her, when his hand made contact with her bottom it was to stroke over her skin with such heat, and such obvious desire, that it held even more impact than it would have if he'd touched her any other way.

He teased her like that for so long that she was about to start begging when he finally moved his hand from her hips to the slick flesh between her legs. She immediately spread her thighs for the sweet slide of his fingers into her. With his other hand, he caressed her breasts, and when he rolled one nipple between his thumb and forefinger at the exact moment that he slid the pad of his thumb over her clitoris, Lori shuddered and came so hard everything went black for a split second.

She was still trying to get her bearings when he lifted her off him so that she was on her hands and knees on the bed and one of his arms was wrapped so tightly around her waist that she didn't need to support her own weight.

Grayson's breath was warm on her ear as he teasingly said, "Have you learned your lesson yet about picking the right paint colors?"

The word, "No," was barely out of her mouth when he bucked his hips into hers. He felt so good thrusting inside of her in what was one of her favorite sexual positions that she couldn't help but loudly cry out her pleasure. He didn't still his movements to make sure she was okay, didn't mistake the sound for anything other than the pure joy that it was as he took her so hard again and again that he ended up having to cover her head with one hand so that she didn't hit it on the headboard.

And with every stroke of his body inside hers, Lori

felt a little more of Grayson's pain leave to make room for pleasure. Pleasure he obviously hadn't thought he deserved for three long years.

"Your wife was beautiful, wasn't she?"

Grayson's first thought, as he lay warm and loose in a tangle of Lori's arms and legs a while later, was that only she would think to ask that question about his wife when anyone else would have gone straight for the morbid, the sad.

His second thought was that, with the birds chirping and the leaves rustling outside his bedroom window, it did, finally, seem the right time to answer her questions about his past.

Lori had just given him so much: wonder, pleasure, laughter.

The very least he could do was give her the truth.

"She was." He was surprised to find himself picturing Leslie as she had been at nineteen rather than as the unhappy thirty-two-year-old woman he'd had in his head since the day she died. "Very beautiful."

"Who fell first?" Lori scooted up so that she could fully see his face while still touching him along the length of his body. "You or her?"

There was no jealousy, no pity, in Lori's question, so it was surprisingly easy for him to reply, "We were in college, and she said no the first time I asked her out. So to answer your question it was definitely me."

Lori looked delighted by the tidbit. "Oooh, you had to chase her?"

Even though their bodies were already touching from

shoulder to toe, he had to reach out to brush the hair out of her eyes, and stroke his hand over her face as he said, "I wouldn't take no for an answer."

"Which I'm sure she found as sexy as I do, by the way," she said, and then, "Tell me more about her, about the two of you."

Amazed to realize that Lori's questions were actually helping him remember and honor his wife in a way he had never been able to since her death, he said, "We got married right after graduation. I went to work in the city for my father's investment firm, and she got a job working for an interior designer. When we bought our first house out in the country, she left her job to focus on decorating the house and working on charity events and the family we planned to have." This time Lori was silent as she waited for him to continue. "We had trouble getting pregnant."

Lori took his hand in hers. She didn't squeeze it, just held on to him. "That must have been hard."

He took a breath, one he couldn't seem to inhale all the way. "Our marriage hadn't been what either of us had thought it would be. The country house had been our first try at making it better. A child was supposed to be our second. When neither of those worked—"

Grayson stopped, knew he didn't have to say anything more, that he'd already given away enough. He'd never talked to anyone about this before, not even his parents or Leslie's.

But, suddenly, being the only one who knew what had really happened seemed like too big a burden to keep bearing all alone.

"Somewhere along the way, she started drinking. But I never knew about what she'd been doing until she crashed into a tree and they told me she was way over the legal blood-alcohol limit. That was when I went home and saw all the signs I'd missed, every last one of the hints she'd been leaving me, just hoping I'd see her. Hoping that I'd be there for her the way I'd once promised when we were young and the world was going to be ours and I refused to have it any other way."

For a long while, Lori didn't say a word. She simply put her arms around him and held on tight.

Until, finally, she lifted her head from his chest and said, "Last night, when you took me to that barn dance and pushed me out onto the dance floor, you gave me back my heart, Grayson." Her mouth was barely a breath from his as she whispered, "And I can't see how a man who could do something that good could possibly be bad."

The birds were still chirping, the leaves were still rustling. The chickens still needed their eggs collected, the pigs their stalls mucked. The crops needed weeding and the CSA boxes needed to be assembled. But as Lori kissed him, and he kissed her back before making love to her yet one more time, Grayson knew that everything had changed.

Because he finally knew what it felt like to hold sunshine in his hands…and when Lori left, it was going to feel like winter all year round, even on the hottest days of summer.

Twenty

The next few days passed in a blur of backbreaking hard work as Lori helped Grayson lay in the boards and beams for the new roof of his cottage while keeping up with all of the usual farm chores. And, of course, there was the wonderful sex they had every night when the animals were finally taken care of and the only thing the two of them needed to focus on until sunrise was each other.

The sex was so good, in fact, that Lori sometimes wondered if she was dreaming. But each morning when Grayson dragged her out of bed at sunrise so that she could make them both breakfast, she knew she wasn't dreaming. A dream would never be so heartless, or make her muscles ache quite so much at the thought of his incredibly long lists of work to be done on the farm.

She was taking a ten-second break, dreaming of a tropical beach and a fruity drink, when Grayson rode up on his horse and said, "I need your help with something on the back forty." He pulled her up onto his horse without so much as a "please."

"You know," she said as he wrapped his arms tightly around her waist and rode off with her, "I'm sure I could learn to ride if you could spare a few precious minutes to show me how."

"Of course you could," he agreed. "You'd be a natural on horseback. But I want you here with me."

With his surprisingly lovely words echoing all through her heart, she snuggled deeper against him. "I'd rather be here with you, too." She honestly couldn't think of anywhere she'd rather be than out on this beautiful green pasture with Grayson. "So, what are you going to do to work me to the bone now?"

"Are you sure you want to know?"

He sounded way too happy with himself and she groaned while stewing in all the possibilities of the torturous work he had planned for her—maybe digging a ditch or hauling heavy rocks. But when the grass started to turn to sand and he didn't stop the horse, her suspicions suddenly shifted in another direction.

"Do you own the beach out here, too?"

"Technically, no," he answered as he finally tied up his horse to a nearby tree and helped her down, his big hands warm on her waist as he stole a kiss. "But since the only way to get to this part of the shore by land is through my property, we're not going to have to worry about anyone seeing you here naked."

"Naked?" Her body heated up even as her eyes narrowed. "Are you saying you brought me to the beach to seduce me?"

He pulled a large foil wrapper and a thermos out of one saddlebag. "I brought lunch, too. For later."

She loved seeing him like this. Smiling. Playful. Happy. It was how he deserved to be.

Lori wanted so badly to heal Grayson. He obviously blamed himself for what had happened with his wife. And she hated that he did. She wanted to clear away his pain and fill up the empty spaces with love.

But life, she knew, wasn't always that easy. And sometimes having some fun despite the pain was all you could do.

She looked down at the picnic he'd packed, and teased, "Well, if you've got lunch, then I suppose you could have me as an appetizer first."

The next thing she knew, he was throwing her up over his shoulder, pulling a thick blanket out of the other saddlebag and carrying her down to the beach. She could easily have gotten back down on her feet, but what was the point of pretending she didn't love this?

Just as she was going to let herself pretend, at least for the next few days, that this was a life she could stay at and live forever.

They'd barely spread the blanket out on the sand before they were both reaching for each other.

"I don't know how you do it," he murmured as they stripped off each other's clothes and he sat on the blanket and pulled her over him. "All I know is that I can't stop wanting you."

"I'll show you how," she said as she wrapped her arms around his neck and straddled his naked body. She loved the feel of the hard and fast beat of his heart against her own bare chest, proof that she affected him as much as he affected her.

She found his mouth with hers and kissed him softly, the salt spray from the ocean already on his lips. She knew she'd never forget this—making love to Grayson on his beach, his arms tight and warm around her. She could feel how much he wanted her, but he didn't rush her, didn't roll them over on the blanket and thrust into her, even though both of them would surely enjoy that, too.

He'd given her so much pleasure while also giving her back her confidence in herself as a beautiful, desirable woman—and now she wanted to give him back just as much. Lori knew she couldn't fully heal Grayson, that she couldn't change his past. But she could give him a few moments of sweet perfection in her arms.

Moments just like this.

She licked out against his tongue and he groaned his pleasure into her mouth as his tongue licked back. He made her smile, her rough and gruff farmer, even as she rocked her pelvis into his, his erection thick and throbbing against her slick skin.

But there was so much more of him she wanted to taste, to run her tongue, her lips, over. She rained kisses across his jaw, his five-o'clock shadow scratching her lips in the most delicious way, then down beneath his jaw into the hollow of his neck where she had licked the rain from his skin just a week before.

The storm hadn't only been brewing outside; it had hit both of them just as hard, just as suddenly. He said she made him forget, but he made her forget, too. Because one kiss, one caress, at a time, Grayson had taken the place of every other man she'd ever been with—all of them nothing more than a prelude to the real thing.

To love.

She'd planned to run her hands over his broad shoulders, to kiss every inch of him, but the intensity of their passion for each other ran too deep for her to do anything but grab the condom he'd dropped onto the blanket, tear it open and lift her hips up so that she could slide it onto his absolutely gorgeous erection.

Grayson's entire body stiffened while her fingertips grazed his hard flesh, and she understood how hard he was working to keep himself in control for another few seconds—because she was doing the same thing herself.

"You'd better go faster than that," he growled.

Lori was both grinning and panting as she decided to mess with him just the teeniest bit. "I'm going as fast as I can," she said, even as she let her hands linger across him, her hips bump just a little against his, the tips of her breasts slide over his rock-hard pecs as she fiddled with the condom.

"Like hell you are," he said, and then he was taking the job away from her, his hands moving to her hips a moment later to hold her tightly as she finally took him inside, sliding down over his thick length one perfect inch at a time.

Her eyes fluttered closed, her breath rushing from her body as pleasure overtook her. When she finally figured out how to breathe again and opened her eyes, she found Grayson staring at her with such desire—and such wonder—that her chest clenched so tight she could actually feel her love for him throbbing between them.

The only way she could keep from saying the words aloud to him was to cover his mouth with hers and focus every last cell, every last muscle in her body, on pleasure, on filling herself with his hard heat again and again and feeling him grow even bigger, even harder, inside of her with every stroke.

"Grayson..." She couldn't see anything but him, couldn't think anything but his name, couldn't feel anything other than the deepest pleasure she'd ever known in her life. And as the ocean waves crashed behind them into the jagged rocks along the coast, Grayson was her anchor as he held her so tightly on his lap that she could no longer move. She could only hold on as he thrust up into her again and again until she was crashing hard into a climax so beautiful she was nearly sobbing at the pleasure he gave her.

And as he called out her name, then exploded inside of her as she held him just as tightly as he'd been holding her, she didn't have to wonder if her body had just told him of the love she hadn't let herself speak aloud.

All that was left to wonder was whether he'd heard it, too.

The next afternoon, the sun was already starting to set by the time Grayson found her in the pigpen. "You're just getting their stalls mucked out now?"

Lori remained amazed both by the way he managed to infuse each word with so much irritation, and by how cute she found it. Not rushing as she finished the final stall, she carefully washed off her rake and hung it up before saying, "I would have finished earlier, but someone made me late for work this morning by not letting me get out of bed."

As she walked over to him at the gate, he made a face. "You *really* need a shower."

"Well, you *really* are cranky," she retorted even though she completely agreed with him about how nice a shower would be right about now. "Think a shower can wash that away, too?"

"You think this is cranky?" he growled as he took hold of her and dragged her around the side of the barn. "I'll show you cranky."

Before she knew it, he had her standing fully clothed under the outdoor shower. He stripped the wet clothes, hat and boots from her so fast that all she could do was stand there in shock and let him. Only to be doubly shocked when she realized his jeans and boots were already off, too, and he'd put a condom on.

A moment later, he picked her up and drove into her, both of them utterly ravenous for each other despite the fact that it had barely been eight hours since they'd last made love. She didn't need foreplay, didn't need anything but his strong arms around her and his fierce desire to drive her straight to the edge, and then all the way over as his lips landed on hers and he drove his tongue into her mouth just as he thrust his hips forward.

Later, when he soaped her up, then made her feel good all over again with his hands and mouth, Lori made a mental note to remember to call Grayson names more often than she already did.

* * *

A few days later, Grayson had just stepped in the back door when he heard Lori's voice coming from the kitchen.

"Hey, Soph, time for my daily check-in so that you don't think an ax murderer has gotten to me."

He hadn't realized Lori and her sister spoke every day. Despite opening up to each other about their failed relationships after their first night together, by tacit agreement since then, they hadn't pushed each other hard for anything. Instead, they'd both simply enjoyed their time together.

But it was getting harder and harder for Grayson to deny that he was starved for more of Lori. Not just her body. Not just her laughter. But to know her better.

All of her, inside and out.

So even though he knew he shouldn't listen in without her knowledge, he didn't head back outside to let her finish her call in private.

"Oh!" he heard Lori exclaim. "Is that a baby laughing? Really, it's two babies laughing at the same time?" He felt the wonder in her voice deep in the center of his heart. "What could be better than that?" she asked on a sweet little laugh of her own. "I can't wait to see them on Sunday. I've missed my little niece and nephew so much."

He'd known since that day he'd taken her to the General Store to pick up boots that she'd be leaving him for a family lunch this Sunday.

Unfortunately, he also knew that the odds of her coming back to his farm—and to him—after that were slim to none. Because once she reentered her real life, she'd see how ridiculous hiding out on his farm really was. Lori was a world-class dancer. She had a family who loved her. As much a part of the land as she seemed to be every time he looked at her, the truth was that she didn't belong on his farm.

It was why he'd been careful not to get too close, telling himself again and again that it was smarter just to fill up on pleasure so that he wouldn't hurt as much once she was gone.

But Grayson knew better: it would hurt like hell.

And he would have to let her leave, anyway, because keeping Lori hidden away on a farm would deprive the world of her truly special gift. He'd known from the first second she showed up that she wouldn't last very long. But he'd always thought she would leave because she couldn't hack the hard work.

Now he knew the truth. Lori Sullivan could do anything she set her mind to. But while there were plenty of great farmhands out there, only a few people were meant to be dancers.

"Yes," she said to her sister, "I do feel better." She gave a contented little sigh. "Lots better. What can I say? Being a farmhand obviously agrees with me. Oh," she added on a playful note, "and lots of super-awesome sex with a hot cowboy doesn't hurt, either."

She laughed at whatever her sister said. "Don't worry, Soph. You'd like Grayson. He's nothing like Victor." Lori was silent for a few moments as her sister spoke again. "I don't know. I'm still working that out."

What didn't she know? Grayson asked himself. Was

she finally going to confront the douche bag she used to date? Or was she telling her sister that she thought there was a chance of a future with the cowboy?

Shit. This was why it was a bad idea to listen in on a conversation. Especially only half of one.

"I love you, too, Soph. Kiss each one of Smith's and Jackie's perfect little fingers and toes for their aunt, okay?"

Grayson slipped back out the side door and stood in the driveway, staring up at the moon, wondering when in the hell he'd managed to completely lose hold of his heart. A few minutes later, Lori came outside to join him and slipped her hand into his.

"I swear," she said in a voice filled with wonder, "the moon looks prettier here than anywhere else. Everything does."

"It's even better from the middle of the pasture."

Hand in hand, they started slowly walking out across his land, the night air clean and crisp, the sky an inky blue. For once, she was quiet as she stared up at the sky and he knew he should be appreciating the rare moments of silence.

Only, more than he wanted a return to the quiet he'd grown so accustomed to over the past three years, he wanted *Lori.*

"Tell me about your family."

He felt her start in obvious surprise, but she quickly covered it with a laugh. "The sun will probably be back up by the time I finish doing that. There are eight of us, remember?"

"You only have one sister, right?"

She nodded. "We're twins."

"There's two of you?"

"Don't sound so horrified. We're nothing like each other. In fact, I can guarantee you would *love* my quiet, calm, librarian sister. Everyone does, especially Sophie's pub-owning, tattoo-covered husband, Jake."

He raised an eyebrow. "How'd they possibly end up together?"

"Sophie and Jake have been in love with each other since they were kids, but neither of them wanted to admit it until they finally gave in and had a one-night stand at my brother Chase's wedding. Sophie got pregnant with twins and the rest is history."

By now, he wasn't terribly surprised at the way Lori acted as if something like that would be a perfectly natural progression for a relationship. She didn't expect life to be normal, or by the book.

"My brother Gabe is just a little older than me and Soph. He's a firefighter in the city and recently married Megan after saving her and her daughter, Summer, from a bad apartment fire last year." With barely a breath between sentences she explained, "Summer is an amazing eight-year-old who made my brother Zach take her new puppy for a couple of weeks while they were gone on vacation. He ended up meeting Heather, who's a dog trainer, and she wanted nothing to do with him. But then her dog fell in love with his puppy, and Zach realized he couldn't live without Heather, either, so now they're engaged."

His head was spinning with names and details. "The

dogs are engaged? Or are you talking about your brother and his dog trainer?"

"Oooh," she exclaimed, "Summer would *love* it if we had a little ceremony for the dogs, too. Good idea!" She paused for half a second before jumping to what seemed like a totally random question. "Do you like baseball?"

He gave her a look that said she should know better. "I'm a red-blooded American male. Of course I like baseball."

"But since you're from New York, you're probably more of a Yankees fan than a Hawks fan, right?"

"Are you kidding? After seeing Ryan Sullivan pitch up close, I—" The last names suddenly clicked into place. "Don't tell me your brother is the guy responsible for the Hawks winning the World Series this year?"

"Last year, too," she confirmed with a happy smile. "He just got engaged to his best friend from high school. Vicki is an awesome sculptor. So awesome, in fact, that one of my other brothers hired her to work on his last movie."

Grayson had thought he was catching up, but now she was losing him again. "You have a brother who works on movies?"

"I should make you guess this one." She waited expectantly for him to figure out who the hell in Hollywood she could possibly be related to, before finally scrunching up her nose and sighing. "I don't know why *nobody* ever sees the family resemblance. I'll give you a hint." She pretended she was holding a gun with her free hand and pointed it at him. *"All the right friends in all the right places can't save you now, can they?"*

"Jesus," he said as he realized her brother was Smith Sullivan, one of the biggest movie stars in the world. "Is there anyone you *aren't* related to?"

"Well," she said just slowly enough that he realized she was going to hit him over the head with yet another whopper of a sibling, "you know the wine we had with dinner the other night? My brother Marcus owns Sullivan Winery, and—"

"There's an *and?*"

Lori started humming a song he'd heard on the radio approximately a thousand times in the past year. It was catchy and well written enough that somehow he wasn't sick of it yet. "You know that song, right?"

"Who doesn't?"

"Marcus's fiancée, Nicola, wrote it. And sang it." She lifted her hands to his chest. "But before you totally start freaking out—"

"I'm not freaking out," he said, but she ignored him, of course.

"—since I haven't noticed that you're all that into photography, you probably haven't heard of my brother Chase."

"I was on the board of directors for the International Center of Photography in New York City. Of course I know who Chase Sullivan is."

Had he really been stupid enough to think that he could have uncomplicated, no-ties sex with Lori *Sullivan?*

Hell, in everything he did or saw or listened to for the rest of his life, he'd think of her and her family.

"And you know that my father died. I was only two,

but my mother and older brothers tell the most wonderful stories about him, so it feels like I have memories of him, even though I really don't."

He pulled her against him, into the place he always wanted her, with her body pressed close, her cheek soft in the crook of his neck. When she'd told him about her father before, he hadn't been kind, hadn't told her, as he did now, "I'm sorry."

"I am, too," she said as she wound her arms around his neck. "Now will you tell me about your family?"

"It's pretty much the opposite of yours. I don't have any brothers or sisters. My father is still working the stock exchange and my mother helps run half the charities in the city."

"They must be so amazed with your farm, with everything you've done here to make such a difference in feeding an entire community."

He shook his head. "They haven't seen it."

"How could they not want to come see what you've created here?" She looked extremely insulted on his behalf. "I mean, I know it's different from what they're used to in the city, but a little mud isn't going to hurt them."

She was such a fierce defender of him, so ready to take his side. When, what, how had he ever done anything good enough to deserve this time with her? And how could he possibly find a way to keep her here with him for longer than two weeks without her resenting him for keeping her from her family, her career, her real life?

"I've never asked them to come," he admitted.

"Oh, Grayson." She lifted his hand to her lips and pressed a kiss to his palm. "Don't they know better than to wait for an invitation when the only thing that works with you is just showing up and refusing to leave? How come Sweetpea and I are the only ones who have ever figured that out?"

All day, all night, Grayson had wanted to kiss her, but never more than he did right then, with her sweet emotions clear as the night sky in her beautiful eyes.

Leaving the hand she was holding between their chests, he threaded the fingers of the other through her soft hair. She was already tilting her mouth up to his as he lowered his down onto hers.

Every time he kissed Lori and tasted how fresh and sweet she was, Grayson felt as though he was being bathed in warm sunlight on a perfect summer day. And even now, as he kissed her beneath the moon and the stars, that warmth moved through his veins, pumping through a heart that had been cold for so long.

He never wanted to stop kissing her, never wanted to let go of the beautifully warm and sweet woman in his arms. A week ago, he would have made himself let go of her, anyway. But her conversation with her sister was a reminder that she'd be leaving soon enough… and he wasn't even close to having his fill of her yet. So instead of letting Lori go, Grayson pulled her closer.

And when she gasped her pleasure against his lips, it was the most beautiful sound he'd ever heard.

All the next day, Lori thought about the kiss Grayson had given her in the moonlight.

She wasn't surprised to find that he had a deeply romantic side. Not when he'd been revealing himself to her in bits and pieces over the past two weeks without even realizing it. How gentle he'd been in coaxing a baby goat out of the blackberry bramble he'd gotten himself stuck in. The way he spoke to his horses in low, soothing tones as he groomed them. The care with which he picked up his prize hens to stroke their feathers. And, of course, his romantic side was even more fun when contrasted with his cranky-pants attitude during the work day.

Truth be told, there wasn't a side of him she didn't like, and more and more often she found herself wondering about the future…and if it could be possible for them to have one together. Could she figure out a way to combine the life she'd had before Grayson with the new one she'd found with him in the rolling pastures of Pescadero?

In two days she'd be heading to her mother's house for the Sunday lunch she'd promised her sister she would attend. They'd want to know everything, and she knew she'd have to tell them about her ex, the farm, the work she'd done these past two weeks.

But what would she say about Grayson?

And how could she possibly explain what she'd found here with him without them seeing that she'd fallen head over heels in love with a man who couldn't love her back?

Yes, she knew none of them had had an easy road to their own happily-ever-afters. Nonetheless, being the only one left in a family of joyously-in-love siblings wasn't easy.

* * *

Later that day, going with Eric to help with the CSA pickups was bittersweet. This time she wondered if it would be the last time she got to do it. After he dropped her off and drove back down the driveway, she found Grayson on top of the cottage roof.

"Hey, cowboy," she called up to him, "you make a girl want to stare up at the blue sky forever."

And it was true—even looking at him from a distance made her heart clench and her stomach twist and her breath come faster. She might only have loved him for a week, but that love ran so deeply through her that she could barely hold the words back sometimes, especially when he was kissing her and holding her in his strong arms at night.

He grinned down at her, the smile she so loved making her heart flip-flop around in her chest like crazy as he said, "Looking good down there, too, cowgirl."

"Good enough to take a little break?" she said with a playful little flounce of her chest and hips.

"Hell, yeah," he said in such a hot, sexy voice that her head spun and her knees grew weak. "Grab the small hammer from the kitchen counter for me and I'll nail down these last couple of shingles." He stripped her with his eyes. "And then I'll nail you."

Boy, did he know how to motivate her as she all but ran into the kitchen to get his hammer. But when she saw Sweetpea lying halfway off her bed of pillows and blankets, with her head turned in a slightly strange position, Lori immediately forgot about Grayson waiting for her on the roof.

"Baby, are you okay? Please be okay."

She ran a gentle hand over the cat's side and was beyond relieved to find her still warm and breathing. She immediately scooped her off the floor. Despite the special meals Lori had been making and hand feeding to her, Grayson's cat had become terribly thin, so that every one of her ribs was showing. Even her tail, which had remained thick despite her illness, was now nearly hairless.

Lori was still sitting on the couch rocking the cat in her arms when Grayson came in the side door. "How long were you planning on making me wait for the—" He stopped cold as he saw her with Sweetpea. "Did something happen with Mo?"

For once, Lori didn't correct him on the cat's name. "I don't think she feels very good tonight. But we're just going to cuddle it out."

Grayson sat beside them on the couch and ran a large hand over the cat's skinny frame before placing it over Lori's. They stayed just like that until long past the moment the cat fell peacefully asleep—the loner and the two strays who had refused to let him be alone.

Twenty-One

Early the next morning, Grayson forced himself to get up with the sun, despite having the most beautiful woman in the world in his bed, warm and soft and always ready for him. But when he went out into the kitchen to pound back a quick cup of coffee, he immediately knew something was wrong.

It was Mo. She wasn't making her little snuffling noises. She wasn't blinking her eyes open to acknowledge his presence for a split second before going back to sleep away the rest of the morning.

She was gone.

His heart broke knowing he'd lost the furry friend who had been with him every step of the way as he'd built a new life on the farm. At the same time, he'd come to accept life and death for his animals. It was nature. It was the cycle of things.

But Lori was going to be absolutely devastated.

Taking a blanket off the couch, he carefully bundled up the cat in it. He could bury Mo before Lori woke up and spare her the painful goodbye, but he knew that would be worse.

Carrying the cat in his arms, he walked back into the bedroom. He simply stared at Lori for a few seconds, drinking in the sight of her in his bed, her dark hair spread out across the pillows, her beautiful face calm, her endlessly energetic body finally still for a short while as she slept. Her mouth was tilted up slightly at the corners and he hoped she was dreaming of him.

Crap. He couldn't do this to her, couldn't wake her from her happy dreams and break her heart. He was moving away to deal with the cat himself when she stirred.

"Grayson?"

He swallowed hard before turning back to face her. She immediately noticed the bundle in his arms.

"Is it Sweetpea?" Lori's voice was surprisingly steady.

Grayson, on the other hand, couldn't seem to find his voice as he nodded instead.

Silently, she drew back the covers and got dressed. She wasn't crying, but he could feel sadness radiating out from her with every single movement. Together, they walked outside, both of them automatically heading past the barn. Lori walked over to the spot with the most sweeping views of his land.

"Here. Sweetpea should be right here. Right by the barn, where you found her."

He handed Mo to her and got the shovel. It didn't take long to dig the hole and, soon, Lori was kneeling and placing the cat into it. One tear slid down her cheek, and then another.

"Thank you for making me feel so welcome here, Sweetpea. I love you."

Somehow, just barely, Grayson kept his own tears from falling as Lori stepped back and he shoveled the dirt into place. She found a rock and some flowers and laid them down over the grave.

When she looked back at him, her face awash with tears and her shoulders bowed with grief, Grayson finally pulled her into his arms the way he'd wanted to from the start. They stood like that for a long time, until she started shivering in his arms. Gently, he brought her back inside, Lori crying harder with every step away from the cat's grave.

"Love is too hard." She fit the words in between sobs. "I'm too weak for love." She shook her head against his chest. "I'm never going to love anything ever again. Never. Ever. Again. Not anyone or anything."

Grayson pulled her closer, held her tighter. He'd known she would cry and he would have done anything in the world to make it so she didn't have to.

But she had to. Because she had loved his balding, foul-breathed cat with everything she had.

He knew now that this was how Lori Sullivan loved. All the way. Every single time.

Even when she knew that her love wouldn't be able to save anyone or anything.

"You have the softest heart of anyone I've ever known," he said, whispering the words into her hair as he rocked her. "And it's exactly what makes you so strong."

And it was why he loved her. One of the reasons,

anyway. Because he also loved her bratty comebacks. He loved the way she put her entire self behind whatever she was doing, even if she had no idea what she was doing and was getting it all wrong. He loved the way she danced as if she was connected to the clouds and the sun and the rainbows.

And he loved that she'd stormed into his life and turned everything upside down before he even had a chance to stop her.

Maybe it wasn't fair to lay this on her now, to combine love and death into one moment. But if there was one thing Grayson had learned during the past three years, it was that life wasn't fair. The weather could take out his crops overnight. A healthy animal could fall sick so suddenly that there was no time to call the vet.

And a beautiful woman could show up on his doorstep and change his life with no warning at all, leaving him no time to figure out how to guard his heart from her.

"I love you."

She was still sobbing, her tears soaking his shirt, as she lifted her head to face him. Her eyes were red and her nose was running...and she'd never looked more beautiful to him.

"What did you just say?"

It figured that when he finally lost his heart again, it would be like this. To a woman who had driven him crazy from the moment he set eyes on her.

"I said..." He paused so that she wouldn't miss it this time. "I. Love. You."

Her sobs receded as she blinked at him in shock. "You love me?"

She said it as though it was the craziest idea in the world. As though there was no way he could possibly love her.

Frustration—the familiar frustration he'd felt since that first day, when she'd told him she was going to be the best farmhand he'd ever had—started to eat at him.

"Yes." He tried not to growl the words at her. "I love you."

He waited for her to smile. To throw her arms around him. To declare her love right back to him.

Instead, she said, "Are you sure you're not just saying it because of Sweetpea? Because if this is some crazy idea you have to make me feel better…"

Damn it. Couldn't a guy declare his love to a girl without getting twenty questions thrown back at him, not to mention heaps of disbelief?

Not trusting himself to speak—he'd yell at her and then she'd yell back and then the next thing you knew, there'd be doors slamming, and none of that would be fair when she was still sad about the cat—he picked her up and headed toward the bedroom.

"Where are you going? What are you doing?"

"I'm going to prove to you that I love you, damn it," he said between gritted teeth.

He tossed her onto the bed. Hard enough that she caught air.

"I just bounced." She looked utterly amazed by it.

He ripped his clothes off and then came at her. "You're going to bounce again if you're not careful."

Damn it, this wasn't the sweet, careful wooing that he should be doing to prove that he loved her. But she drove him so crazy he couldn't think straight, couldn't stop himself from yanking her shirt and jeans and boots off, too.

"I love you," he said as he threw her boots across the room, where they hit the wall and fell with a satisfying thud to the floor. "So that means you're going to have to love something again. I know you hate doing anything I say, but this time you're going to have to. Because you're going to love me back. I'm going to make sure of it."

She only had on her bra and panties now, but suddenly it was irrelevant that he was naked and she was nearly there when she said yet one more time, "You really love me?" as if it couldn't possibly be true. But behind the disbelief, he heard something else.

Fear.

She'd always acted so sure about everything, even when she wasn't. His chest clenched at the thought of his proud, brave girl ever being afraid again. He wouldn't stand for it, wouldn't let her be scared of anything just because she'd made some crappy choices about men before she met him.

Lori Sullivan had been born to face life down, to laugh and to dance.

And to be *his*.

"I'd say it again if I thought you were finally going to believe me," he said as he pounced on her. He threaded his hands into her incredibly soft hair. "Now be quiet so I can prove to you that I love you. And that you love me, too."

Of course she opened her mouth to say something, so he covered it with his and kissed the words away.

No more words. He wasn't any good with those, anyway.

But by the time he was done with making love to her, she'd understand exactly how he felt about her.

He'd make absolutely sure of it.

Lori remembered the first dance lesson she'd ever had. Her mother had taken her to the studio in downtown Palo Alto and she'd been afraid. She hadn't let on, of course, that she was scared. Not even when her legs were shaking so hard she was afraid she'd embarrass herself in front of the beautiful teacher. Because one day when she grew up, she wanted to be just like Madame Dubois, tall and slim and proud, her hair pulled back into a bun, her limbs so graceful simply crossing the room to shake hands with her mother. Madame had smiled down at her, then reached out a hand and drawn her into the middle of the room. There were other girls, older ones, stretching along the barres that were placed in front of the floor-to-ceiling mirrors.

"Dance for me, Lori," was what Madame had said, and then, suddenly, she hadn't been scared anymore. Because dancing was who she was, the very core of her. She'd started leaping and twirling, closing her eyes so that she could dance to the music in her head, a symphony of emotion and beauty.

Now, as Grayson drew her into him and kissed her

so sweetly, so perfectly, she remembered that little girl who had danced because she loved it. She hadn't been trying to please anyone, hadn't danced for any other reason than because it made her feel whole and perfect and beautiful and so wonderfully alive.

It was just how Grayson made her feel, even in those first days when she hadn't wanted to feel anything at all.

He loved her.

Disbelief had come first, but that was because she hadn't been expecting it. And also because he so loved being cranky, even when he was saying he loved her.

But then, there had been fear. Such big fear it threatened to swallow her whole.

Fear that she couldn't love right this time, fear that she didn't know how to put love in its place and keep it there safe and pretty and simple, fear that she'd just end up making all the same mistakes she always had.

Lori clung to Grayson as he kissed her and she spun deeper into him, into everything he'd given her without ever wanting to.

She felt so raw from losing Sweetpea, and she knew she would for a long time, but she could also feel Grayson's kisses already healing her where she was torn and hurting.

He rained kisses over the rest of her face, her eyelids still damp from her tears, and then her forehead and the curve of one ear, before taking her lobe between his teeth. She shivered at the sweet pleasure of the small bite, and then the slow swipe of his tongue over the sensitive skin on her neck.

He was so big, so strong, so tough, and yet no other

man had ever been this gentle in bed, this intent on drawing every ounce of pleasure out of her. He moved lower then, his tongue dipping into the hollow of her throat, and she moaned aloud as he laid her back against the pillows so that his hands could follow the devastating path of his mouth and tongue and teeth all along her skin. She arched into his kisses, his caresses, gasping at every perfect kiss.

The morning sun was coming in now through his bedroom window and bathing them both. Where she'd been so cold outside just a short while earlier, now she was warm and safe.

And loved.

He was pressing kisses to the upper swell of her breasts, and she reached out to stroke his cheek. His stubble was thick as it rubbed across her breasts and beneath her fingertips. He licked out across one of her nipples through her bra before catching lace and flesh between his teeth and she wrapped her legs around him, no words necessary to tell him what she needed. She arched her back so that he could undo her bra clasp, and a heartbeat later her chest was completely bare to the most wonderful mouth any man had ever possessed.

She couldn't catch her breath, but it was just as well, because a moment later Grayson was crushing his mouth to hers again and they were rolling over so that he was on his back and she was lying across his big, hard body. His hands cupped her breasts as she sat up to straddle him while pressing the V of her legs into his enormous erection.

"Come for me, Lori. I need to see you come apart for me."

His kisses had heated her up so much already that his erection throbbing between her legs and a handful of sexy words were a potent combination. So when he leaned up, pressed her breasts together and took both nipples into his mouth at the same time, she went spiraling all the way over into a mind-blowing climax.

Long before she had her breath back, he had her lying back on the bed again, and was peeling off her panties. She shook with continued need as he brushed his fingertips between her legs, then lowered his mouth to press as soft and gentle a kiss to her sex as he had to her mouth.

Lori had never been so overwhelmed, so completely swamped, with desire—and pure, sweet emotion—for anyone. She'd always thought she'd given all of herself to her family, to her friends, to dancing. But when she was in Grayson's arms, when he was loving her so beautifully, she knew she hadn't even come close to the true depths of what she had to give.

Until he'd come into her life—or rather, before she'd forced her way into his—she hadn't known it was possible to feel this much.

She opened her mouth to tell him he was right, that she loved him, when he slid his fingers into her at the exact same time that his lips and tongue amped up their seduction of her most sensitive flesh. And if he hadn't been there to gather her into his arms and hold her steady as she shook from the force of the pleasure of yet another powerfully strong climax, she would have slid all the way off the bed.

But nothing was forever. Sweetpea had taught her that. So she couldn't wait another second to tell him how she felt, couldn't take the time to find her breath, her voice, to wait until they weren't naked and sweaty and wrapped up in each other.

"I love you." She slid her arms around his neck but she didn't kiss him again, not until she'd said it at least one more time. "I love you so much."

His grin came fast, and was so darn beautiful that she was already grinning back as he said, "I knew it."

How could she declare her love for him in one breath and want to growl at him in the next? "I wouldn't if I could stop myself."

His smile grew even bigger. "You never stood a chance."

She used her dancer's strength to roll them over to straddle him once again. "Of course I did, you *farmer.*"

"Oooh, baby, you know I love it when you call me names. What else have you got?" he taunted.

"Big bully."

He stroked her breasts and cupped her hips with his deliciously big and calloused hands. "So hot. Give me more."

"Blockhead."

"You sitting on me naked, calling me all those names, is better than porn."

She laughed despite herself and had to poke him in the chest to try to show him he hadn't gotten the better of her. "You're the one who never stood a chance."

She expected him to laugh again, to tease her again. Instead, his expression grew serious.

"I never did, Lori, not for one single second."

No matter what happened from here forward, she knew she'd never stop loving Grayson. It wouldn't matter that their lives didn't fit together. It wouldn't matter that he deserved someone who could be a full-time farmer with him. It wouldn't matter when she was three thousand miles away from him on a stage in a big city, dancing for a crowd of strangers.

She would still love him with her entire heart.

"Dance with me, Grayson." Love was forever, but not everything else could be. So she'd take *now*...and she'd hold on to it for as long as she could. "Please, dance with me."

Their bodies were poised to come together, and any other man would have been beyond frustrated with her for wanting to get up on their feet. Fortunately, Grayson had been frustrated with her from minute one, so at least he was used to it.

She climbed from his body even as he swung his feet to the rug beside his big bed. She loved that he'd built nearly everything in this room, that she could feel his touch in every surface, in the wood posts of the bed, in the welded ironwork of the head- and footboards.

And then she was in his arms and they were dancing. There wasn't much space on his bedroom floor, but they didn't need it. Not when it was enough just to be in each other's arms and to sway to the music she was sure they both could hear.

Tears came again, falling as fast, as thick, as they had before and, for the second time in one morning, he let her cry against his chest.

"It will be okay, Sweetpea," he said into her hair, using the same name for her that she'd used for the cat. "I promise it won't hurt like this forever. One day you'll feel better."

But didn't he know? "You've already made everything better."

His mouth captured hers, and then he was lifting her up off the floor altogether so that her legs were wrapped around his hips and he was pressing her back down onto the bed and coming into her with slow, perfect heat.

"So have you," he told her as he thrust into her and she met each thrust with the press of her hips against his. "Everything's better now. So much better than it's ever been. So much better than I ever thought it could be."

His cheek was pressed up against hers and that was how they loved each other, with her smooth skin rubbing into his stubble, her hands holding on to him just as tightly as he was holding on to her.

Lori had always been loved by her family. She had seen the love between her siblings and their husbands and wives. She knew how it was to hold a baby niece and nephew in her arms and stare into pure wonder.

But it wasn't until she was in Grayson's arms, and he was kissing away her tears and caressing her so gently, so sweetly, until they were both shuddering with pleasure, that Lori finally learned what love truly was.

Addicting.
Selfless.
And entirely without bounds.

Twenty-Two

Two days later, Lori still couldn't believe Grayson had agreed to come to Sunday lunch with her. They'd dropped her rental car off first, and now, as she sat in the front seat of his truck, she couldn't sit still. Taking him to meet her family was a really big next step for her. Thinking of all the men she thought she'd been in love with before, she now knew none of them had ever meant anything to her, because she'd never once been tempted to bring them home to meet her family.

When Grayson put his hand on her knee, she told him, "You don't have to worry with my family," even though he hadn't said anything about being worried. "They're amazing."

"From everything you've told me, I'm sure they will be," he said, but the muscle jumping in his cheek betrayed his obvious reservations.

"They're going to love you," she insisted.

"They're going to take one look at me and instantly see that I'm not good enough for you," he countered.

"And six older brothers means I'm going to have to let each of them get at least one punch in." He rubbed his jaw as if he could already feel the pain. "But don't worry," he said as he squeezed her knee and gave her a lopsided grin, "I won't let them damage any of the good parts."

She knew it was his way of telling her everything was going to be okay but, for the first time, she didn't feel like teasing him back.

"All your parts are good, Grayson." She covered his hand with hers. "And I would never let anyone hurt you."

Grayson couldn't imagine actually wanting to have a family lunch once a month. His father had always been busy with his career, his mother equally so with her charities. As a kid he'd learned not to count on them being there for much more than the requisite recitals and graduations. And the formal meals they did have together had been full of long silences and awkward questions about school and girls.

But evidently Lori and her ridiculously famous and successful siblings willingly met up all the time. Grayson had been a cynical bastard before she'd barged into his life and now that cynical voice inside him was telling him that there had to be some family dysfunction Lori hadn't mentioned. Like jealousy. Or competitiveness.

Only, whenever Lori talked about her family, she was always happy. Laughing. And full of nothing but love.

Still, that didn't explain why she hadn't gone home

to them when her world had fallen apart, rather than driving out into the middle of nowhere and insisting that a grumpy stranger put her up.

Lori directed him to a ranch house on a suburban street in Palo Alto. He could feel her excitement growing with every mile they got closer to her mother's house.

"I can't wait to see how big the babies are." She'd told him all about her new nieces and nephew—one niece from her brother Chase, and a niece and nephew from her sister, Sophie. "They're so cute, it's crazy. And Summer is the perfect older cousin for them. She even changes diapers," Lori added with a scrunch of her nose at the thought of it. "The three dogs take it up to the perfect level of craziness, just like when we were kids." Her smile faltered slightly as she said, "I wish Sweetpea could have come with us today. She would have loved being in the middle of it all."

He reached up to stroke a hand over her hair. "I wish Mo was here, too, because then I could have used her as a big furry shield."

She smacked his hand away in mock irritation, but she was laughing again as they got out of the truck. Walking hand in hand down the sidewalk, he could hear the laughter and conversation coming from her mother's yard. Lori sped up and pulled him toward the front door. She didn't ring the doorbell, just walked in. The living room was empty and the French doors out to the back were open wide.

Of course, the second they walked into the backyard, every eye in the place turned to them—even the babies and animals sensing something big was up. Grayson was glad for those stressful years on Wall Street when he'd learned not to let anyone see him sweat, no matter how bad the pressure.

Crap, he thought as he saw just how big each of her brothers was in person. He was screwed.

"Everyone," Lori said, "this is Grayson." She rattled off the names of her siblings and their other halves and children one after the other.

He hadn't been expecting a warm welcome from her brothers, and he wasn't disappointed when they all scowled at him. In perfect contrast, a beautiful, gray-haired woman came forward with open arms and a ready smile.

"Grayson," she said in a warm voice that sounded so much like Lori's. She reached for his hand with elegant fingers. "I'm Mary, Lori's mother. I'm so glad that you could come today."

He stared at her, stunned as he realized he was looking at a picture of Lori in forty or so years...and that she would be even more beautiful than she was today.

In that moment, he wanted to tell Mary that he was in love with her daughter. But as he looked into Mary's eyes and said, "Thank you," something told him she already knew exactly what he felt.

Lori, of course, immediately ran off to lift one baby after another into her arms. Grayson stood with Mary and watched her shower them with love.

"She's missed them," he said to Mary in a low voice. "She's missed all of you. I tried to get her to come back home, but she wouldn't leave my farm."

"Of all my children, Lori's always been the most stubborn, even when she's wrong about something." He felt Mary's eyes on him, wise and surprisingly calm, considering the chaos all around her. "She isn't always the easiest personality for everyone to like," Mary admitted, "but she's impossible not to love."

A baby reached for Grandma Sullivan, and as she moved to pick her up, Grayson remained apart from everyone for a moment to better take in the scene in front of him. Everyone in Mary's backyard was paired off. Some had children, some had pets, some were engaged, some were pregnant, but all of them were clearly happy.

But even crazier was that, instead of making him uneasy, he realized why Lori had been so irresistible from the start. Love—pure, unconditional love—was all she'd ever known.

And that same love was what she'd given him, even when he hadn't deserved it, and hadn't believed he'd ever be capable of giving it back to her.

But he did love her. So much that even though there was nothing more he wanted than to keep her holed up with him on his farm until they were old and gray, he knew he had to set her free.

Grayson didn't have one single doubt that she was right for him...but he couldn't ignore the question of whether *he* was right for *her*.

When it was just the two of them, working to mix oil and water was a challenge they both relished, and it meant that they'd certainly never lack for spark. But they couldn't hide out on his farm forever. Lori would need to dance in cities with crowds and strangers, and she deserved to have a partner who could support her, she deserved to be in a relationship with a man who could be there for her. Not a man who, since his wife's death, hadn't been able to go back to New York, and had completely avoided San Francisco, as well, since the people from his old world shuttled easily between the two.

The women were now chattering and playing with the babies, while her brothers were silently glaring at him.

Fuck.

If these guys had been anyone else, he would have just waited out the silence. But for Lori he moved toward the group and said, "Lori talks a lot about all of you."

Smith spoke first. "She hasn't told any of us about you." The movie star's expression was glacial. "Why do you think that is? Our sister isn't exactly the silent type."

Grayson shook his head and agreed, "No, she's not."

"Then what the hell has gone on the past two weeks?"

He understood her brothers' anger, their frustration. If Lori had been his sister, he would have felt exactly the same way. "I can't tell you what your sister is thinking or feeling. I can only tell you what I feel." For years he hadn't spoken of feelings, even when he was married and life had still been rolling forward normally. It wasn't until Lori came and kept poking him with her sharp stick of a tongue that the floodgates had burst open. "I love her." Clearly, her brothers were stunned by what he'd just told them. "I want what's best for her, just like you do."

Just then, Lori's twin came over to save him. Grayson had always pictured himself with women like Sophie—quiet, sweet, soft. Much like his wife had been, in fact. Whereas Lori laughed too loudly, talked too much, moved too fast…and yet, now he couldn't imagine himself with anyone but her.

"You look like you could use a beer." Sophie took his arm and gently led him away from her brothers. "Ignore them. They're just upset that Lori didn't confide in them, and they've always thought it was their duty to play mean-and-scary with our boyfriends." She reached into the ice chest and handed him a bottle. "But you should know that if you hurt one hair on my sister's head, they won't get a chance to take you down—because I'll have already done it myself."

Despite how elegantly pretty and soft Sophie looked, Grayson had no doubt at all that she would tear him to shreds if he messed with her sister. "She's lucky to have you."

He was surprised when she sighed. "I don't know if she'll agree with that, especially once she finds out that Jake and I made a couple of calls to Chicago and pulled in some favors to deal with her ex before she could do it herself."

"What are you two whispering about over here?" Lori asked, suddenly appearing beside them without making even the slightest sound.

Her twin jumped. "How many times have I told you," Sophie said, her hand over her heart, "don't *do* that!"

Just then, Mary called out, "Lunch is ready," and everyone went to take a seat. But the second everyone's plates were filled, Lori's brothers started in again. Only, this time, Lori was their target.

"Where have you been for two weeks, Lori?" Ryan asked her, point-blank. On the pitcher's mound, he was as easygoing—and lethal—as they came. Now he was just lethal. "What the hell happened to make you pull out of your show in Chicago like that and not tell any of us?"

Grayson's first instinct was to protect her. He put his arm around her waist and pulled both her and her chair as close to him as they could get. Instead of answering her brother's question, she turned to Grayson and pressed a soft kiss to his mouth.

"It's okay," she reassured him, before finally turning to her brother. "All of you warned me for two years to stop dating scumbags. Now's your chance to say I told you so about Victor."

"None of us wants to say that, Lor," the brother with the radio turned down low on his belt said. Just a little bigger than the others, he had to be the firefighter. "What we want to do is kill the scumbag."

Grayson agreed wholeheartedly with her brother, but Lori shook her head. "Victor wasn't worth my time, and he definitely isn't worth any of yours." Grayson caught the look that passed between Sophie and her husband. He owed them big-time for avenging Lori. "And, honestly, it wasn't even what he did that was the last straw," she admitted. "It was realizing I didn't want to dance anymore, because all the fun had been squeezed out of it. So I walked out—not just on the show, but on all of it."

"You? Not dance?" Judging by the baby girl happily rattling her soft toy on his lap, Grayson guessed this came from Chase, the photographer. "That's crazy, Naughty."

"Don't worry," she told him before turning back to Grayson with a smile. "I'm not quitting, after all, because Grayson helped me realize that I do love it—I figured that out while I spent the past couple of weeks on his farm being a farmhand."

He hated the way she was being put on the spot, but when she looked at him like that, with such trust and love, how could he do anything but forget that they weren't the only two people in the world, and smile back?

"*You* have been working as a *farmhand?*"

Grayson didn't like the note of disbelief in her brother Zach's voice, even if it was exactly the same reaction he'd had when she showed up that first day in her rental car. "My CSA customers love her, and so do the chickens and the pigs."

Lori looked adorably smug. "They really do, don't they?"

"Yes, they really do," he said with a quick kiss to the tip of her nose. He knew her family was watching them closely, but he didn't care what anyone else thought. Either they'd like him or they wouldn't. But her family wouldn't be the reason he and Lori didn't work out.

No, the two of them had plenty of other reasons already stacked up against them.

Leaning into his chest, she contentedly laid her head against his shoulder as she told them, "The country community is really cool and it's so incredibly beautiful out there. You should see the stars and the moon at night."

He stroked his hand over her hair and upper arm as she spoke, and as the conversation slowly turned from Lori's past two weeks to baby milestones and budding vines and movie sets and concert tours, Grayson was surprised to realize that he was enjoying being part of the large group, even if it was only temporary. The women, for the most part, were far more welcoming as they asked him questions about his farm, while her brothers continued to treat him as though he was on probation.

He couldn't blame them for that. Not when he completely agreed that their sister was precious beyond measure.

And that she deserved nothing but the very best.

Lori was trying not to be frustrated with her brothers. It was just that they were being so unreasonable! Especially her oldest brother, Marcus, who hadn't yet said a word to Grayson. If anyone should have something in common, it was the two of them, since they both earned their livelihoods from working with the land, and she and Nicola both had very public careers as a dancer and a singer.

She'd been glaring at Marcus all throughout lunch, trying to make it clear that she expected him to bend a little and accept the man she was in love with. But when all he did was ignore her in the most irritatingly big-brother-like way, she shoved out her chair and said, "Marcus, we need to talk."

Grayson pushed his chair back as if he planned to come with her, but her mother quickly held out her arm and said, "Grayson, could you take a look at my vegetable bed? I'm having some trouble with my artichokes."

Lori and Marcus had always been especially close, and she loved and respected him for all he'd done to help raise her when their father had died, but she refused to let him act as if he knew what was best for her.

"I love Grayson," she said to Marcus as soon as he walked into her childhood bedroom and closed the door. The room that had held the contents of her and Sophie's entire world as little girls now seemed so small. And yet, it was still comforting. "You're not even trying to get to know him."

"You met the guy on the rebound, Lori, and you've only known him two weeks. Less than that. How can you actually believe you're in love with the guy?"

"His name is Grayson," she growled, "not *the guy*. And are you seriously saying that to me?" She raised an eyebrow. "Isn't what you just described exactly what happened with you and Nicola in *way* less than two weeks? You didn't tell any of us about her, either, not until you showed up at Sunday lunch and declared your love to her in front of everyone." Lori was a foot smaller than Marcus, but that didn't stop her from facing him down, toe to toe. "We all accepted her. We all made her feel welcome. Why can't you do that with Grayson?"

"Because I love you and I can't stand to see you make

another mistake!" His booming voice cut through her frustration like a foghorn.

She could easily read between the lines of what he was saying: He was not only worried about her heart being broken, he was also worried about her giving up her own career and dreams for the man she'd fallen in love with.

"You and Nicola have made it work, being on the road for her music and also having to take care of the vines and your winery. Don't you think Grayson and I can, too?"

"Even if he loves you and you love him, it's obvious that he's damaged, Lori. Badly. We can all see it." He drew her into his arms. "I know how softhearted you are, that you want to take care of everyone and shower them with love. But sometimes love isn't enough to heal a person. I don't want to see you get hurt again."

"I love you, too, big brother," she told him as she wrapped her arms around him, "but I wouldn't walk away from Grayson when he was hell-bent on trying to make me leave, and I won't walk away from him now, not even for you." She drew back to give him a stern look. "So when we go back outside, I expect you to be nice."

Of course, Marcus was just as stubborn as she was, so instead of agreeing, he said, "Tell me more about the farm."

It wasn't much, but it was something, so she grabbed it with both hands as she told him all about her first time in the pigpen.

* * *

Her siblings were all used to the way Lori blew in and out of a room so fast that if you blinked you might miss her, but what they weren't used to was seeing her with someone she was obviously very much in love with.

Especially when he was the kind of guy none of them would ever have thought to pair her up with.

After she and Grayson had headed back to the farm, Smith looked around the table. "So?"

Sophie immediately jumped in with, "I like him." Though she and Lori had had a slightly rocky couple of years, no one was surprised to see Sophie stick up for her sister. Not when they'd always been especially close to each other. "She's never been with a guy like him before, but somehow he's perfect for her."

Gabe nodded grudgingly. "They did seem to be a good fit."

But Zach was shaking his head. "Okay, so maybe he's a good guy. And maybe he does really care about her." All of them had been able to see that in every look, every touch, the way he'd instinctively wanted to protect her when they'd been grilling her on what had happened to her in Chicago and why she'd disappeared on them all. "But he lives on a thousand-acre farm and runs a CSA that supports an entire community. He can't walk away from that for her."

"Who says she's asking him to walk away from it?" Sophie shot back, no longer the quiet little sister they'd nicknamed Nice when she was a little girl.

"Can you really see Lori living on a farm?" Ryan asked.

Marcus had stepped up to take care of all of them after their father died, but they all knew he and Lori had a special bond. "Actually," he said, "she has always loved to help me in the vineyards."

But Ryan was holding firm. "I'm sure being out on a farm is fun for a week or two—something different, especially after what happened in Chicago. But she's Naughty," he reminded them all.

"You're right, Ryan," Chase said. "It's Lori we're talking about here." He gave them all a considering look. "She's not like other people and never has been. So why are we all thinking her love life needs to make sense?"

Only one person hadn't spoken up yet: their mother. They all turned to her now to see what she thought about the man her daughter had brought home today. As they had done so many times before, they looked to her for answers.

Mary Sullivan smiled at her children and at the men and women and children who had also become a part of her family during the past two years. "Lori loves Grayson. And he loves her."

With a few simple words and her calm smile they knew she was right: there wasn't anything else they needed to know about Lori and Grayson's situation. Because there was nothing they could trust in more than love.

"Now," Mary said as she stood up, "who's hungry for dessert?"

Summer ran back to the kitchen to help bring out the chocolate cake with the extra rainbow sprinkles they'd made together. Each of the couples squeezed one another's hands just a little tighter. They'd all been where Lori was right now, in a place that didn't necessarily make sense, but at the same time was more right than anything else had ever been.

And love, as Mary had gently reminded them, had prevailed each and every time.

Twenty-Three

"So?" Lori said to Grayson as they headed north toward her San Francisco apartment in his truck. "Did you survive my family?"

Grayson knew the clock had been ticking from the moment she'd crashed into the fence post on his driveway two weeks ago, but now it felt as though time was racing at warp speed. Days had become hours. Hours had become minutes. Too soon, they'd be left with mere seconds.

"You've got a great family." His words came out a little too raw but, Lord, he was going to miss her.

"What did I tell you?" she said with a jaunty little grin. "And no one even punched you, so that was a plus."

Sunday lunch hadn't exactly been comfortable for him but, even so, he knew her family really was great.

"Believe me," he told her, "it was close there for a while. If your sister hadn't saved me from your brothers, I would have been a goner for sure."

The sound of Lori's laughter filled up all the places that had been dark and cold and empty before, and as he drank it in, he wished like hell that he'd done more joking with her and less grumbling.

Then again, she'd pushed every last one of his buttons, hadn't she?

Lori reached for his hand and rubbed her thumb over his palm as they drove. Affection was such a simple thing for her, and now he knew where she'd learned her capacity to love: from her family.

"I'm the yellow two-story apartment on the corner," she said, pointing half a block ahead. He found a spot just outside and grabbed her suitcase, and when she opened the door, he wasn't surprised by the color, the energy, the exotic sculptures and paintings displayed on every possible surface. Where everything in his farmhouse was there by necessity, nothing Lori had would ever be called *necessary*...and yet, it all was. Because everything, from the clay figurine of dancing girls to the tribal masks hanging from the walls, made up the incredible woman that she was.

"I got this in South Africa," she told him when she found him looking at a vibrant, brilliantly stitched wall hanging. "And this one," she said, pointing to a painting of a young boy and girl about to kiss, "came from Paris." He recognized city scenes from London to Sydney, all places she'd danced in and would again.

The chasm between his life and hers grew deeper from moment to moment. Because that was all they had left now.

Moments.

And every one of them was precious.

Lori was holding his hand and pulling him down the hall, saying, "It shouldn't take me long to grab some T-shirts and jeans, and then we can—" when Grayson tugged her back toward him.

He took her beautiful face in his hands and kissed her with a desperation he couldn't control. She immediately melted into his arms, her strong body so sweetly pliant in passion. They quickly ended up against the wall, one of her legs coming up to wrap around his hips, her hands threaded into his hair.

They were just seconds from having a hot and dirty quickie in her apartment. But that wasn't how Grayson wanted to say goodbye, damn it.

"What's wrong?" She reached up a hand to cup his jaw. "You've been on edge for the whole drive." She gave him a crooked little smile. "And not just your normal level of edge."

He stared into her eyes, so full of life, so bright— brighter than any star in the sky. Brighter even than the sun. "I love you."

She stroked his cheek. "I love you, too."

Her smile this time was soft. And so sweet he nearly broke right then and there and fell to his knees to beg her to stay with him. And to never, ever leave.

"Now, spit it out," she demanded.

Once before he hadn't talked to her, hadn't let her in. But now he knew he had to. Even if every word he said was going to rip his heart out of his chest.

"We both know we're not here so that you can pick up new clothes."

A flash of fear passed through her eyes, but she quickly masked it with a wicked little smile. "I planned for us to tangle up my sheets, too."

Ruthlessly shoving back the vision of stripping off her clothes and making love to her in her bright and sunny apartment, he said, "You've got to deal with what happened in Chicago."

"You're right. I do have to go." She tilted her head back enough so that she could look up into his eyes. "But while I'm gone, I don't want to leave you on the farm by yourself."

"I was alone for three years." He'd never forgive himself if he was the reason Lori didn't take her life and career by the horns again and show it who was boss. "I'm pretty good at it, you know."

She shook her head. "You're too good at it. That's what worries me."

"Don't worry about me."

"All this time you've been looking for a way to make me leave," she said, clearly trying to tease him, but sounding more sad than anything else. "But just as you couldn't get rid of Sweetpea, you're not getting rid of me this easily, either." She looked deeply into his eyes, as if to make sure he really saw the truth of what she was saying to him.

I'm coming back to you.

He kissed her then, long and sweet and soft, before saying all the things he should already have said to her a thousand times over. "I've never had food as good as what you make, the chickens don't want to eat scraps from anyone but you, the crops have been growing twice as fast since they first felt your green thumbs… and Mo and the pigs and I have never loved anyone more than we love you."

"Oh, Grayson." Her face finally crumpled, her beautiful mouth wobbling, tears running down her cheeks. "It would be so much easier if you'd just be cranky and bossy right now."

God, the hardest thing he'd ever done in his life was giving up what *he* wanted so that the woman he loved could get what *she* needed. "Now that you've whipped my farm into shape and taught everyone in Pescadero how to line dance just like they do it in Nashville, it's time to go show that idiot in Chicago what you're made of."

She sniffled, nodded, hugged him close and held on tight. They stood together in her hallway, two people who should never have been together…but who couldn't ever have found what they'd found with anyone else.

When she suddenly pulled back, her eyes were dry and filled with the resolve and determination that he'd seen on the farm every time he'd challenged her—and she'd challenged him right back. "Before I head off for Chicago and you go back to your farm to feed your chickens, I think that I should teach you a new dance."

"What's the dance called?" he asked as she led him into her bedroom.

She was already pulling him down over her on the bed as she answered, "The tangle."

Twenty-Four

"Lori!" The minute she walked into the Chicago dance hall, her friend Alicia ran over and threw her arms around her. "I'm so glad you're back." Alicia pulled away and did a quick once-over. "You're gorgeous and glowing. I hope that means you've found someone to replace the scumbag."

Scumbag? "What do you know?"

Alicia scowled. "That Victor is a pathetic excuse for a man *and* a dancer."

"Who else knows?"

"Everyone." Her friend's scowl deepened.

"But—" Lori didn't get it. How, after nearly two years of hiding the truth about Victor from everyone, did they all suddenly know the score? "How'd you find out?"

"Didn't your sister tell you?"

Lori raised an eyebrow, at once filled with love for her meddling twin and annoyance that she'd felt she had to step in to deal with Lori's mess. "My sister didn't tell me anything. What did she do?"

Alicia looked a little worried now that maybe she'd stepped into something she shouldn't have. "Just made a couple of calls, I think...."

"And?"

"And, uh, some people came by to talk to Victor. Some *big* people. With lots of tattoos."

Perhaps it wasn't nice of her to laugh at the picture of her ex having to deal with Jake McCann's Irish-pub-owning friends, but she couldn't help it.

"Besides," Alicia added, "when you walked out like that, we guessed something had to be up. The only reason anyone ever put up with Victor was because of you. We love you, Lori. But him?" Her friend made a face. "It's been *horrible* since you've been gone."

Lori had done a lot of thinking over the past two weeks, not only about what Victor had done, but about what she'd done, too. It wasn't her fault that he was an asshole, but hadn't she shielded her friends and family from his true personality? Because if they had known what he was really like—that he was selfish, and demanding, and unfaithful—then she would look like an idiot for sticking with him.

"Thank God you're back to take over for the last week of the show."

Lori wasn't planning to stay, and she tried to form the words to explain to her friend that there was somewhere else she needed to be...but she couldn't. Not when she felt terrible about leaving her dancers in a bad situation in the first place.

And not when she knew that staying to shepherd her dancers through to the end was the right thing to do.

"I'm sorry I left you with Victor."

"None of us blame you for going. And trust me, no one has any plans to work with Victor or Gloria again. Please say you're going to chew him to pieces."

"Oh, don't worry," Lori assured her friend, "I've learned a lot these past couple of weeks about dealing with animals."

Victor couldn't hide his surprise when Lori walked into the small office upstairs.

"Get out of my seat. I have a show to fix."

At the clear command in her voice, he immediately stood before realizing he should have stayed right where he was. Holding on to the back of the chair as if to keep his claim on her show intact, he gave her a hurt look.

"How could you have walked out on all of us like that, Lori? If anyone is responsible for the show going downhill these past two weeks, it's you."

If she hadn't gotten mad and disillusioned enough to walk away, she never would have found Grayson. Which, she was more than a little shocked to realize, meant that if she had to do it all over again, she would hope it all played out exactly the same…if only so that she could finally learn what true love was.

But even if everything she had been through had been worth it just to get to Grayson, she still deserved her pound of revenge. Ten pounds would be even better.

"You're right," she admitted. "Walking out on the show wasn't at all professional. I shouldn't have done it. But," she added in a calm tone that did little to hide the ice behind her words, "you shouldn't have been a lying, cheating douche bag who slept with the lead dancer I hired for *my* show." She smiled, baring her teeth at him. "So I guess we were both wrong, weren't we?"

They'd had more than their fair share of arguments while they were together, but Lori had focused more on the make-up sex than what was behind the fights. She had told herself it made their relationship exciting. Really, though, all it had done was make her a fool. Because in all the time she and Victor had been together, she couldn't think of one kind thing he'd done for her that hadn't been for his own gain.

Whereas Grayson had taken her to that barn dance, and then to her family's Sunday lunch, when they were both the very last places he'd wanted to be. He'd even pushed her to return to her own world despite his obvious belief that she wouldn't come back to him, back to the farm. All because he loved her, and wanted the best for her, rather than himself.

"We were on a break," Victor protested. "You could have slept with someone else if you wanted to."

"Funny," she said, though there wasn't even a trace of humor in her voice, "I wonder how many other breaks we had that I never knew about? And I'm assuming that's also what you told Gloria when you took her to bed? Did you also tell her she was a better dancer than I am? And was she stupid enough to believe your lies the way I always did?"

She watched his face carefully as she spoke. Now that she was no longer desperate to convince him to love her the way she'd thought she loved him, she could finally see her ex for what he was. A handsome, charismatic, underhanded snake. Right now, she guessed, he was trying to decide between hurling insults or turning on the charm. When she saw his half scowl turn to a smile, she knew he'd decided on charm.

Grayson may have been short on charm, she thought with a secret smile, but at least she could always count on him to be honest. He would never say he loved her just to get her back into bed. And he was no slouch in the handsome department, either. If the two men were to stand side by side, Victor would look like a glossy, pint-size poser compared to Grayson, who had earned every one of his muscles, every glorious inch of tanned skin, from good, honest work beneath the sun.

"I made a mistake, baby. I got caught up in the heat of the moment during rehearsals."

Lori knew all about heat now, about how strong a pull another person could have on your life. That when you were meant to be together, no amount of common sense, no attempts at self-control, made any difference.

Grayson had told her that she forgave too easily, but she couldn't imagine going through life holding on to grudges that would eat away at her. Even when someone clearly deserved it.

"I forgive you," she said, and relief immediately moved across Victor's features. He was opening up his arms for her as she said, "Now, get out of my way."

He stood there, his arms still reaching toward her, a stunned look on his face, but she was done with him now, so she simply sat down and started to go through the paperwork laid out across the table.

Just as quickly as he'd put on the charm, her ex

stripped it away. "You're the one who walked out on the show, not me," he sneered. "Instead of admitting it was too big a production for you to handle, you ran off crying like a little girl who got her feelings hurt in the sandbox. No one thinks you're good enough to manage a show this size. And no one wants you back."

Without acknowledging anything he'd said, she pulled out her cell phone and dialed the show's producer. "Neil? Hi, it's Lori Sullivan. Yes, I really am sorry for leaving so suddenly, and I promise I'll make it up to you, but now that I'm back, I just wanted to do a quick check-in with you about firing V—" When she was cut off, she listened for a moment, then said, "Yes, I'll take care of it now and then I'll see you backstage tonight after the show."

She disconnected. "Looks like it's time for you to take another break," she told her ex. Then she really did put him completely out of her head as she started calling her dancers one by one to let them know about the emergency rehearsal she was scheduling for that afternoon.

Now that the nearly two-year break *she* had taken from clear and rational thinking was finally over, Lori Sullivan was back.

And she was going to be better than ever.

Ten hours later...

God, she missed Grayson so much.

Lori had wanted to call him all day, but it had been one thing after another. When she realized that everything really had gone off the rails on her show, she'd known she had to spend as much time with her dancers as possible, both to reassure them and to get them excited again about their performance. And of course she'd had to deal with Gloria's tears and apologies ad nauseam, too.

Lori was just pulling her phone out of her bag to finally call Grayson and tell him she loved him, and that she was going to miss him every single second of the week it took her to come back to him, when it rang in her hand. The name on the screen was one of the biggest producers in the business.

"Hi, Carter. How are you?"

"I'm *freaking* out!"

Lori grinned. Carter was always losing it over something. A man he had a crush on. A slightly pulled muscle. The sky not looking quite blue enough to suit him. He was flamboyant and funny and brilliant. Getting to work with him a couple of times this year had not only been the highlight of her career but, even better, she'd made a very good new friend, too.

"Poor baby," she murmured, "how can I help?"

"The International Exhibition of Modern Dance is next week and the lead in the central piece came down with *mono*." Lori was already racking her brain for someone she could call to help him out when he said, "I need you to come to New York immediately and save my exhibition."

"Me? But you know modern dance isn't my specialty."

"Trust me, you'll be perfect for the piece. And I'll be sunk without you!"

"I'm flattered," she told him, and she really was, "but I can't leave Chicago until my show's over next week. And then there's somewhere else I really need to—"

"I just emailed you the videos," he said, cutting her off before she could actually get to the part of the sentence where she said no. "You can rehearse in Chicago, and then the second your show wraps, we'll get you on a jet and into dress rehearsals with the rest of the troupe. You'll have forty-eight hours to fine-tune before the show. It's one night only. One very important night where I *need* you."

Everything was happening so fast, which was just the way Lori had always liked it. And she still did, she realized. Only, it felt like she was spinning farther and farther away from Grayson with every minute.

"Well," she finally said to her friend, "I suppose I could look at the videos and let you know if I think I can do the piece justice."

Carter whooped and told her he adored her to pieces before hanging up.

Lori had told herself it would be easy to head straight back to Grayson, that she had simply come to Chicago to tie up some loose ends. But look how easily she'd been pulled back into not just one show but two. She could have said no, but the truth was, she wanted to dance. Of course, she wanted to be with Grayson, too. And now she felt like she was being yanked in two completely opposite directions.

Grayson had clearly seen this coming, had obviously thought they wouldn't be able to put their two worlds together. She'd sworn he was wrong.

But was he?

Two weeks ago, she'd avoided going to her mother for advice, simply because she hadn't been ready to hear it. Now, as she dialed the top name on her cell phone's favorites list, she prayed her mother was home.

"Hi, sweetie," her mother said as she picked up. "I was just out in the garden thinking about you."

"The garden? How could that possibly make you think of me?"

"When you were a little girl, you loved to come outside and help me with your little plastic shovel. You'd pick out worms and be so thrilled with every carrot, every potato and tomato. Do you remember the dance you used to do around the vegetable bed?"

Lori smiled as she thought back to those wonderful summer afternoons out in the backyard when she had her mother all to herself and lots of nice, soft dirt to play in. "I can't believe I thought that dance I made up would help the plants grow faster and bigger."

"It *did* work," her mother told her. "Nothing has ever grown as well since you moved out of the house and into your own apartment. Ever since then, I've always thought what an unexpectedly perfect fit gardening and dancing are."

"In that case, I'll make sure to do a little dance for your veggies at the next lunch," Lori said, her voice thicker now as she soaked up all of the love her mother was giving her...and the renewed confidence in the power of love to transcend absolutely anything. "I'll bet Summer and the babies would love to dance around your garden."

"Your father," Mary said suddenly, "was a great dancer, too."

Lori could so easily picture her mother in her father's arms, elegant and oh so beautiful as they moved across the dance floor. It was, she knew, just the way she and Grayson must have looked at the barn dance as they'd waltzed.

She knew he didn't think she was coming back. And it wasn't because he didn't love her. On the contrary, he loved her so much that he couldn't stand the thought of making her live any way but exactly as she wanted to. But didn't he realize, she thought with a little shake of her head, that she *always* got what she wanted? And since she wanted both him *and* dancing, somehow, some way, she was going to work out a way to have both.

Especially now that she'd found her unexpectedly perfect partner.

Grayson had never been happier about all the things that could go wrong on a farm. Today, it had been the water mister in his pigpen going out. He'd spent the day covered in mud and swearing at plastic pipes and tubing. But frankly, he wasn't sure how he would have gotten through the day in one piece otherwise. Not when every single thing on his farm reminded him of Lori. The way the pigs had snuffled around him all day, wishing he was their beautiful friend coming with special treats and pats for their little heads. The way the chickens had run to the gate when they saw him coming, only to back away when they realized he wasn't Lori.

When the plumbing job was finally done and even

he couldn't take his stench anymore, he showered out by the back of the barn, but that reminded him of the first night when he'd had to come out to shower to try to escape her and the feelings he couldn't contain. He'd wanted her so much, but more than that, he'd already begun to admire and like her. And then, of course, there were the many sexy showers they'd shared after that....

When the water grew cold, he wrapped a towel around himself and went back into the house.

God, it was quiet. Too damned quiet. But there were flashes of color all around now from where Lori had brought out a vase that she'd found up in the attic, along with the bright yellow quilt she'd bought in town at the General Store because she said it made her happy just to look at it.

His phone rang and when he saw her name on the screen he leaped at it. "Lori."

"Grayson."

Even for a man of few words, he'd never realized that so much could be said with so little.

"I've missed you so much," she said. "Tell me about your day. Even if it has to do with something boring about a tractor or fertilizer, I want to hear it."

He laughed, the sound not nearly as rusty now as it had been for most of his life. All because of her. "I spent the day knee-deep in pigs and mud and broken water pipes. Your basic average dream day on a farm."

How he loved the sound of her laughter, could picture her holding the phone up to her ear, probably twirling around on her jaw-droppingly perfect legs as she spoke to him.

Always moving.

Always laughing.

And so full of love she never failed to stun him.

"Wow, two sentences was one more than I thought I'd get out of you," she teased. "You must really love me."

"I love you so damned much," he confirmed for her before saying, "Now it's your turn to talk my ear off."

"I did it, Grayson. I got in Victor's face and told him to get out of mine. I fired him with the full support of everyone in the show. It turns out that after I left, they put two and two together and found out what he'd done. But honestly," she said in a far more chipper voice than he would have thought after having to deal with that slime, "squashing that bug only took a few minutes. The rest of the day I was working with the troupe, and that was really great." She barely paused for breath as she barreled ahead and said, "I'm going to need to stay here for the rest of the week to take them through to the end."

"Of course you are. They need you." And she needed them just as much. It was something he'd never doubted for a minute.

It wasn't until she was finally silent for a long moment that he knew something else was up.

"I want so badly to come back to you and the farm the second the show is over, but…"

Another pause came and he had to grab a kitchen chair and sit down to brace himself for it.

"A friend of mine needs me to go to New York City to be a last-minute replacement for the lead in his show, which means I'll need to fly from Chicago to New York to perform at the International Exhibition of Modern

Dance the following weekend before I can catch a red-eye to come back to you."

Grayson wanted to beg, even wanted for a minute to be bitter that she'd chosen dancing over him. But how could he do either of those things when he *knew* she was making all the right choices?

Of course she had to do both shows. And of course she'd have to do all the other shows that would come next, opportunities she couldn't possibly turn down. Not only because so many people in her industry depended on her, but also because she was meant to dance, and to keep dancing.

But she was also meant to be with him, damn it.

Grayson wanted to see her dance. And he wanted to be as brave for her as she'd been for him. Not only in the way she'd insisted on loving him after he'd tried so hard to push her away, but by confronting the man who had hurt her so that she could love again with a whole heart.

Lori had been brave enough to face down her past.

It was long past time for him to do the same.

Twenty-Five

Grayson stepped off the plane in New York and found the driver waiting for him by the luggage carousels. For a moment, it felt as though the past three years hadn't happened. As though this were just another business trip, and he was simply heading home to Westchester to shower and change and have a predinner drink with Leslie, where both of them tried to act interested in things they didn't actually care about at all.

When he gave the address to the driver, to the man's credit, he barely betrayed a response. In the backseat of the town car, Grayson took out the picture of Lori as a little girl that Mary Sullivan had given to him at Sunday lunch. He'd kept it with him every second since she'd been gone, and it never failed to bring a smile to his face, even now.

Both of her front teeth were missing, she was wearing ripped boys' jeans and a T-shirt that were both at least two sizes too big and she was hands-down the prettiest thing he'd ever seen in his life as she leaped through the air, dancing in the middle of her crowded backyard. He could see the way, even at eight, that she'd blossom into such a striking beauty. He could also see that she was too determined, too stubborn, to ever allow anything or anyone to take away her joy, her love for life.

Grayson wanted to be worthy of sharing that life with her, but he wanted something else, too. He wanted, one day, to take pictures of his own little girl as she danced and laughed and loved just like her beautiful mother.

Noticing a flower stand out the window, Grayson asked the driver to stop, tucking the picture of Lori into the pocket above his heart as he opened the door and stepped out of the car. He didn't buy the biggest, flashiest bouquet. Instead, he bought a small bouquet of bright tulips, Leslie's favorite flower.

"I'll walk from here," he said to the driver, who nodded and pulled over to the curb to wait.

The cemetery looked the same as it had three years ago during his wife's funeral, the last time he'd ever been here. The grass was perfectly green and meticulously mowed. The sky was full of dark clouds that looked as if they would burst with rain at any moment, the gray, cold sky so different from the clear blue over his farm.

As he approached Leslie's gravestone, he could see that it was polished clean and bright, with an enormous bouquet of flowers in a vase beside it that he knew had to be from her parents.

The last time he'd been here, he'd been stunned…and racked with guilt. The shock had eventually lessened as he accepted that she really was gone. But the guilt and the blame he'd placed on himself for not knowing his own wife better had deepened. Every day he struggled. He'd put on his suit and tie and go into work and field questions and sympathy from colleagues and friends and people he only knew from cocktail parties. The guilt and blame and disgust he felt toward everyone who said they loved her and missed her but who hadn't done a damn thing to stop her self-destruction grew to the point where he knew he couldn't stay there another second. He'd needed to start over in a world that was as far from New York society as possible, so he'd gone west and, just like Lori in her rental car, had stumbled onto his farm. The real estate transaction had been completed by nightfall, and Grayson had never planned on looking—or coming—back.

"Leslie." He knelt down and laid the flowers on her grave, putting his hand over the cold stone as if that would help them finally connect again. "I'm sorry I haven't been back for so long."

It was so awkward—it was as if they were having one of their superficial conversations again, where both of them spoke, but neither of them said anything. Lori, he knew, would never have stood for that. Cemetery or not, she would have said exactly what was on her mind…and in her heart.

Suddenly, he could picture her there, egging him on: *Come on and grow some balls, farmer. Why are you still so afraid of baring your soul?* Unconsciously, his hand went to the picture of her in his shirt pocket. *They're all good parts,* she'd told him. *And I would never let anyone hurt you.* Even now, he could feel her protecting him, his fierce and beautiful dancing farm girl who had the biggest heart of anyone he'd ever known.

Grayson sat down on the grass beside Leslie's gravestone and ran his fingers slowly over the engraving of her name. "I'm sorry I was a bad husband. And I'm sorry that I wasn't much of a friend by the end, either. I knew you were unhappy. I was unhappy, too. But I didn't know how to fix any of it, so I ignored it instead. I ignored you, Leslie, and I'm so, so sorry."

He'd apologized more in the past two weeks than he had in his entire life. And yet, just as he had with Lori, he couldn't see how his wife could ever forgive him for the mess their lives had become before she died. No amount of apologizing would change that.

But since his big mistake had been that he hadn't talked to her—really and truly talked to her—when she was still alive, he figured, at the very least, he could change that now.

"After you died, I pretty much lost it. I turned away from every last person, every last piece of our life, and decided to start over. I'm in California now, on a farm. A big one, right by the ocean. Whenever the fog rolls in, I think of how much you loved to walk along the coast on stormy days. I wasn't searching for happiness, just for an escape, but the amazing thing is that I found happiness, after all. Not just in the land, and my animals, but with the last person on earth I would ever have expected.

"You would have liked Lori, Leslie, and I know she would have liked you, too. She never stops asking questions, and when I try to ignore them she just asks more, so I've told her all about you. About when we were in college, how we used to go to the tree-lighting and yule-log ceremonies, and that one year we were so excited about being the big winners of the bad-poetry contest. I even told her all about the way I asked you to marry me and ended up dropping the ring into a storm drain because I was so nervous."

He thought he heard something then, a rustling of the leaves above him that sounded like a question: *Is she pretty?*

Before he knew it, Grayson was laughing and crying at the same time. Of course it was what Leslie would want to know.

"Yes," he said as he finally let his tears fall for the woman who had been such an important part of his life for so long. "She is."

And during the next hour, as he sat and finally talked to his wife, the thick gray clouds blew away one by one until there was nothing but bright, blue sky above the two of them.

Lori stood backstage at the Joyce Theater in New York City in a circle with her dancers, all of them holding hands as they got ready to go out onstage. It had been the craziest forty-eight hours of her life, but she'd loved every second of it.

Carter had brought her in to take over on choreography that had been set in stone for months. But the vision she'd had was so clear and pure that she'd choreographed a brand-new dance barely one step ahead of the dancers learning the movements.

"Thank you so much for going on this journey with me," she told them now. "You're all amazing and wonderful and I love you guys for trusting me with this dance and putting your hearts and souls into something that means so much to me." She grinned at them. "Now, let's go make some magic happen."

One by one, they took their places on the darkened stage and when the lights slowly came up the audience saw them not as dancers, but as beautiful wildflowers in red and orange, yellow and purple. All around the flowers the wild green grasses swayed in the breeze. The score the orchestra played sounded like the ocean on a clear day, of children playing with buckets and pails in the sand and seagulls flying above the gently crashing waves.

On a crack of thunder from the percussion section, the bright, sunny lighting gave way to a sudden storm, blue lights and whisper-thin streamers beginning to rain down from above the stage. To the crashing sound of the waves and the hard pellets of rain, the flowers and grasses gave in to the wildness of the storm, even more beautiful now as they were blown hard by the wind, soaked by the rain.

And then, suddenly, the smallest wildflower was ripped from the ground by the wind. She was blowing away from the rest of them, when from the center of the group, the largest, most powerful blade of grass reached for her.

He cradled her against him in a beautiful dance of

protection and love as the storm continued to rage, and then, when the storm waned and the sun emerged again, he finally set the brightly colored flower free to fly away.

Oh, how beautiful that wildflower was as she flew, higher and higher in that bright, pure sunlight. The other flowers, the grasses, watched her dance through the sky, as they knew she'd dreamed of doing all her life.

The sun was setting and the flowers were closing their petals, the grasses already collecting dew in the cool night, when the wildflower emerged again in the dark sky. She'd always dreamed of flying, but one perfect dance in a storm had given her new dreams.

She still wanted to fly…but she no longer wanted to do it alone.

And then the wildflower and the blade of grass were coming together again, wrapping themselves around each other in a dance of love that was just as beautiful beneath the calm moon as it had been in the rain and the wind.

That was when the lights came up enough for Lori to see the ruggedly beautiful man in the front row. Grayson was surrounded by men in tuxes and women in sequins, but in his flannel shirt and dark jeans and cowboy boots, he was the one who shone.

She'd choreographed this dance to celebrate the beauty of his land and to bask in the passion they'd discovered together on a stormy afternoon. Now, she danced only for him, the wildflower that had been blowing off course, until his love had shown her exactly where she needed to be.

With him.
Forever.

Grayson was waiting in the wings when Lori came off stage, and she flew into his arms.

She'd said *I love you* to him in a dozen different ways during the dance, and now he was the one saying, "I love you. You're everything to me, Lori. Everything."

He didn't let go of her hand as she went to congratulate her dancers on the phenomenal job they'd done. He couldn't have stopped touching her for anything in the world, even when she went out of her way to embarrass him by saying, "Everyone, this is Grayson, the hottest farmer you'll ever—"

Of course the only way to shut her up was with a kiss, so right there in front of thirty strangers he tugged her close and covered her mouth with his.

Everyone was applauding and hooting and hollering by the time he finally let her up for air, and while Lori worked to get her breath back, he said, "It's nice to meet you all. I was blown away by your performance."

Just then, a slim man dressed in a silver-blue suit rushed up and threw his arms around Lori. "Amazing, Lori. Simply amazing! Just as I knew you'd be. People can't stop talking about your program." When he realized that Lori's hand was connected to Grayson's, the man pursed his mouth into an appreciative *O*. "And who is this gorgeous hunk of yours?"

Seeing the gleam in Lori's eye that told him she would say anything she needed to if it would egg him into giving her another kiss, Grayson held out his hand.

"I'm a big fan of yours, Carter. And even more so now that I know what great taste you have in choreographers."

The man's eyes widened as he blushingly thanked Grayson for the praise. He air-kissed them both on both cheeks in his characteristically dramatic way before running off to keep watch over the rest of his production.

When the two of them were finally alone again, Grayson stroked his hand over Lori's cheek and said, "I know a great pizza place around the corner. Best pepperoni you'll ever have."

She quickly changed and they headed outside. Holding each other in sweet silence they walked down the crowded sidewalk and turned into a smaller side street. They passed the jewelry store where Leslie had exclaimed over diamond earrings and he'd surprised her with them on their first anniversary. They'd often eaten at this pizza place during finals in college.

But instead of being followed by a ghost, it felt more like Leslie was an angel watching over them.

Grayson knew he'd never be a man of many words, but from here on out he planned for every one he said to Lori to matter. Once they were sitting on stools at a tiny booth with dripping, steaming slices of pizza in front of them, he told her, "I never thought I could be in the middle of New York City and my farm at the same time. But as you danced I was there in both places, Lori, right back in that storm, holding you in my arms, wanting to keep you safe and knowing you needed to fly free again. All this time, I thought one had to give way for the other, and that it was impossible for them to connect."

There was so much more he wanted to tell her, so much he had to say, but he'd never had much practice at it, and the words got stuck in his throat. Thank God Lori had always heard everything he didn't know how to say.

"According to my mom, when I was two—" She picked up her slice of pizza and jammed a huge bite into her mouth. "Oh, my God!" she exclaimed after she'd chewed and swallowed in clear rapture. "This really *is* the best pepperoni in the world!" She mmm'd and aah'd over the pizza until, finally, she continued her earlier sentence. "I used to think the word *impossible* was actually two words. Evidently I would dance and twirl around the house declaring, 'I'm possible!' over and over until everyone was going crazy."

"I know how that feels," he said in a low voice that clearly didn't scare her in the least, because she stuck out her tongue at him in response.

"So," she asked as she picked up what was left of her enormous slice and gave him a soft smile, "how is she?"

Of course Lori would know where he'd been today without his saying a word. It was one of the many reasons why they were so perfect together. He was a man who didn't say much, and she was a woman who knew how to listen to a look, a touch, a glance. A kiss. And tonight, he knew exactly what she was doing, talking and teasing and eating as though his being here with her in the city that held all of his personal demons was perfectly normal. He'd never met anyone who was so openly emotional, or so willing to share her heart.

He could see how much every one of her dancers, and the show's producer, adored her. And for good reason. Lori was completely adorable, even with grease dripping from the corner of her greedy mouth.

He wiped it away with the tip of his finger before saying, "She asked if you were pretty."

Lori looked absolutely delighted with that, even as her eyes grew soft and a little misty with emotion. "You really do have great taste in women, you know."

Grayson knew he hadn't done everything he needed to do yet. He still needed to sit down and talk with Leslie's parents, and his parents were in Europe, so he couldn't introduce Lori to them. But while talking to Leslie at her grave hadn't been easy, it hadn't destroyed him, either. He'd come back, soon, to say the rest of what he should have said so many years ago, to everyone he should have said it to.

But this time, he'd have Lori by his side every step of the way, along with an angel watching over both of them.

He reached for his pizza, but his plate was empty. Of course, he knew just where to look for it: in Lori's mouth.

"You weren't eating it," she said with her mouth full.

Even as he growled at her to give up his slice or else, he knew she was right.

He really did have great taste in women.

Twenty-Six

Grayson didn't know if he'd ever get used to being with a woman so beautiful that she turned heads everywhere they went, and so friendly that half the people on the plane home from New York now had an invitation to come visit the farm. But even though there was no question that life with Lori would be a hell of a lot to handle, he did know one thing for sure: just as her mother had told him, she was worth all the struggles and frustrations that came with loving her.

Smart woman, that Mary Sullivan. No wonder she'd raised eight great kids. Grayson looked forward to spending time with her over the coming years.

He'd figured Lori would want to go by her apartment to pick up some of her favorite things, but when she said she was antsy to get back to the farm—and that moving their sister's stuff was what big brothers were for—they headed straight to Pescadero from the airport. Although they did make one quick stop at the airport's rental-car office, where she smacked a kiss straight on the lips of the very surprised woman behind the counter.

"You were right. Pescadero was amazing!" Lori had gestured to Grayson, and he would have kissed her to shut her up again, but she'd been having such a good time that he let her say, "Look what I found there."

The woman looked from Lori to him in confusion for a moment, before her lips curved up into a big smile. "And to think, all I ever came home with from Pescadero was a sack of organic carrots and some pretty pictures of the coast."

In his truck, Lori had turned on the local country station way too loud and was singing along in an equally loud, off-key voice, when she suddenly cried, "Stop the truck!"

The dire tone of her voice had him slamming his foot on the brake. Before he knew it, she was scrambling out of her seat and running across the road after what looked to be a white plastic bag.

He leaped out of the car and hollered, "Get off the road!" Of course, she didn't listen, not until she'd finally caught the tumbling bag in her hands.

When she turned back to him, her expression broke his heart. "It's a kitten." She tore open the bag all the way and scooped out a little ball of fur, telling it, "You're safe now."

Grayson kept an eye out for oncoming traffic on the two-lane farm road as he went to her. Lori was already sneezing, but he knew that wasn't why her eyes were wet.

"Sweetpea sent her to us." She kissed the fluff between its ears. "She looks like a Millie, don't you think?"

"Actually, I was thinking he looks like a Bob."

She grinned at him and nodded, and for a moment he thought maybe she was going to agree with him. That is, until she said, "Come on, Milliebob, let's go home."

For the rest of the drive, she chattered to the kitten— whom he swore he'd never, ever call Milliebob, even as he knew he'd be breaking the vow by week's end—telling the little cat all about the farm and the other animals and how much she was going to love it there. As soon as he pulled up, Lori jumped out of the truck to take the kitten to meet the pigs she'd named after her brothers and sister.

Later that evening as they walked outside, hand in hand, to be together in the cool, dark silence that one could only get on a thousand acres, Lori told him, "I really missed it here."

Her voice was full of awe at the beauty all around them. An hour ago, she'd been covered in mud and had been as happy as a pig in it. Now she was fresh from the shower he'd given her out by the barn, one that had started with soap and ended with pleasure.

Lori stopped short as they passed the large grove of oak trees and she saw the new foundation he'd been putting in. "What's this?"

He'd missed her like crazy every second she'd been in Chicago and New York City, so much that he'd thrown himself into this huge new project, praying with every board he'd cut for the forms, every nail he'd hammered, that she'd actually come back to him.

"A studio. For you. And your dancers."

She threw her arms and legs around him and was about to kiss him when the night sky suddenly lit up so much that they both turned to look up at it.

"A shooting star!" Her eyes shone with excitement and happiness as she gazed down at him. "What did you wish for?"

Standing in the middle of wildflowers and blades of dark green grass beneath the stars, Grayson pulled a ring out of his pocket. "I wished for you to be mine. *Always*."

As Lori told him she'd always been his, and promised that she always would be, the two of them danced together on a thousand-acre stage beneath the spotlight of the moon.

Three months later...

"Now that every Sullivan from around the world has arrived for our family reunion," Lori said to Grayson, "do I need to get you a bag to hyperventilate into?"

Despite the dozens of Sullivans and spouses and kids and animals running loose all around them, Grayson wrapped a lock of Lori's long hair around his fingers and tugged her closer, as if they were the only two people in the world. "I've got a much better idea for what to do with my mouth."

Even though they'd kissed approximately a trillion times during the past three months, it felt like the first time all over again as Lori's heart raced, she lost her breath and her toes tingled in her cowboy boots while her fiancé showed her, yet again, just how much he loved her.

"Seriously, though," she said when he finally let her come up for air and her synapses had begun to fire again, "you're amazing for agreeing to have so many people here on your farm."

"Not *my* farm. *Our* farm." He stroked her hair one last time, then moved his hand down past her shoulder and over her arm to leave a path of tingles all across her skin before he slid his fingers through hers. "And you know I like your family." He lowered his cowboy hat against the bright sunlight as he looked out at the huge group of Sullivans. "Even if there are a whole hell of a lot of them."

Just then, she saw one more rental car pull into the makeshift parking area they'd set up by the side of the barn. Grayson's mother and father got out. His hand tightened slightly in hers and she lifted it to her mouth to press a kiss to it before saying, "I'm so glad your parents happened to plan their trip for this weekend, too." It had been a surprising coincidence of timing when he'd told her about their travel plans, but of course she'd been thrilled by the news.

Not wanting the Tylers to feel at all out of place around her big family, she made sure to hurry over to give each of them a warm hug. "I'm so glad you could come for a visit." When she and Grayson had visited them on their estate in New York a month earlier, she'd been able to see just how much they loved their son, even if they weren't great at saying the words aloud. Just as she'd known better than to wait for Grayson to invite her into his heart, she knew she couldn't let him and his parents wait any longer for each other, either.

He shook his father's hand and put his arms around his mother, and Lori happily noticed that they all held on just a little bit longer than they had a month ago. People said miracles couldn't happen overnight, but wasn't that how quickly love had blossomed between her and Grayson? And hadn't life always been one miracle tumbling and leaping after another, from her family to dancing to her little nieces and nephews to the man standing beside her?

A few moments later, her mother was there to welcome Gina and Brent Tyler. Lori loved watching the effect her mother had on people—the way she immediately made them feel relaxed and appreciated.

"You raised a wonderful son," Mary Sullivan told the Tylers. "Every single day I'm so happy that he and Lori found each other."

As Grayson drew Lori even closer and pressed a kiss to the top of her head, his mother's eyes grew damp. "Yes," she agreed, "they are a perfect match, aren't they?"

Funny, right then, it looked as though his parents and her mother and then Grayson, too, were all sharing a secret look. Suddenly, her mother turned to Lori and said, "Did you hear about the great surprise your sister put together for the girls? She brought in several hairdressers and makeup artists to fix all of us up before the big family pictures are taken. They're all set up and waiting for us in your new dance studio."

"That sounds fun," Lori said, even though she

couldn't figure out why her twin would have any interest at all in something like that, considering Sophie wore almost no makeup and rarely needed to do anything to her long, glossy hair to make it look great. "Can you let her know I'll head over later? First, I'd like to give Grayson's parents a tour of the—"

Grayson cut off her sentence in his favorite way: with a kiss. Sometimes she would run off at the mouth even when she had nothing whatsoever to say, just to score more kisses.

"Go with your mother," he told her. "I'll show my parents around."

She had thought he'd want her there with his parents as a buffer, just in case things got awkward again, but now she realized he probably wanted some alone time with them. "Okay." Only, when she went to walk away, he didn't let go of her hand.

She looked down at their entwined hands and was about to make a funny comment about his needing to let go of her when she looked up into his face.

The sheer depth of the love in his eyes had her forgetting everything except her own love for him. Her mother's arm around her waist was the only reason she could have walked away from him just then.

"You really did find a wonderful man, honey," Mary said as they headed off toward the studio Grayson had built for her. "It's hard to believe he hasn't always been a part of the family, isn't it?"

Over the past three months, Lori had watched a truly special bond develop between her fiancé and her mother. She figured part of it was that they had both lost a spouse and understood each other's pain in a way that other people never would. But just as her mother had said, their relationship went deeper than that. Grayson was already family—a total guy with her brothers, the sweetest uncle-to-be ever to the babies and Summer and always there to help out a Sullivan in need.

"I can hardly wait to marry him," she told her mother. "If I could, I'd do it today."

A few moments later, the two of them stepped in through the door of the studio. Several of the best hair and makeup artists that her brother Chase had worked with over the years were already working their magic on Sophie, Nicola, Chloe, Megan and her eight-year-old daughter, Summer, Heather, Vicki and Smith's fiancée, Valentina. Growing up, Lori had always longed for more than one sister, and every day she gave thanks for the amazing women her brothers had found.

Summer clapped her hands and said, "Lori's here!" Megan's eyes got big for a moment before she leaned over to whisper something to Summer that had her daughter smiling and zipping her fingers across her lips.

"Your farm is amazing," Nicola said as she handed Lori a glass of champagne and led her over to an empty chair. "What a great place for a family reunion."

Lori knew how much Marcus's pop-star fiancée loved his vineyard in Napa, and that her brother loved touring the world with Nicola just as much. "Just wait until you get out there with the pigs," Lori teased her soon-to-be sister-in-law. "You're going to love the one I named Marcus. He keeps all the other pigs in the pen safe and sound."

She'd taken pictures of each of the pigs and given them as gifts to their namesakes in special frames, knowing her siblings would love it. Her brothers and sister hadn't let her down—each of the pictures were now displayed on their mantels along with their other family pictures.

There were few things Lori loved more than being surrounded by her friends and family. This family reunion had already made the short list of the best days of her life. Meeting Grayson was, of course, at the very top.

As the makeup artist and hairdresser both got to work on her, Lori sipped her champagne and listened in on the half dozen conversations going on around her—about dogs and kids and car races and new sculptures and movie sets. Clearly, she thought as she took in the extra-big smiles and happy voices, everyone was having just as much fun at the reunion as she was. And the farm had been the perfect place to host it.

"Wow," Summer said as she came over a short while later when her hair and makeup were done, "you look so beautiful, Aunt Lori."

Lori smiled at one of her favorite kids in the whole wide world. "You do, too. I love your crown of wildflowers. It's so pretty."

Summer was holding something behind her back and gave Megan a quick glance. When her mother nodded, she held it out to Lori. "I made you one, too."

Lori was beyond touched. "You're the best! Can you put it on me?" She bent her head down so that Summer could reach the top of it.

When Lori turned to face the mirror again, she barely noticed how glossy her hair was, or the way her features had been perfectly played up with mascara and blush. All she knew was that with the wildflowers in her hair, she'd never felt prettier.

The room grew quiet and she noticed all of the women looking at each other in a particularly serious way. And her mother was gone. When had she left the studio?

"Hey, is something wr—" But she never got a chance to finish her sentence, because just then her mother walked back into the room holding a dress.

A wedding dress.

It was the most beautiful wedding dress Lori had ever seen…because it was the one that her mother had worn at her own wedding. And Lori knew it would fit perfectly.

"Oh, my God." She tried to stand, but when her legs were too wobbly to hold her up, she had to grip the arm-rests and sit down again instead. "What—" Her brain wasn't working. "How—" Her mouth wasn't working either. "You—"

Her mother smiled at her and said one word. The only word that mattered. "Grayson."

Lori Sullivan wasn't a woman who cried. But she'd broken that rule on this farm in Pescadero again and again. Out of despair on her first night in Grayson's house. Out of pure sadness after Sweetpea died.

And now, out of pure joy.

"From the first moment I met Grayson," her mother told her, "I knew he was the man for you, sweetie. But if I'd ever had any doubts, his asking me to help plan a surprise wedding for you would have put them immediately to rest. Only a man who truly knew and loved you would think to do something this perfect for you."

Sophie put a Kleenex in one of Lori's hands and then pulled her out of her chair with the other. "Your groom is waiting. Rather impatiently, I believe."

Lori laughed even as her tears continued to spill. Everyone she loved was here with her today and they were all so amazing to help Grayson surprise her with this wedding.

"I love all of you so much." The women gathered around her in a group hug, all of them crying and laughing now.

Lori was notoriously steady, both onstage and off, but now her fingers were shaking so much that her mother and sister had to help her get her clothes off. After she'd put on the gorgeous silk lingerie Sophie handed her, her sister showed Lori the fabulous heels they'd bought to go with the dress. Lori shook her head. "I'm going to wear my boots." They were her new white ones with colorful wildflowers stitched up the side, after all. Then she lifted her arms and they slid the silk-and-lace wedding gown on, her mother lacing up the back while Sophie readjusted the flowers on her hair and dabbed at the tears under her eyelashes without smearing her new makeup.

A knock sounded on the door and her mother went to open it. Lori's oldest brother, Marcus, was standing there in a tux. He was smiling at her, but she could see his eyes grow a little glassy as he said, "You're absolutely beautiful, Lori." He held out an arm. "Ready to take a walk down the aisle?"

More tears threatened to spill as she put her hand in Marcus's. "Did you know about this?"

"All of us did." He brushed a lock of hair from her eyes and added, "You were right not to give up on Grayson. Talking with him these past few months has proved to me that he truly does love you the way you deserve to be loved. With absolutely everything inside him."

She hugged her brother, his support meaning more to her than he could ever know. Everyone else moved past them to go take their places at the surprise wedding set up in the middle of the open field. She knew she should have been amazed that they had been able to pull all this off without her guessing something was up, but she'd always known how wonderful her family was.

Her hand tightly grasped in her brother's, the two of them made their way to where the country band from her first-ever barn dance was playing a waltz, and Sullivans from all over the world, along with Grayson's parents, were there to celebrate with her and Grayson.

And then she saw him, standing at the end of the wildflower-strewn aisle, gorgeous in a tux, black cowboy hat and boots. She didn't think before letting go of her brother's hand, lifting up her skirts and running to him.

She no longer saw anyone else, no longer heard the band playing. All she could see were Grayson's dark eyes filled with such hunger, such passion, such love. And all she knew was that he was everything she had ever wanted, everything she had ever waited for, as she flew into his arms and wrapped hers around his neck.

Laughing with her, he swung her around, her hair flying behind her as they did yet another perfect dance together. Their mouths found each other a moment later and the crowd of Sullivans cheered them on.

"I love you," she whispered when she was finally able to pull her mouth from his.

"I love you, too," he whispered back against her ear. "And I can't wait another second for you to be mine."

With that, he put her back on her feet and took her hands in his as the officiant began the ceremony.

"I'm very pleased to welcome everyone to what has to be the most unique wedding I've ever been a part of." Everyone laughed and then the man said, "Lori, Grayson, do either of you have anything you'd like to say to each other before I continue?"

Lori nodded. She moved closer to Grayson and looked up into his beautiful dark eyes. "I love you. Always. Forever." All her life, she'd talked and talked and talked. But today, standing with Grayson in her mother's wedding dress in front of their families, there was nothing else she needed him to know.

Grayson grinned down at her, somehow not at all surprised by the fact that she'd chosen this very moment to stop being a motormouth.

"Grayson?" the officiant asked. "Is there something you would like to say to Lori?"

"Yes, there is." His deep voice rumbling over her skin felt as good as the sweet caress of his hands always did. "When your mother and your siblings and I planned this wedding to surprise you, I wanted to be able to stand here and tell you the exact moment I fell in love with you. But I can't do that."

"You can't?" A pin could have dropped in the grass and it would have been heard in that moment as everyone grew perfectly silent to listen for his reply.

"No, I can't. Because every single moment I've spent with you is that moment, Lori." With a collective *"Aww"* and *"Isn't that sweet?"* sounding from their audience, he told her, "I fell in love with you when you crashed into my fence post and chased after my chickens and fell down in the mud with the pigs. I fell in love with you when you taught everyone in town to line dance. I fell in love with you when you put Mo's feelings before your own and stayed with her for as long as she needed you." One fat tear slid down her cheek as he said, "And, most of all, I fell in love with you when you showed me that it was safe to love again. I keep falling in love with you again and again. Just like I'm falling right this second."

She had to kiss him again before they both said, "I do," and then Grayson was sliding a beautiful ring onto her finger and Lori was picking up one of the wildflowers on the ground to twine it around his ring finger.

The man who claimed he wasn't good with words— and who had thought he wasn't capable of loving again—had just proved himself irrevocably wrong. On both counts. She couldn't wait to tell him every single little thing she loved about him, of every possible way he'd pleased her with this surprise wedding today. But all that talking would have to wait.

Because she wasn't nicknamed Naughty for nothing.

And right now was the perfect time for the new bride to drag her new husband off to a secret corner of their property to show him *exactly* how much she loved him, body and soul.

* * * * *

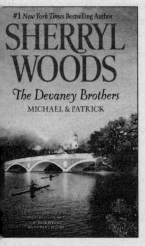

National Bestselling Author

Dakota Cassidy

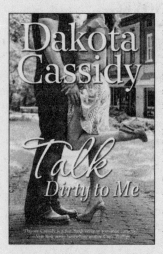

Notorious mean girl Dixie Davis is flat broke and back in Georgia. Her best—make that only—friend Landon, has thrown her a lifeline from the Great Beyond. Dixie stands to inherit his business…*if she* meets a few conditions:

She's got to live in Landon's mansion.

With her gorgeous ex-fiancé, Caine Donovan.

Who could also inherit the business.

Which is a phone sex empire.

Wait, *what?*

Landon's will lays it out: whoever gets the most new clients becomes the owner of Call Girls. Can Dixie really talk dirty *and* prove that she's cleaned up her act?

Available now, wherever books are sold!

Be sure to connect with us at:
Harlequin.com/Newsletters
Facebook.com/HarlequinBooks
Twitter.com/HarlequinBooks

HARLEQUIN® MIRA
www.Harlequin.com

MDC16

REQUEST YOUR
FREE BOOKS!

2 FREE NOVELS
FROM THE ROMANCE COLLECTION
PLUS 2 FREE GIFTS!

YES! Please send me 2 FREE novels from the Romance Collection and my 2 FREE gifts (gifts are worth about $10). After receiving them, if I don't wish to receive any more books, I can return the shipping statement marked "cancel." If I don't cancel, I will receive 4 brand-new novels every month and be billed just $6.24 per book in the U.S. or $6.74 per book in Canada. That's a savings of at least 22% off the cover price. It's quite a bargain! Shipping and handling is just 50¢ per book in the U.S. and 75¢ per book in Canada.* I understand that accepting the 2 free books and gifts places me under no obligation to buy anything. I can always return a shipment and cancel at any time. Even if I never buy another book, the two free books and gifts are mine to keep forever.

194/394 MDN F4XY

Name   (PLEASE PRINT)

Address   Apt. #

City   State/Prov.   Zip/Postal Code

Signature (if under 18, a parent or guardian must sign)

Mail to the **Harlequin®** Reader Service:
IN U.S.A.: P.O. Box 1867, Buffalo, NY 14240-1867
IN CANADA: P.O. Box 609, Fort Erie, Ontario L2A 5X3

Want to try two free books from another line?
Call 1-800-873-8635 or visit www.ReaderService.com.

* Terms and prices subject to change without notice. Prices do not include applicable taxes. Sales tax applicable in N.Y. Canadian residents will be charged applicable taxes. Offer not valid in Quebec. This offer is limited to one order per household. Not valid for current subscribers to the Romance Collection or the Romance/Suspense Collection. All orders subject to credit approval. Credit or debit balances in a customer's account(s) may be offset by any other outstanding balance owed by or to the customer. Please allow 4 to 6 weeks for delivery. Offer available while quantities last.

Your Privacy—The Harlequin® Reader Service is committed to protecting your privacy. Our Privacy Policy is available online at www.ReaderService.com or upon request from the Harlequin Reader Service.

We make a portion of our mailing list available to reputable third parties that offer products we believe may interest you. If you prefer that we not exchange your name with third parties, or if you wish to clarify or modify your communication preferences, please visit us at www.ReaderService.com/consumerschoice or write to us at Harlequin Reader Service Preference Service, P.O. Box 9062, Buffalo, NY 14269. Include your complete name and address.

ROM13R

BELLA ANDRE

31608	COME A LITTLE BIT CLOSER	___ $7.99 U.S.	___ $8.99 CAN
31600	LET ME BE THE ONE	___ $7.99 U.S.	___ $8.99 CAN
31560	IF YOU WERE MINE	___ $7.99 U.S.	___ $8.99 CAN
31559	I ONLY HAVE EYES FOR YOU	___ $7.99 U.S.	___ $8.99 CAN
31558	CAN'T HELP FALLING IN LOVE	___ $7.99 U.S.	___ $8.99 CAN
31557	FROM THIS MOMENT ON	___ $7.99 U.S.	___ $9.99 CAN

(limited quantities available)

TOTAL AMOUNT	$ _____
POSTAGE & HANDLING	$ _____
($1.00 for 1 book, 50¢ for each additional)	
APPLICABLE TAXES*	$ _____
TOTAL PAYABLE	$ _____

(check or money order—please do not send cash)

To order, complete this form and send it, along with a check or money order for the total amount, payable to Harlequin MIRA, to: **In the U.S.** 3010 Walden Avenue, P.O. Box 9077, Buffalo, NY 1426-9077; **In Canada:** P.O. Box 636, Fort Erie, Ontario, L2A 5X3.

Name: _____
Address: _____ City: _____
State/Prov.: _____ Zip/Postal Code: _____
Account Number (if applicable): _____

075 CSAS

*New York residents remit applicable sales taxes.
*Canadian residents remit applicable GST and provincial taxes.

HARLEQUIN® MIRA®
™ www.Harlequin.com

MBA0514